# Shades of Stars

## Lola Pink Mystery Series, Volume 2

### Gina LaManna

Published by LaManna Books, 2018.

SHADES OF STARS

**First edition. April 21, 2018.**

Written by Gina LaManna.

To my wonderful husband who inspires every hero. :)

# Acknowledgments

**SPECIAL THANKS:**

To Alex—This one's for your Datsun. я тебя люблю!

To my family—Thanks for giving me inspiration (that I never use in books! ;-)).

To Stacia—For making sure I always feel like a star. :-)

To you, readers!—For making every book feel so special. You're the real stars!

# Synopsis

LOLA PINK IS IN ALL shades of trouble. Her shop is still under construction, she's sort-of-fired from her job, and her hottest date this week is with a microwave burrito. However, when Dane Clark finds himself at the center of a murder investigation, Lola slips on her gorgeous vintage sunglasses and takes the case.

She's determined to prove that her sometimes-boss, sometimes-boyfriend is innocent, even if that means dealing with Dane's "charming" parents and planning a "splendid" charity gala in under two weeks. However, it doesn't take psychic powers for Lola to see that the closer she gets to uncovering the murderer, the more danger she's in—and this killer isn't afraid to strike again.

With Lola struggling to piece together love, career, and a murder investigation, she wonders if her relationship with Dane Clark is destined for failure, or if maybe, it's been written in the stars all along...

# Chapter 1

"ARE YOU LOLA PINK?"

I cinched my fluffy pink robe tighter around my body and rubbed sleep out of my eyes. "No."

"You're lying." The man blinked in surprise, then stuck a finger in my face. "*You're* Lola Pink."

"I don't turn into Lola Pink until I've had three cups of coffee and the sun is all the way up," I said pointedly, nodding toward the first fingers of sunrise in the distance. "It's not even seven o'clock in the morning."

"You're the psychic, right?"

"I'm not psychic. My grandmother was psychic."

The man on the front steps—a short guy with fire-engine red hair—stepped back, scanned the sign on the door, and shook his head. "It says right here: *Psychic in Pink. Are you searching for something? Have you lost your way in life and need a little direction? A clue to what's next? Well, we'll help you find whatever it might be that you're looking for—*"

"Stop, stop, *stop*!" I spoke louder with each word. "I know what the sign says."

"Well, I need some help with a few problems. May I?" Without waiting for a response, he brushed past me into the shop. "*Whew*, this place is a mess."

I scanned the cozy, oceanfront hut, taking a long minute to gather my sleepy thoughts. It was true—this place *was* a disaster: plastic hung from rafters, half-sawed hunks of wood were spread everywhere, and so much dust lined the floors I now needed to shower three times a day. "We're in the middle of a remodel."

"Huh," he said. "Maybe you should just tear this place down?"

"Did you come here for help, or did you come here to criticize my home? I'm warning you, I haven't had coffee; the latter option is *not* a good idea. Neither is the former, for that matter, but you seem pretty insistent."

"Hear me out, lady," he said. "My name's Richard. I need some help with the ladies."

"No kidding," I said on a breath. Crossing my arms, I spoke louder. "You can start by not calling me *lady*."

"Oh, good grief. That's what I'm talking about! A guy can't win these days." Richard ran a hand through his red hair and began pacing between two partially finished countertops. "Everything would've been fine if it weren't for Stephanie."

"Who's Stephanie?" I would've sighed, but that required energy. At this point, it was easier to go along with the man than shove him out the front door. Plus, he looked sweaty, and I wasn't in the mood for sweaty man germs on my fingers.

"Stephanie's my soulmate!" He shook his head, looking supremely agitated. "She's meant for me, and I'm meant for her."

"Great. So get married."

"She doesn't want to! That's the problem. She just doesn't see things yet the way that I do."

"I wonder why."

"I know, right?" He faced me, missing the sarcasm completely. "I mean, I'm a catch. Ain't that the truth?"

I surveyed his sort of buff, small body and wild jade eyes, and attempted a smile. It didn't work, judging by the look of disappointment on his face.

"Am I that bad?"

"Define what you mean by *bad*."

"Lady, you couldn't even smile at me. Don't lie. I'm here for honest help."

I sucked in air and held my breath until my cheeks ballooned out. Then I let it hiss between my lips until I'd reached a point of Zen that would allow me to speak without growling. "Fine. You want a psychic reading? Sit down."

"Where?" He watched as I took the only seat—a plastic-covered, squashy red armchair that had once belonged to the real psychic of the Sunshine Shore, Dotty Pink.

I gestured vaguely to the room, but there was no other place to sit. "Okay, you can stand. What do you need help with?"

"Stephanie dumped me last night. She said I don't treat her like a lady."

"Well, do you?"

"Of course I do! I just told her last night she had a great tush. Best I've seen."

"Oh, gee whiz. You're a real Romeo."

"And I mean look at me..." He did a weird thrusting motion with his hips. "Do you see this body? I work out."

As he massaged his biceps, I let my head fall into my hands. I chanced a look up once his dance was complete. "When's the last time you took her on a date?"

"Well—"

"A real, live date," I said. "Drive thru milkshakes from McDonald's don't count. I'm talking reservations, corsage, a fancy dress."

"A cor-*what*?"

"Flowers, Richard! Do you buy her flowers?"

"They just die on her anyway. Her thumb's blacker than ink."

I struggled to keep my eyes from rolling to the ceiling. "Do you know what? Maybe I am psychic. I'm getting a vision."

"I knew it!"

"*Nothing's* changing in your future."

"Really?" His face crumpled. "You can't be serious."

For the first time, I caught a glimpse of despair behind his muscle flexing and name calling and overall brashness. It was this emotion that I latched onto as I leaned forward, trying not to inhale the coconut scent of his tanning lotion. "I'm going to ask you one question. Do you love Stephanie? I mean really, truly love her. You'd do anything in the world to have her forever?"

This time when he spoke it was softer, the vowels rounded and thoughtful. "Yes, I do," he said. "I'll do whatever it takes to get her back."

"Okay, then here's what you need to do," I said, launching into a twenty-minute long discussion that covered basics such as flower-buying, date-making, and other respect-filled ways to try and win Stephanie back. "I can't promise this will work, but it's a start."

Richard stared at me with an open-mouthed expression. "Uh, can you write that down?"

"Lo, we're here—oh, good *morning*!" Johnny called through the front door as he unlocked it. He looked at me in the chair, as if seeing a ghost. "Is that you, Lola?"

"The one and only," I said. "People seem to be confused this morning about who I am."

"What'd you do with the real Lola Pink?" he asked, feigning surprise. "Usually you don't wake up until we get the sledgehammer out."

"Well, I'm a new and improved woman," I said. "And I have company. Meet Richard."

Johnny looked at the man, raised his eyebrow, and seemed unimpressed. "Okay, well—do you mind if we get started? I'd like to keep cracking on the renovations."

"Go ahead," I said, pulling a notebook toward me. I made a list for Richard to follow, handed it over, and wished him luck. As parting advice, I waved and called after him. "Remember: Buy a nice bottle of wine, not the box of it. And not beer—it's not as romantic."

"Thank you, Miss Pink," he called over his shoulder. "I owe you one. Don't worry, I'll call if I have any questions."

"Please don't," I whimpered, leaning against the doorframe.

"Another nut looking for a psychic?" Johnny asked, appearing next to me.

Johnny DePaul owned a construction company one town over, and he'd come highly recommended to me from Mr. Dane Clark, the king of Castlewood. After a horrible last attempt at remodeling this place, I was more than happy to report that Johnny was efficient, honest, and skilled at his job. Unlike Luke Anderson.

"Yeah," I said. "They seem to flock to me, though I don't know why."

"You should really take the sign down."

"I should, actually. You have a point."

"But she *can't*!" A familiar female voice piped up from behind Johnny. "She misses Dotty too much."

I peered over Johnny's shoulder toward my front steps.

Babs stood there, a huge smile on her face. "I thought I smelled coffee while I was walking past, so I stopped by."

"Right," I said, watching as Babs's eyes left mine, flicked over to Johnny, and drank in his broad shoulders and sturdy build. Johnny seemed too surprised to speak, so I tapped him on the shoulder. "Babs, can you join me in the kitchen for a second?"

"Of course." She twirled dreamily after me as she danced through the construction zone until she stubbed her toe against a ladder and cursed like a sailor the rest of the way.

"You're a real poet," I said, pulling filters down from the cupboard as Johnny rejoined his other work buddies on the front lawn. "Now, do you want to explain why you felt the need to swing by my house this morning?"

"I smelled coffee."

"I haven't made coffee yet. I always come to *your* office to get coffee—so nice try on *that* one." I gave her a stern look and added a note of warning to my voice. "Babs, Johnny is not going to find you attractive if you're stalking him."

"He's beautiful, okay? I just wanted to say hi."

I looked to Johnny. Most people wouldn't think of *beautiful* when they saw Johnny—he was sort of big all over, tall and broad and strong. He came from an Italian family and looked it—dark hair, dark eyes, loud voice. He wore a gold chain around his neck with a small cross on it, and he had about six siblings and nineteen cousins. He was a nice guy, he just wasn't... *beautiful.*

"Beans," I said for the third time. "Can you hand them to me?"

Babs had been clutching the bag of coffee to her chest like it was a teddy bear. "Oh, right," she said, handing it over. "Sorry."

"I have to get dressed and head to work," I said, as the coffee pot gurgled to life. "Don't get any ideas about making out with Johnny while he's supposed to be working. I can't go on living in dust like this for much longer, and I can't have you distracting him."

"Why don't you live with your boyfriend?" Babs now focused her full attention on me. She never tired of talking about love and men—whether it was her life, or someone else's. "You can hardly say you're going to *work* if you're sleeping with the CEO."

"I'm not sleeping with him! We had a few sort-of dates. I don't know what you'd call us. We're not putting labels on anything yet."

Babs didn't look convinced.

"At least I'm not stalking him."

"I'm not stalking Johnny," she retorted, looking the slightest bit sheepish. "I'm just visiting my friend. *You.* You're *welcome.*"

"This is why you make a great lawyer," I told her. "Turning my words around like that. Do you want coffee before you go?"

"No way," she said. "I've already had three cups. Plus, your coffee sucks."

I poured some into a mug and took a sip. *Dirt.* "Can I stop by your office on my way to work?"

"Bring your own mug this time."

"I don't steal your mugs."

"You borrow them. Permanently." Babs pointed two fingers at her own eyes, then made the *I'm watching you* gesture as she stomped out the front door. As she passed Johnny, she gave him a giggle, a wave, and then ran smack dab into the doorframe.

"Are you okay?" Johnny asked as she stormed out in a flurry of ex-pletives. When she didn't answer, he turned to me. "What's up with her?"

I rolled my eyes. "Men."

# Chapter 2

"LOLA!" MRS. DULCET'S eyebrows bent in surprise as she pulled open the door to the sprawling castle-like manor that served as a home for Dane Clark and his staff. "I didn't expect you for another hour at least."

"Well, I got up early," I said with a smile. "All that construction makes it hard to be lazy."

"I imagine." She shifted her weight from one foot to the other, looking uncomfortable with my presence. "Do you have time scheduled with Mr. Clark?"

I gripped the mug I'd borrowed from Babs's office a little tighter and studied the exquisite hallway behind her, one decked out in rich old woods and gorgeous art that probably belonged in the Louvre. "Well, I imagined we'd have our usual breakfast meeting and go over the itinerary for the day. Unless Mr. Clark's schedule has changed?"

"Oh, well, he's busy at the moment."

"Busy?" I glanced at the mug, thinking I should really return it. I'd noticed at least seven of Babs's mugs stashed in various locations around my house after she'd mentioned it. "Should I come back?"

"Dear me, I've been so rude." Mrs. Dulcet stepped off to the side of the doorway. "You'll understand I'm just not used to seeing you before nine in the morning. We run on a very regimented clock over here."

I matched her forced laugh. "If Dane is busy, maybe I can just pop by his office to run through the itinerary? I won't keep him long. But I was supposed to help with some paperwork, and he said he'd have it ready first thing this morning."

"He's not in his office."

"Oh, okay."

We stood there, eyeing each other for a moment. Lucy Dulcet had a head of hair as red as The Little Mermaid, and on most days, she was the warmest, gentlest soul in the entire castle. In fact, the only time her claws came out was when Mr. Dane Clark—CEO of Clark Company—needed protecting.

"Sorry, I shouldn't have come this early," I said finally. Then I thumbed over my shoulder toward my bicycle. "I'll just wait on my...uh, vehicle."

"Hey there, Pink! How's it going?" Gerard, the keeper of Mr. Clark's famous garage, appeared behind Mrs. Dulcet in the doorway. He carried a shiny apple in hand, a single bite missing. "Are you busy?"

"Me? No. In fact, I've got an hour to kill if you want to put me to work."

"Come on down to the garage!" Gerard was a handsome older man—one of Babs's many crushes, due in part to his exotic Australian accent. She'd run into him several times during my calamity-filled first gig for the Clark Company. "We've got the shoot in action. You're missing all the excitement."

I glanced first at him, then at Mrs. Dulcet. "Shoot?"

Mrs. Dulcet's face turned pale. "I must have forgotten. Mr. Clark didn't mention it to you?"

"No, I didn't see it on the schedule." I said slowly. "Could it be that he doesn't want me there?"

"Don't be silly," Gerard said. "Come with me. You can meet Andrea."

"Andrea," I repeated. "Sure."

"They're on a break right now. If we hurry, you can beat the hair and makeup folks before they steal them away."

When Mrs. Dulcet didn't offer any advice, I shrugged. "Sounds good. What's the shoot about?"

"Clark Company has been working quietly on a chip that'll go into self-driving cars. The PR team thought it'd be good publicity to get a few shots with Dane in his garage—his collection is well known and admired among car enthusiasts."

"And Andrea?"

Gerard gave me a wry grin. "Guys like cars. Guys also like beautiful women. She's a model we stick in the front seat—PR team's orders."

He told me this as we strolled through the grounds of the beautiful estate. All the bushes, trees, and flowers were kept in gorgeous displays. The lawn was a piece of art, each trellis a perfect bouquet of sweet smelling flowers.

"I've gotta do the rounds on the Datsuns," Gerard said as we reached the garage. "Dane and Andrea are in the main room. Go on around the corner and you'll find them."

The garage was less of a *garage* and more of a showroom. I'd never been in it before, but I'd seen a few magazine pictures of his legendary collection. White walls lined every corridor, bright lights flashing off cars in every shade of royal blue, poison black, vibrant red. It was a car enthusiast's dream come true.

Voices filtered from up ahead, so I strolled forward around the corner. And came face to face with Business Barbie. Dressed in a pencil skirt tight enough to cut off the circulation in her legs, the woman I guessed was Andrea stood three inches away from Mr. Dane Clark. Her lips were the color of strawberries, her hair the shade of flames. Her boobs were like two perfect cantaloupes sticking out of her chest, landing really, really close to Dane.

"Wanna feel them?" she was asking Dane. "They're brand new."

"No, thank you." Mr. Clark coughed, looking extremely uncomfortable, his gaze veering toward the ceiling. "Maybe someone else around here would be interested?"

Business Barbie snapped her gum. "Go on! Don't be a prude. One squeeze."

I hovered awkwardly in the wings, wondering when the appropriate time to announce myself would be. Should they know I heard Andrea's *very generous* offer or should I opt for the playing it cool route?

While I waited, I watched my boss—my sort of boyfriend—the socially inept and technological genius owner of the Clark Company, a billion-dollar company that had been passed down through his family for generations, as he stalled. His face turned the color of the shiny red convertible next to him, and I winced as he tried to step backward, stumbled over himself, and then in an attempt to redeem himself, leaned a hip awkwardly against the side of the vehicle.

Despite the lack of grace around women, this generation of the Clark family was decidedly stunning. Hair the color of ink, eyes the color of sapphire, the combination was startling upon first sight. Though he wasn't movie star handsome, there was something about him—the way he walked, talked, moved—that turned the heads of women as he entered a room. He was rich, and he was recognizable. He just didn't understand how to talk to the female species.

I took another step forward, but before I could announce my presence, Business Barbie reached out and grabbed Dane's hand and pulled it toward her, giving a bubbly laugh as she did.

I let out an involuntary gasp, and both parties turned to look my way. Mr. Clark's eyebrows shot up while Business Barbie's drew together in skepticism.

"Who are you?" she asked. "I thought they were sending *Janet* to do hair and makeup."

"I'm not hair and makeup," I said. "Are you—"

"Oh! Are you the janitor Gerard called to clean up the mess?" She frowned mid-sentence as Dane yanked his hand away as if he'd been seared. "Sorry about the coffee spill. I swear I'm such a klutz."

Footsteps sounded behind me, and then Gerard appeared at my side. He came to a hard stop at the picture before us. "Am I interrupting?" he asked in the awkward silence.

"I think maybe we both are," I told him, then offered Dane and Andrea a wave. "It was nice to meet you Andrea—Dane, just come grab me if you need anything. I'll be in the house."

"Wait!" Finally, Dane blinked to attention. "Lola, don't go. I didn't—she just..." Frustrated, he turned to Business Barbie while pointing to me. "*She's* not the janitor," he finally snapped. "She's my personal assistant."

The words *personal assistant* hit my back like a dagger. Which was ridiculous because that's exactly what I was hired and paid to do. Paid very handsomely. I wasn't here as Dane's date, his girlfriend, or anything close. Not *really*.

"Lola." Dane's voice rolled across the open garage floor. "May I speak to you?"

"Why don't you finish up your shoot," I said evenly, "and I'll go ahead and get started on the papers you wanted me to work on this morning. I'd hate to miss my deadline, Mr. Clark."

# Chapter 3

FORKS CLINKED AGAINST plates, the sound loud in the deafening silence of the dining hall.

"Coffee?" Mrs. Dulcet asked, scurrying from the kitchen with a silver pot in hand. "It's a new batch."

I nodded. "Thank you."

"My, aren't we a chatty bunch this morning?" She looked up, her eyes sliding from one end of the long dining hall table to the other. "Excellent. I'll be out of your hair in a second. Let me know if you need more biscotti, Lola."

"Thank you," I said, reaching for my third cookie. I bit down, crunching into it while holding firm eye contact with Dane. A health nut and exercise fanatic, he hated when I overdosed on sugar. Which was an essential daily occurrence. "I think five will be plenty."

"*Five?*" Dane raised his eyebrow and looked pained. "With the nine strips of bacon you ate, that's more than two hundred percent of your daily—"

"Don't say it," I said. "Ignorance is bliss."

"—fat," he finished.

"Andrea probably doesn't eat fat," I mused. As soon as I said it, I heard the pettiness in my own voice and frowned. I searched for something positive to focus on instead. "She seems very outgoing, and she's obviously beautiful."

"Lola, you *must* know I wasn't—am not, and never was—interested in her. I didn't even meet her before the PR team started using her for the new campaign. We're launching a chip for self-driving cars, and...it doesn't matter." He folded his hands on the table in front of his plate and concentrated on me. "Is that the reason for your extended silences?"

"No."

Mr. Clark sighed long and loud. "I sense your agitation, Lola—please don't try to hide these things. You know I can't read your mind."

"I'm feeling *focused*." I jerked the stack of papers he'd brought to the table towards me and pretended to read through them. "Interesting stuff."

"It's in Chinese."

"Oh," I said. "Well, I'm practically fluent."

The next words to come out of Dane Clark's mouth were decidedly not English.

"What?" I asked.

"I asked if you understood Chinese. *In Chinese*." He stared at me intently, looking curious. "Why haven't you stayed here recently?"

I took my time sipping the coffee before responding. "I've been busy at the shop. New construction crew and everything."

"We're keeping the bedroom at the ready in case you should require its services. Mrs. Dulcet just went shopping for an entirely new wardrobe."

"Huh," I said, pretending to be unimpressed when really I wanted nothing more than to take a nap in the bed, soak in the spaceship shower, and outfit myself in the high-quality thread counts that Mrs. Dulcet kept stocked in the walk-in closet I'd inherited during my first job for Mr. Clark.

Dane had initially required that I live on the premises while we searched for a stolen blueprint. However, when he'd hired me on full time, I had asked Babs to read the contract and make sure it allowed for nights away from the castle. Just in case anything went south.

"I promise you, Lola, Andrea is nothing but a business acquaintance."

I sighed. "I know. I shouldn't feel jealous anyway—I was just surprised, I guess. You didn't do a thing wrong, and I swear I'm not mad at you."

"Then what are you?"

"Women are sometimes just irrational," I said. "Well, probably men too. But you guys don't have so many freaking *hormones* to put up with; it's not fair!"

"What?"

I shook my head and gave him a quiet smile. "Andrea is a beautiful woman. She's a *model*. She's stunning, and bubbly, and fun, and...the two of you look really good together. It's easy for me to be a little jealous, even if I know there's nothing between the two of you."

"But Lola—"

"I know I work for you, Dane, but I still really like you," I confessed. "I know we're not officially dating, and we're sort of seeing where things go, but—"

"Would you like to be officially dating?"

I wrinkled my nose. "I'd sort of prefer if you don't ask me over breakfast like a business contract."

"Fine." He processed that tidbit, most likely filing it away for later. "I like you too, Lola—a lot. Not only as my personal assistant, and I'd like to see where things go if you're up for it."

"I am." I smiled, my mood vastly improved. "I'd like that a lot."

"Just promise me next time you feel uncomfortable about anything, you'll tell me about it. It's *so* much easier for me if you just talk to me instead of making me guess."

"I'll try," I said a bit growly. "But I can't promise I'll always be good at it. Sometimes I'm just crabby, and I want you to guess."

"That hardly seems fair."

"I'll work on it," I promised. "And you can work on reading my mind."

Dane looked intensely concerned, so I put him out of his misery and explained I was joking. That brought on an extensive sigh of relief.

"Speaking of uncomfortable, I'm sorry I showed up early to work. I think I made Mrs. Dulcet uneasy because I didn't have an appointment, and she didn't know what to tell me."

Dane frowned. "She was probably confused, as am I, actually. You were supposed to receive an updated itinerary with the photoshoot included and a request to move our breakfast meeting to ten a.m. The PR team called late last night with the last-minute details for the event, and I instructed them to send you a full sheet of information."

"Oh, well, I didn't receive it. Sorry."

Dane's eyes flashed a shade deeper blue, and I was briefly reminded of balmy Mediterranean waters. "I'll have a word with them."

"Oh, there's no need to get anyone in trouble—"

I was interrupted as the bubbly redhead popped herself into the dining room at that very moment. "There you two are," Andrea said, leaning into the doorway and wrinkling her nose at the cookies on my plate. "Oh, I wish I could eat those and not have them go straight to my ass."

I forced a smile back. "Call it my special talent."

"Anyway, I just came up here to apologize." The model winked at me, and then Dane. "I didn't know the two of you were dating. You should know you have nothing to worry about, Lola. Dane and I are just business acquaintances."

"Thanks for saying that, but...don't worry. Things are all good here."

"Great! Anyway, do *you* wanna feel? Dane wasn't interested," she said, puffing up her chest like a penguin. "I'm really in awe of these things. They're new since the last photoshoot I had with Dane."

"I'm good." I waved a hand. "Really. Thanks for the offer though."

"No problem. You two enjoy your breakfast now. I'll see you in a few weeks, Dane."

Dane nodded, and I waved goodbye. Dane's eyes never left my face throughout the entire exchange.

"I am truly sorry if any miscommunication on my part hurt you, Lola," he said. "I've nothing to hide. In fact, the only reason for the abrupt change in schedule is because my father is coming to dinner tonight, and he asked to see the prints."

"You really don't have to explain, Dane."

"We didn't even have a shoot on the calendar—the images aren't needed for another few months, but my parents decided to come to town for two weeks to enjoy the Sunshine Shore festival. While here, my father will—*I'm sure*—attempt to run the business for me. He insists on having a hand in things despite his retirement. In fact, I doubt they want to enjoy the festivities at all and are merely using it as an excuse to check up on the company."

"Your father?"

"Randall Clark." Dane hesitated. "Do you have plans for the evening?"

"Actually, no. Would you like me to bring something?"

Dane cleared his throat. "Bring something where?"

The silence was suffocating as I realized Dane had simply asked about my evening plans...to be cordial. He hadn't invited me over to join his family—which made *complete and total sense*—though I'd somehow invited myself anyway. *Insert desire to die.*

"Um, actually, forget it. I totally forgot I am loaded down with dinner plans tonight. So many offers I don't know *who* to hang out with." I tapped my finger against the stack of papers, willing my mouth shut. "I'll have these back to you by four this afternoon."

We exchanged awkward goodbyes as I heaved the stack of contracts out of the dining room. As I left, I heard Mrs. Dulcet re-enter the room. Then I heard something that sounded like a smack to Dane's head and a muted exclamation of pain from my boss.

"Did I say something wrong?" he asked his butler, their voices trickling through the halls. "Why on earth would Lola want to come to dinner with my parents? I thought I did her a *favor* by not inviting her. She said she had plans anyway."

"Oh, Dane," Mrs. Dulcet said on a sigh. "Sometimes I want to shake you."

I hid a smile, and despite the barrage of emotions swirling through me, I couldn't help the piece that warmed at the sound of his voice, the look in his eyes as I pictured his confusion, the curve of his lips during one of his rare smiles. If I didn't care so much about Dane, surely nothing about this morning would have upset me—which only proved my suspicions correct.

I was falling, and I was falling fast for Dane Clark.

# Chapter 4

*DINNER PLANS MY ASS*, I thought, staring deep into the microwave as a frozen burrito circled round and round and round. When it finally *dinged*, I put a slab of cheese on top, sent it for another spin, and then cut in in half.

"Perfect," I muttered upon finding the inside frozen solid while the outside was hot enough to scorch my taste buds. "Thanks for your cooperation, beans."

I took the burrito over to the psychic shop area, yanking the plastic off Dotty's most favorite cherry-red, fluffy chair as I settled in for my fine dining extravaganza.

It was blissfully quiet. When I wasn't woken at the crack of dawn by someone named Richard looking for help with the ladies, I rarely saw this place uninhabited by workers these days. Johnny and his crew were doing a fabulous job, but they were around a lot—*all the time*—and it had the side effect of making me feel like I was never truly alone.

*Until now.*

I did have my burrito to keep me company, though a single bite into the edge sent me reeling for the fire extinguisher.

Returning the burrito to the plate, I sat back and surveyed the plastics dangling from every surface. Here in the quiet, I could almost picture the finished product. The ghosts of Dotty's old place mingled with the promise of new life, and the effect was jarring. As if this very building was caught between life and death.

I'd instructed Johnny to keep the bottom level of the house as open as possible so the rooms positively filled with light. We'd agreed on a small coffee bar off to the corner that'd lead into the sunglasses shop on the other side of the back wall.

We'd leave most of the furnishing styles untouched, including Dotty's chair and some of her beads because I wasn't yet ready to rid the room of her things. Eventually, I'd have to take the *Psychic in Pink* sign down from the door and update it to *Shades of Pink*, the name of my soon-to-be beachy shop.

If all went well, the place would retain the warmth, the openness of Dotty's psychic practice, without the whole *seeing into the future* thing, since I was the worst at seeing into the future.

Just last week I'd told my neighbor there was no chance of rain all weekend. He'd gone out of town and left his windows open only to come back and find everything in his apartment completely drenched. *Whoops.*

My stomach growled, and I decided to give the burrito another chance. "Fool me once, shame on me. Fool me twice..." I took another bite and burned my mouth again, swearing off the pain. "*Shame on me.*"

Since my dinner was not cooperating, I opted for a more productive use of my time: sunglasses shopping. Sliding the computer onto my lap, I clicked through the usual sites looking for deals. Lately, I'd been into antiques and retro-themed sunnies, enjoying the individuality of each design. Not all of them were even functional, but that's what a collection was all about: people gathering junk they'd never use but enjoyed nonetheless.

I'd clicked purchase on a variety of antiques, along with the newest design from Angelo—a current genius in eyewear—when the phone rang, startling me just in time to save myself from certain debt.

Checking the time before answering the unknown number, I realized it was only quarter to eight. "Hello?"

"It's me," the low voice said from the other end. "Dane Clark."

"What's wrong?" I sat up straighter. "Why are you calling me instead of eating dinner with your parents?"

"Dinner doesn't start until nine."

"Oh."

"I need to ask a favor of you."

"Sure. Name it."

"Can you come pick me up?"

"On my bicycle?" I frowned. "Where's Semi?"

"He'll meet you at the castle and drive you. Just get into Castle-wood."

"Okay." I'd started heading toward the stairs to change out of my embarrassing pajamas but stopped mid-stride. "I'm confused. Where did you say you are?"

"I'm at the police station."

The news hit me like a two by four, and I sat down on the stair-case. "You're kidding. Has there been a mistake?"

"Andrea's dead," he said. "And they think I killed her."

SEMI, THE TALL, DARK-skinned, super strong man in charge of keeping Mr. Clark safe, opened the back door to a black SUV after the two of us had sprung Dane from the police station.

"Climb in," Semi instructed. "The media will be here soon, if they're not already."

I climbed into the vehicle after Dane, shutting the door behind me as the car began to move. Semi had spared me a bicycle ride by swinging by my house to pick me up while I'd scrambled into the appropriate clothes (and backup sunglasses) that were required for such an event.

As we drove toward the castle in silence, the gravity of the situation, along with the curiosities of it, broke me. I needed to know what had transpired between the time I'd left the castle and the time I'd clicked *purchase* on the Angelo shades and received a call that flipped my night upside down.

"So," I said, struggling to find the best way to word my next question. "Do you know what *really* happened?"

Dane's eyes flashed first to the rearview mirror where he watched Semi, then over to me. "Do I know who killed her? *No.*" His eyes glittered as he looked directly into my gaze. "Are you asking if I killed her? The answer to that is also *no.*"

"Dane, I wasn't asking that." I reached my hand over and rested it on his. "I trust you—I know you'd never do anything like that. I mean, *how* did everything happen? Why did they arrest you?"

"They didn't arrest me—they simply brought me in for questioning." Dane sighed. "As per her contract, Andrea gets a say on which photos make it into the media. She stuck around most of the day to review pictures as the photographer edited them, like she always does."

I nodded. "When did she leave your house?"

"Around four in the afternoon," he said. "I don't remember an exact time because I was upstairs in my study—alone."

"You don't look at the photos together?"

"I could care less what I look like in the media. It's all a game, and I have better uses for my time. I let the photographer pick the best images."

"She didn't come up to say goodbye or anything?"

He shook his head. "We have a business deal, Lola, we are not—" he stopped, looking surprised as he cleared his throat. "We *were* not friends."

"Of course. I understand."

"Around six o'clock, I heard a knock on my study door. I assumed it was Mrs. Dulcet, though aperitifs weren't scheduled until eight o'clock to account for my parents' late arrival."

"It wasn't Mrs. Dulcet coming for you?"

"It was the police, announcing they'd found Andrea's body on the side of the road. She was dead. Blunt force trauma to the head."

I flinched. "And the murder weapon?"

"A paperweight from my office."

"How did they find it?"

"Find what, the murder weapon?" Dane looked aghast at the very mention of it. "It was hidden on the scene of the crime, but poorly. You are familiar with Route 1, obviously?"

I nodded. It was the single road that ran along the coastline. It connected Castlewood, Sunshine Shore, and many of the other small towns in our little niche of beachfront property.

"Someone threw it from the side of the cliff." He shook his head, glancing down at his hands. "I can only assume they expected it to fall into the water, but it didn't. Its fall was stunted by a twisty bunch of bushes ten feet down, and that's where it landed."

Clearing my throat, I stepped cautiously over my next point. "Do you have any idea how it got there?"

"I didn't kill her." His voice was soft, eerily calculated. "I already told you that."

"I know," I said. "I'm just asking about any suspects."

"It makes no sense for me to kill her!" Dane was talking to himself now, agitated. "If I had killed her, I *certainly* wouldn't have left her body there. I wouldn't have left a murder weapon—*from my office*—at the scene of the crime." With each passing word, his voice rose in volume. "That makes no sense. It's all wrong. If I'd done it, I would've—"

"Stop right there." I gripped his hand tighter in mine. "I know you didn't kill Andrea. It's probably not a good idea to explain how you *would* have, since we both know you'd never do anything of the sort."

"Of course. I'd never be so careless."

"That's not what I meant, Dane. I meant that I *know* you. The inside of you." This time my voice was quieter, gentler. "Forget about the how or the why and let me explain. I know you as a *human being*, and I know you wouldn't kill another person in cold blood."

He blinked. "How can you know that?"

"Because. I just do. Call it my psychic intuition."

"You told me you're not psychic."

"I'm not, Dane, it's just..." I trailed off and switched to a new tactic. Resting a hand on his heart, I let his pulse beat against my palm. "You may be many things, Mr. Clark, but I know you're not a murderer. That's it. That's all. No explanation necessary. I trust you."

"She's right," Semi agreed from the front seat. "Mrs. Dulcet, Gerard, Nicolas—we all know you're not guilty. But laying out plans for the perfect murder ain't gonna help your case. With all due respect, boss, keep your damn mouth shut."

Understanding dawned in Dane's eyes. "Ah, I see. Point taken."

A bit grudgingly, I removed my hand from Dane's chest, pretending that it hadn't sent tiny bolts of lightning skittering through my elbow, up to my shoulder, the electricity winding its way into my heart.

"Next question," I continued, before I could get distracted by the fluttering sensations. "Do you know who *might* have killed her? Did anyone have a motive?"

Confusion flashed through Dane's eyes. "I have no idea. She seemed like a perfectly pleasant woman to me."

"Fair enough, but it doesn't sound like she was killed on accident. A blow to the head? It sounds like someone wanted her dead."

"Or someone got carried away in a heated argument and conked her over the head," Semi said. "Maybe they hadn't meant to kill her."

"True," I agreed. "But either way, someone popped her on the head with a paperweight. Why? Who? Also, why would they have had Dane's paperweight if they weren't trying to frame him for murder?" With horror, I turned to look at Dane. "It must have been someone who knew you were with her most of the day. Someone who had access to your schedule."

"I suppose it's possible she was murdered in the castle and her body was moved," Dane said. "It wasn't clear when the police were questioning me whether she was murdered on the side of the road or merely dumped there."

"Either way, it's bad news," I said. "A murderer was in your office, Dane. When did you notice the paperweight missing?"

"I didn't. I had no clue what the detectives were referencing when they asked me about it. It was a Christmas gift from someone in my family. If it's the one I'm thinking of, it was horrible. Ugly. After I opened it—and yes, my fingerprints are likely on it—I stuck it in the bottom desk drawer and never bothered to look at it again. Of course, I looked in the drawer for the paperweight when the police arrived, but it wasn't there."

I shook my head. "Why would someone want to kill Andrea with a paperweight? And why would they make it look like you killed her?"

"I don't know," Dane said. "But I imagine we'd better find out."

# Chapter 5

WE RETURNED TO THE castle in somber silence, all our initial thoughts culminating in one conclusion: Dane didn't kill Andrea, we knew that—so who did? And *why*? And perhaps the most important question of all: *Who was close enough to Dane Clark to frame him for murder?*

"Do you mind giving me a ride home?" I asked Semi as we pulled up the castle drive. "Unless—Dane, do you want me to stay?"

Dane's eyes flicked to mine. "Yes, please—I'd like that."

As he helped me down from the SUV, he didn't say a word more, but he clutched my fingers tighter than necessary, and I didn't mind one bit.

Despite the horrible circumstances, my heart pinged with warmth toward Dane, and I savored him leaning on me in whatever way he needed. Even Dane Clark—master of stoicism—shouldn't have to face murder charges alone. He was an innocent man, I knew, even as his blue eyes stared emotionlessly ahead.

"I'm so glad you're back!" Mrs. Dulcet rushed out to greet us the second our feet hit the walkway. She pulled Dane into a hug, kissed him on both cheeks, and then whispered in his ear loud enough for me to hear. "By the way, *they've* arrived. What horrible timing, dear, I'm so sorry."

I blinked between the two, suddenly realizing who *they* were. Dane's parents. *Dinner*. In the rush of the evening's events, I'd totally forgotten about my lack of invitation to the castle for the festivities. I also idly wondered why the event hadn't been cancelled in light of recent circumstances.

"Dear, you'll want to get going." Mrs. Dulcet reached out, clasping my hands in hers. "Trust me. I'm saving you a headache—it's not

that we don't want you here, I swear it. Not to speak disrespectfully
of my former employer, but after all you have been through tonight, I
urge you to go home and leave this to us."

"No." Dane returned his hand to mine. "She'll be staying."

"I will?" I looked over to him. "You don't have to do that, Dane.
You probably want to be alone."

"Unless you don't want to be here," he said, a flash of uncertainty
crossing his eyes. "I would love to have you by my side."

"If you want me to be here," I said softly, turning to face him, join-
ing both of our hands into a small circle, "I'll be here."

His eyes roved over my face hungrily, as if it were the last time
he'd see me. He leaned forward, his lips brushing just slightly against
mine. "I *need* you to stay."

"Then I'll stay." My heart fluttered at the touch of his lips against
mine. "For as long as you want me here."

I turned in time to see a small smile twisting the corners of Mrs.
Dulcet's lips. She hid it well and switched back to business mode as
she gestured for us to follow her inside.

"Keep in mind, Dane's parents can be a bit intimidating," Mrs.
Dulcet explained softly. "I would've given you more warning,
but...well, I told Dane he shouldn't invite you to dinner. It was my decision, not his. I thought I'd spare you the headache of meeting them.
I'm sorry, I was wrong."

She left us in the entryway, excusing herself before I could respond. The next thing I knew, I was buckling under the weight of
what felt like a sandbag tossed at my chest. When I looked down, I
found one huge man's jacket and a woman's fur coat draped across my
forearms.

"Thank you, darling." The woman who'd tossed me the coats
looked to be close to Mrs. Dulcet's age, but a little more well preserved. As if money had bought her the finest things in life, including

hair care and facials and manicures. "What a pretty new housekeeper you've got, Dane."

"She's not—" Dane started, but he was interrupted before he could finish.

"I'm Dane's mother, and you may call me Mrs. Clark." She stuck her hand out to shake mine, but I had no idea how she wanted me to move when already my arms were trembling under the weight of the jackets.

Dane took the jackets from me, frowning at his mother. She frowned right back at him. During the silence, I reached out and returned the handshake.

"It's a pleasure to meet you, Mrs. Clark," I said swiftly. "I'm Lola Pink. You can call me Lola."

"Lola," she said, her voice a bit husky as she spoke. "I don't suppose you could take these jackets off my son's hands? We have urgent matters to discuss."

"*Mother*, Lola is not the—"

"Dane, hand over the coats and tell me how you got into this mess—we heard all about the little incident on the way down." The other half of Dane's parental unit stood taller than all of us, broad shouldered with a bow tie on his neck and glasses on his nose. "I have my lawyers on standby. I don't appreciate the hassle, but we'll do what we must to make this woman's murder go away."

"That's not necessary," Dane said. "And mother, Lola is *not*—"

"You won't be staying, will you?" Mrs. Clark asked me pointedly. Then turning to Dane, she clucked her tongue. "I swear they don't teach the maids anything these days. Why is she still hanging around?"

"She's not my *maid*!" Dane finally broke through the noise, his eyes flashing. "This is my personal assistant, Lola. She's here because I asked her to be here, and she's staying. She's also a *friend*."

"Really, Dane." I rested a hand on his arm. "If this is a family matter, I can leave. I can call Babs for a ride back."

"That would be lovely," Mrs. Clark said, finally smiling at me. "And can you *please* take care of these jackets for us? What's happened with the help around here, Dane?"

Dane didn't respond, only turned to the closet and hung up the jackets himself. A calmness settled on the room—silent, tense, almost worse than the barrage of questions and unsolicited advice that'd begun the second we entered the house.

"There," he said quietly. "The jackets are taken care of, and dinner should be ready. Shall we take our seats?"

Mrs. Clark must have sensed the warning notes in her son's voice because she settled for a glance down her nose at me as we entered the dining room.

Three seats were set. One at either end of the table, and a single place in the center.

"Oh, my. I can see *one* of us wasn't expected," Mrs. Clark said to Dane. "Was it me or your father? Would you like me to wait in the car while you dine with your *help*?"

"Mother, please. It'll take all of two seconds to get another place setting ready. Mrs. Dulcet, do you mind setting a spot for Lola, please?"

The butler must have been listening from just around the corner because she appeared with another plate, napkin, and utensils not three seconds later. "Hello, Mr. and Mrs. Clark," Mrs. Dulcet said. "I hope your travels were comfortable."

"The train ride was obnoxious and the seats were *ridiculous*," Mrs. Clark said. "We pay a premium for first class. You'd think they'd at least ensure our comfort."

"Now, Amanda, please," Randall said. "The seats weren't so terrible, but I agree the food was abysmal."

"You don't even understand." Amanda Clark rolled her eyes. "It was like sitting on a tractor for three hours."

"Next time we'll take the helicopter." Randall rested his hand soothingly on his wife's shoulder, giving Dane and myself an apologetic stare. "The pilot had requested the week off to spend time with his family or whatnot, so we decided to be adventurous and take the train."

"Oh, yeah, that's tough," I said, feeling the blush on my face as the words slipped out. "No helicopter—*yikes*."

The Clarks all stared at me, and I willed myself to melt into the ground.

"Appetizers!" Mrs. Dulcet trilled, saving the day as she waltzed around the corner with a sizzling platter of grilled vegetables. "We're dining Italian tonight, so I hope that's all right. I've had the cheese flown in straight from Parma as you like, Mr. Clark."

"That sounds lovely, Lucy," Amanda said. "Now, I suppose we should take our seats."

Without realizing it, I'd rested my hand on the back of the chair that I normally adopted for breakfast. Apparently, it was no longer *my* chair, judging by Amanda's pointed stare. Moving quickly out of the way, I settled into the newest place setting while Dane sat across from me. His parents took both heads of the table.

"Tell us what happened this evening, Dane," Randall instructed as he reached for the cheese. "Every detail. My lawyers—"

"Your lawyers will stay out of this," Dane said, patient but firm. "I have my own team, as we've discussed, and they will handle it according to my instructions."

"This is a potential murder charge," Randall argued, his gray hair a strange intersection between fluffy and stiff as it waved atop his head. "This is not something to take lightly."

"Is that what you think I do here?" Dane had picked up his fork and knife, but he laid them down before speaking. "Ever since you left the company, you can't admit that a single thing has gone right. We had our most profitable period—ever—and still it's not enough for you."

"Things are going... *fine*," Randall said, implying that *fine* was the equivalent of rotting fish. "I just think business could be better."

"I know what you think," Dane said. "But with all due respect, *father*, you've retired. Any hand in the business you have now is merely a courtesy. If I'm to run the business as discussed, I need to have complete control."

"If you'd released the extended prototype like I'd counseled you on three months ago, you would've been building revenue for months. *Instead*, you're sitting here frolicking with your help, playing with your cars, and—"

"*Boys*!" A vein pulsed in Amanda's forehead. "What did I say about business talk at dinner?"

"We're talking about murder, dear," Mr. Clark said all too calmly. "We need to make this unfortunate incident go away."

"Dane, you didn't kill that woman, did you?" Mrs. Clark watched her son through narrowed eyes. "Tell me the truth."

"Of course not," Dane said, his voice as sharp as jagged glass. "You know I'd never do anything of the sort."

"Exactly. I know it, your father knows it... I'll even bet *she* knows it." Mrs. Clark jabbed her butter knife in my direction. "So from here on out, I don't want to hear a word about it—it's *business*, you men sorting out your legal mess. What is my one rule at dinner?"

"You have several," Dane said dryly. "No phones at the table—"

"No papers at the table," his dad continued. "No serving dessert without coffee."

"No laptops, uninvited guests, or sweatpants," Dane said, the two men beginning to chuckle as they continued the list. "No red wine when fish is present and absolutely no martinis after cocktail hour."

Amanda Clark cleared her throat then, and both of the men in her life looked toward her end of the table like the apocalypse had arrived—all wide eyes, parted lips, terrified expressions. "No more business talk. End of the conversation."

Both Clark men nodded, bowed their heads, and dug into the appetizers.

I inhaled a piece of grilled eggplant, mostly to keep from snorting in laughter. Then Mrs. Dulcet appeared with the rest of dinner, and apparently, if business wasn't to be discussed at dinner, there was nothing else to say. Three courses passed without so much as a whisper, save for one quick and instantly regretted *pass the salt.*

By the time dessert arrived, the room had sat in silence for so long my ears were ringing. I found myself wishing time had turned back and I *hadn't* been invited to dinner. It now made complete sense why Lucy Dulcet had considered it a favor to warn me away. *But no*, I'd had to come and witness this whole miserable shebang for myself.

The minute dessert wine was poured, the two Clark men leapt at each other's throats with talk of legality, contracts, and other jargon that I had no hope of understanding. Apparently, discussion of business was allowed over dessert.

While they talked, I drank a little bit too much wine, mostly because my hands were bored, and I needed something to do with my fingers. Pouring wine worked well, so I let the fuzziness suck me in and drown out the conversation. I'd already polished off my personal-sized cake, and I doubted asking for another would look good on my resume.

As the men talked, Amanda looked me over critically and offered a tight smile. "You have nice skin."

"Thank you," I said. "I like your dress."

"Thank you."

That was the end of our conversation.

An hour and a half later, I'd made a good dent on the cookie plat-ter. I was a little too tipsy to care about Amanda's judgmental stares as I swirled the last dregs of my cappuccino with the cookie.

When Mrs. Dulcet arrived sometime after my coffee had disap-peared and asked if we needed more of anything, Amanda shook her head and gave a pointed look in my direction. "I think we're done with the biscotti."

I froze, my hand halfway to the plate. "Yes, thanks. I'm full."

Mrs. Dulcet hid any expression well as she gathered the plate from my hands and vanished into the kitchen. Somewhere, that must have signified the end of dessert because shortly after, Amanda stood and fixed her gaze on Dane.

"I'm ready to retire to my room. We *are* welcome to stay here, aren't we?"

"Mother, don't be ridiculous," Dane said. "The bedroom has been prepared for your arrival. I gave the maids the list of items you re-quired."

"At least the help has done *something* around this place," she said under her breath. "Goodnight, Lola. It was a pleasure to meet you."

I wasn't sure whether to bow or curtsy or kiss her feet, so I did some combination of a nod and smile. Thankfully, Dane realized it for the cry of help that it was and came around the table to rest a hand on my back.

"I'm going to walk Lola out," he said. "Mrs. Dulcet will show you and father to your room. Goodnight, mother."

Mrs. Dulcet burst through the doorway, all smiles and chipper-ness despite her long day and longer evening working. "Right this way, Mr. and Mrs. Clark."

Dane led me in the opposite direction, through the kitchen where I waved to a few familiar staff members. They all gave me looks of sympathy, and I doled out appreciative nods to each of them. I was low enough on the totem pole to be considered friendly with the staff, and for that, I was grateful.

"Well, that was sure something," I said when Dane and I reached the front hall. "I'm really sorry if I ruined your dinner. I probably shouldn't have been there."

"I asked you to stay with me," Dane said, raising a hand to brush the fine baby hairs back from my forehead. "I'm the one who should be apologizing. And thanking you for everything. I don't know what I would have done without you."

"Oh, it's nothing. I was just microwaving a burrito at home anyway. So really, it was my pleasure. The food was delicious and the company was... well, interesting."

"I thought you said you had plans."

"When do I ever have *plans*?" I paused a second, confused. Then flushed as I realized my earlier lie. "Oh, *right*. I did have plans—with my burrito and a glass of wine. Alone at home."

"Those aren't *plans*."

"Well, I didn't want you to feel like you had to invite me," I said. "So, I fibbed a little. I'm sorry, but I didn't want to intrude on your family dinner."

"Lola, I asked you to dinner tonight because I wanted you here. Earlier...that was a miscommunication. Please trust that I do as I like. If I hadn't wanted you to stay, I wouldn't have asked you."

I bowed my head, my hands coming up to rest on his chest. "Okay."

His hands reached for me, one of them coming to rest on my cheek, the other slipping around my back. "I promise."

"Well then," I ventured, our lips hovering an inch apart. "What do you want to do right now?"

"Kiss you."

"Oh."

The word was a breath. Dane cut me off halfway through, closing the space between us with a hard, fast kiss. An underlying intensity burned between us, the sure product of the overwhelming emotions that'd barreled through us since this morning.

His hand moved from my cheek to the nape of my neck and he pressed me closer, the scent of him all encompassing. Fresh, sharp—I breathed him in like the scent of cinnamon rolls and melted into his arms.

"What is *this*!" Amanda Clark tried to stifle a gasp of surprise and failed as she came around the corner and caught us making out like high schoolers. "Dane Clark, how *could* you?!"

Dane and I stepped back, though I couldn't help but notice his hand sliding down my back, coming to land just above my waist. It stayed there as he met his mother's gaze. Then another silence launched like an attack, and I buckled against it. I leaned against Dane's side, soaking up his warmth like a shield.

"Um," I murmured when Dane didn't seem inclined to speak. "I should probably be going."

"Yes, I think you should. What has this place turned into? A *brothel*?" Amanda huffed. "Honestly, Dane. You have women coming at all hours of the night?"

"She's not *wom-en*, she's one *woman*," Dane said, his voice surprisingly calm. "And you can call her Lola, as she's mentioned."

"Lola," she said the name like a poison. Clunky, filled with distaste. "Well then, goodnight. Lucy, have Randall call Anders, will you? See if he has space for us to stay while we're in town because I haven't felt welcomed here."

Mrs. Dulcet scurried forward and nodded. "I'll have Mr. Clark contact his brother right away, Mrs. Clark."

"Let me walk you out." Dane's fingers tightened their grip on my back as he guided me to the front steps where Semi was waiting.

I could feel Amanda's eyes on my back as I walked, as if she hoped I'd fall right off the plank and get eaten by sharks.

Dane passed me off to Semi after a light kiss on the forehead. "Make sure she gets home safe, will you?"

Semi nodded his big head, and then moved down to the black SUV to give us space.

"Goodnight, Lola," Dane said, bringing his hands to rest on my shoulders. "I can't tell you how much I appreciate you staying for dinner. If you'd like to stay over, you're welcome here. You are always welcome."

"It's probably better if I go for now," I said, though I couldn't deny it felt nice that he'd asked. A happy warmth began in my stomach and brought a smile to my face. "Goodnight, Dane."

He watched me until we got in the car. Then he raised his hand in a stoic wave before disappearing inside. The door stayed closed for one second before Mrs. Dulcet rushed out, a container in hand. "Semi!" she called, rapping her knuckles on the glass even as the car began to move. "Open the window."

Semi rolled down the windows, and Mrs. Dulcet shoved the container into my hands.

"Desserts," she said, gasping for air. "If I don't send them with you, they'll end up in the rubbish bin. Save them."

I hugged the box tightly to my chest. "I'll take good care of them," I promised. "They'll be gone by morning."

Mrs. Dulcet winked. "Just don't make yourself sick, or Mr. Clark will have my head."

# Chapter 6

"WHY DID YOU BRING US here?" Babs, short for Bernadette, the curviest and loudest of the Sunshine Sisters, leaned back against the water tower. She was also the most brilliant lawyer this side of the Rockies, and one giant bubble of energy and pink lipstick—when she wasn't hungover. "The sun is barely up and my head hurts."

"I told you to stop drinking wine before bed," Annalise said. "It really affects your sleeping patterns."

"I brought cookies!" I thrust the leftovers from the previous evening into the girls' hands, then scooted a travel-tray full of cappuccinos toward the girls. "Thanks for meeting me here so early. I try not to take Emergency Meetings lightly."

Emergency Meetings had been happening between the three of us ever since we'd learned how to climb. For a few months, the cops tried to kick us off our meeting place on the water tower, but our persistency won out. Now, people worried if we *didn't* have at least one weekly gathering for the town to see—and not a soul to hear.

"I have news," I said. "Huge news."

"Is it about Mr. Clark?" Babs raised her eyebrow. "You didn't tell us you had a date."

"We didn't," I said. "Well, not a traditional date, anyway. I picked him up from the police station."

Both girls froze. If the situation hadn't been so serious, I might have laughed at their expressions. Babs had a cookie dunked halfway into her cup while Annalise's dangling feet froze in the splits. Where Babs was the boisterous one, Annalise was our petite, anal-retentive gymnast. She might be a tad on the naïve side, but somehow, the three of us balanced each other out.

"*What?*" Annalise asked over the sound of Babs's biscotti breaking in half and plopping into the coffee.

"I had this hot date with a burrito last night," I said. "And halfway through burning every one of my taste buds, I got a phone call from Dane asking if I could meet him at the station with Semi. The authorities think he *murdered* someone—or at least, they were questioning him about it. A model he's worked with on a few occasions named Andrea. I met her yesterday, briefly. She asked me to touch her new boobs."

Babs shook her head. "Confused doesn't even begin to explain what I'm feeling."

"Let me start from the beginning," I said, backing up to the moment I walked in on the photoshoot between Andrea and Dane. I continued the story up to, including, and through dinner, ending with the kiss that had led Mrs. Clark to declare the castle a brothel. "Then Mrs. Dulcet gave me these biscotti, and that's the end of it."

Babs and Annalise both looked shell-shocked. Rightfully so, since it sounded like I'd given them half the plot of a James Bond movie.

"So this kiss," Babs said. "It was dreamy?"

"Is that *all* you care about?" Annalise elbowed her. "What about the poor girl who died? Did he do it, Lola?"

"Dane?" I asked, sharper than I'd intended. "Are you asking me if Dane murdered Andrea? Of course he didn't!"

"You can't deny that's the first logical question," Annalise said. "A woman was murdered. You're dating the primary suspect. I want to know that you're safe."

"Not only are you dating him," Babs pointed out, "but you're working for him, too. Things are complicated. I can't fault Annalise for asking the question we were all thinking."

"I know Dane," I said with a confidence that seemed flimsy when spoken aloud. "Okay, *maybe* I haven't known him for years, but I know enough. He'd never hurt anyone like that."

"He lacks social skills," Annalise said. "Isn't that a sign of a psychopath?"

I slammed my cup down a little too hard on the ledge. "Look, I called the two of you up here to ask for help. Not to accuse Dane of something he didn't do. Plenty of people have already jumped aboard that train."

"She's just trying to protect you," Babs said, resting her hand on mine. "She loves you, I love you, and we hope Dane loves you too. It doesn't hurt to be safe, though, especially this early in the game."

I blew out a long sigh. "Maybe you're right."

"You're developing feelings for him!" Babs pointed out. "Of course you're going to be on his side. You should be; it's *our* job to ask the questions you can't."

"He didn't do it," I murmured. "I know it."

"Then how can we help?" Babs asked. "What's your plan going forward? Don't bother lying. We know you have a plan, or you wouldn't be up here talking to us and bribing us with coffees."

I finally allowed a small smile as I warmed my hands around the coffee mug. "I want to find out more about the victim's closest relationships. Husband, boyfriend, parents, siblings—anything we can find. Babs, can you help gather that information?"

She nodded. "Won't take me long. I'll do some research and call you this afternoon."

Annalise looked expectantly at me.

"What?" I said. "Are you trying to convict Dane or clear his name?"

"I'm not going to apologize for asking the difficult questions." She shook her head, her tight brown bun swaying with her smoothly executed movements. "I am trying to be sensible about this, but I'm here to help if you need."

"Fine," I said grudgingly. "Thank you."

"You said this Andrea is a model?" Annalise asked, waiting for my nod before continuing. "Well, the entertainment community is a small one. I can ask around. I bet some of the performers have heard of her, and they might know the latest on her relationships. The industry is close-knit out here, and if she's a local, I'll hear something."

"You guys are the best," I said, a large weight dissolving from my chest. "Thank you for being there for me. I just needed to talk aloud—I know Dane is innocent, but it's so much to wrap my brain around."

"You know the rules of the water tower," Babs said. "It's a Judgement Free Zone. Up here, you say what you need, and we do what we can. End of story."

"Girls!" Mrs. Fredericks called from below the water tower. "You have two minutes until the brownies are done. Better start climbing down or they'll get so cold the ice cream won't melt on them just how you like."

"Are they special brownies?" Babs hollered back. "Like last time?"

"What, dear?" Mrs. Fredericks loved nothing more than to feed us during our emergency water tower sessions. "Did you say special? Of course they're special—made with love!"

"You heard her," Babs said. "Brownies are done, folks. Time to move out."

BABS DROPPED ME OFF at the castle after we'd filled our tanks with Mrs. Fredericks's specially made brownies with melted ice cream and a pop of cool whip. I was still full to the brim when I knocked on the castle's front door.

While I waited for it to open, I adjusted my pale blue shades to perch on top of my head. I was proud of how well they matched my little pearly stud earrings, my new distressed pair of jeans, and my baby blue flats. I felt like spring in a Target catalogue—with better sunglasses.

"Hi, Mrs. Dulcet," I said with a smile when the door opened. "Good morning. Thanks again for the—"

"Come in, dear," she said in a louder than necessary voice. "Let me take your things."

I didn't have anything to take, which made me frown with suspicion. Before I could ask what was wrong, I caught sight of the reason for Mrs. Dulcet's strange behavior.

"*Lola.*" Amanda stood just inside the front hallway. On the floor next to her were two suitcases. "Good morning."

"Good morning," I said, trying not to sound optimistic at the sight of her prepared baggage. "Leaving so soon?"

Her eyes flashed. Luckily, Dane appeared in the doorway before she could snap a retort, a smile growing on his handsome face as he caught sight of me. "Good morning, Lola."

"Good morning, Mr. *Clark.*"

"Oh, now it's Mr. Clark, is it?" Amanda looked between her son and me. "Last night you seemed quite a bit...*friendlier.*"

Dane looked at her, then strode across the room and brushed a kiss against my cheek before resting a hand on my shoulder. I could've sworn Mrs. Dulcet nearly burst with excitement, her hands clasped across her chest.

"I'm sorry," I said, feeling the strange need to apologize. "I didn't mean anything inappropriate yesterday evening."

"Don't apologize, Lola," Dane said calmly. "You did nothing wrong. Mother, we discussed this last night. If you don't like the way I run *my* household, you can stay somewhere else."

"Dane! I'm your mother!"

"You're welcome here as always. But if you don't like what you see, you're welcome to leave. Lola is a part of my life, and I'm sorry if that doesn't please you. But it's not changing."

A second ago I'd been ready to run out of this house until that woman disappeared, but now, I sunk deeper into Dane's body, warmth spreading from the very tips of his fingers straight to my core. As much as I hated coming between Dane and his family, the way he'd defended me to his own mother—the very powerful, elegant Mrs. Amanda Clark—melted me into a buttery mess.

"But—" Mrs. Clark's eyes blazed as she tore her gaze away from her son, looking to me like I was the witch responsible for his ruin. "Randall get in here. It's time for us to leave. Is the car ready, yet? *Randall!*"

Her shouts faded into an uncomfortable silence in which Mrs. Dulcet simultaneously offered water, coffee, tea, breakfast, lunch, and dinner. Nobody needed anything, so the four of us stared at one another dumbly until Randall arrived.

"Good morning, folks," he said, beaming at the room as he put a hand on his wife's shoulder. "How did everyone sleep?"

Amanda pursed her lips into a tight circle. "Where are the rest of our things, Mrs. Dulcet? And please alert Anders we'll be arriving at his place shortly."

"Yes, of course," Mrs. Dulcet said and scurried away on a breath of relief.

"I don't suppose you've begun planning the event, have you?" Mrs. Clark asked Dane coldly. "The festival has already kicked off, and the gala is on the last day. That's two weeks away."

"Oh, the event." Dane's voice was measured, calculated as always, but underneath was a layer of panic that I could only decipher thanks to the amount of time I'd spent with him recently. "Yes, *the event.*"

"Don't tell me you haven't thought about it?" Amanda's voice reached screeching levels, and her husband winced as she continued.

"If you haven't booked anything, we might as well cancel it now! Any suitable venue will be gone, the caterers booked, and... *oh, dear*. I might as well never show my face at the festival again. Can you imagine the disappointment?"

"Mother, I'm sor—" Dane started, but I took the opportunity to swoop blindly into battle.

"What Dane is trying to say is that he assigned me the task months ago," I said. "I'm on top of the event planning—don't worry."

"I thought you were a new hire," Mrs. Clark said, her eyes beelining toward mine. "Mrs. Dulcet said you've been here weeks."

"He hired me as a freelancer before bringing me on full time," I said, scrambling for logic. "I've got everything under control."

She took a long moment to scan my body from the top down. "Have you ever attended a charity gala in your life?"

I thought back to the one time I'd attended the local church's fall festival. I'd played the basketball shoot and a ring toss where I'd won a goldfish—and I was almost certain a few bucks from that event had gone to a charity. "Yes, I have."

"Which one?"

"Oh, I've been to so many that I lost track."

"Women for Hearts? Breast Cancer? Hearts for the Homeless?" She paused, a finger on her lips as she watched me for signs of recognition. "I thought the latest adoption event was just marvelous. We found homes for hundreds of dogs and raised a significant sum of money for the shelters."

"That was a great one," I said faintly. "I read about it."

"Here are the last of your bags," Mrs. Dulcet said, accompanied by a bigger, burlier member of the staff. "Anything else I can get for you, Mr. and Mrs. Clark?"

"A new personal assistant?" Amanda asked sweetly.

Mrs. Dulcet froze, her hand on one of the suitcases. Next to me, Dane tensed. The pressure of his fingers on my shoulder increased until it became painful, and I had to wriggle out of his grasp.

"This is my—" he started, his tone low, decidedly dangerous.

"I know, it's your home, sweetie." Amanda interrupted as she crossed the room, stepped in the tiny space between her son and me, and patted him on the cheek. Then she kissed him on the other cheek. "We'll be at Anders's place for the next two weeks until the festival is finished. Of course we'll be attending the gala—but then again, you wouldn't know that, would you? I haven't seen a save-the-date card yet, and those should've gone out months ago. Maybe if you stopped locking lips long enough to look at a calendar, you would've noticed your staff wasn't up to par."

"I'm sorry," I mumbled. "It's been a busy few months."

A newly disgruntled Amanda clicked her heels straight out the front door while her husband, looking a little shell-shocked, followed closely behind. Mrs. Dulcet bustled about getting them into an idling limo while we waited inside the hall.

Dane turned to me as soon as Mrs. Dulcet closed the door. "Thank you," he said. "You didn't have to do that."

"How about we have some coffee while you tell me *exactly* what event I'm planning?" I suggested. "The more caffeine the better."

"I'll prepare coffee and a few bites," Mrs. Dulcet said before scurrying off. "Seat yourselves, please."

"I'm sorry about everything," Dane said. "My mother can be difficult."

"You could use that word to describe her, I suppose."

"And many other words that are less kind," he said evenly, a half smile turning his normally serious features into a lighter expression. "But she's my mother, and I do love her, so I'll refrain. She's just very prejudiced against anyone who didn't grow up in her world. Or really, anyone who doesn't believe exactly the same things she does."

"I understand."

"It's a hard line to walk," he said, a hint of uncertainty in his voice. "I am not *glad* she felt the need to go stay with my Uncle Anders instead of remaining at the castle, but if she can't respect my staff, I don't believe she belongs here, either."

I nodded, though I couldn't bring myself to agree. "I'm sorry if I caused any issues between you and your mother. I didn't intend to do anything of the sort."

"Lola, none of this—none of *that*—was your fault. Can we please forget about it and move on? I'd prefer to focus on the busy day we have ahead." Dane looked up as Mrs. Dulcet brought out oatmeal and grapefruit. "We already had a busy schedule, and now there's...Andrea, too."

"Sure," I said. "But first, how about some details on this event I'm supposed to have planned in two weeks?"

"Oh, right." Dane looked at his food. "I forgot about that."

"Dane, you *never* forget about anything business related."

"I don't understand these events, so they're not my first priority."

"Charity dinners? Well, you have a bunch of people pay a boat-load of money to show up and eat fancy green beans off gold-lined plates. Donate money to charity. Rinse and repeat."

He grinned, actually grinned, which gave me a rush. I liked making him smile. "Well, we can start by..." he trailed off mid-sentence. Then he set his fork on his plate and stared into his oatmeal as if it were a crystal ball.

"Dane?" I waved a hand from my end of the table. "What's wrong? Don't let your mother bother you about this. I'll help you get everything pulled together in time, I promise."

"I know, but I haven't even thanked you for what you did in front of my mother. That was generous of you," he said gruffly. "You didn't need to take the fall for my mistake."

"It's no problem," I said, reaching for another piece of grapefruit as a distraction. "She already had it out for me, so it was just easier."

He stood up then, his chair skidding as it flew back from the table. He crossed the room in a few short steps, and before I could take a breath, he had my face in his palms and his mouth on mine. I sighed into the kiss, his lips molded to mine as his warmth spread to every inch of my body.

Dane had never kissed me like that before. It was as if he'd taken whatever rulebook he lived by and thrown it out the window. For the first time, I sensed true passion—real, unbridled energy that he poured into the moment with me.

My arms curved around his neck as I fell mindlessly into him, my thoughts fading to black as I sank a little bit more in love with Dane Clark. *Love.* There was that word again, the word I couldn't, wouldn't yet address. The situation was too confusing, too messy, and all I knew was that his hands against my skin, his lips on my mouth—all of it was right.

"I managed to hide a container of cookies, and—" Mrs. Dulcet stopped abruptly as she entered the room. "Sorry. *Sorry.*"

Dane straightened, an almost goofy smile plastered on his face. His hand never once left my back, his thumb drawing tiny circles against the tender skin at the base of my neck. "Bring in the cookies, please."

Mrs. Dulcet blushed tickle-me-pink, set the cookies on the edge of the table closest to me. "Carry on, carry on," she said, gesturing as she left the room. "I was never here."

"Well," Dane said once we were alone again, his voice rough as he struggled to regain his former composure. "I think we should get started on the charity event."

I nodded. "Dane," I hesitated. "I hate to ask, but what is happening with Andrea's case?"

"The police are looking into it." Dane's shoulders stiffened as he surveyed me. "I intend to fully cooperate with them and lend assistance where needed. I have nothing to hide. In the meantime, I believe the only choice is to continue business as usual."

"Of course," I said, turning my gaze quickly onto the stack of papers he slid before me. "Let's get started."

# Chapter 7

HOURS LATER, I LIFTED my head from a stack of scribbled Post It notes, ready to call it quits for the day. Or longer. Forever. Planning a party of this caliber wasn't for the faint of heart. Setting out paper napkins and grilling a few brats and dogs wasn't on the agenda for an event this size—forty investors, a hundred folks from the charity, press, and more.

My phone buzzed then, preventing me from banging my head against the desk. "Hey, Babs," I said, reading the name across the screen. "You just saved me from a concussion."

"Great," she chirped. "I love when that happens. Do you have a pen?"

"Yes, along with enough Post Its to build an igloo."

"You use snow for that, Pink. Anyway, I've got something for you."

"About Andrea?"

"Yes. It's like you said—she's a local model. Her biggest gig to date has been this PR campaign for the self-driving cars she's teaming up with Clark Company on—she's in a recurring role on it and seems to have drawn some attention to herself. Seems she's made enough of a name that she got a gig in one of the main fashion shows that'll be running during the Sunshine Shore festivities."

"I guess we've got a rising star on our hands."

"That's not all. Her parents? Total wackadoodles," she said. "They've been arrested about twenty times in the last ten years. They're living a very experimental lifestyle."

I raised an eyebrow and scribbled furiously. "What sort of arrests—violent stuff?"

"None of it's violent. In fact, it's very peaceful. I think they're ingesting a few too many special brownies, and we're not talking about Mrs. Fredericks's brownies that are made with love, if you catch my drift. Just last month they spent a night in jail because they wouldn't get out of the highway during a protest."

"What cause do they feel so strongly about protesting to get arrested?"

"Oh, you name it, they've got their hands in it. Women's rights, men's rights, gay rights, black rights, white, brown, yellow, short, tall, animal, human...you *name* it, they care about it. They're just so full of love and brownies they join every protest that comes to the coast."

"It's a lifestyle for them?"

"I guess so. Must get a thrill out of it. Anyway, they don't live on the Sunshine Shore—no surprise there. They live in Glassrock."

"That's far!"

"It's twenty minutes by car."

"I don't have a car, and it's a tough bike ride. There's hardly a trail, and where there is a trail, it is jagged rock."

"I'll go with you," Babs offered. "I don't have a client meeting until five. I can pick you up in fifteen minutes."

"What's the catch?"

"There's no catch," Babs said a little too sweetly. At my extended silence, she sighed. "Fine. They have a Froth & Foam on the way there, and I want a root beer float."

I considered it, but then shook my head. Realizing she couldn't see that, I spoke instead. "No, Babs. I don't want to get you into this. I'm doing it as a favor for Dane—and I haven't even mentioned it to him yet. I don't want to involve you."

"He doesn't *know*?"

"No," I whispered as footsteps approached in the hallway. "He'd never ask for help with something like this."

"What's he going to say when he finds out? Because you know he will."

"Oh, um..." I hesitated, dragging my gaze from the floor up to a pair of bright blue eyes that stared intensely back at me. "You know, nothing much. Gotta go."

"Cough if he's standing over you."

I coughed enough to hack up a lung. I stopped only when Dane's face crinkled in concern.

"Bye, Babs," I said. "Talk to you later."

"I know you'll change your mind. This delay caused my price to increase," Babs said quickly before I could hang up. "When you show up at my office begging for a ride, you better have two coffee mugs you stole from me ready to return and five bucks."

"Why five bucks?"

"Root beer float," she said, and then disconnected.

"Who was that?" Dane entered the room with painstaking patience, his steps slow, deliberate. "Babs?"

"How'd you know?" I squeaked. "Er, I guess I said her name."

"What were you talking about?"

"Life."

"And death?"

I blanched. "What do you mean?"

Silence rang in my ears as Dane made his way across his office, stopping when he reached the mahogany desk. Resting his knuckles on the wood, he leaned over it, his nose inches from mine. "Were you, or were you not, just having a conversation about Andrea's death?"

From my place at the head of the desk, I tried to look confident. But Dane Clark had eyes that could pierce solid metal, and I wasn't nearly that tough. I melted in two seconds flat. "I promise I was going to tell you! We haven't done anything yet except ask around a tiny bit."

He rose to his full height, the lean, strong muscles intimidating in his quiet concentration. "Go ahead then and tell me what you found."

"Dane, don't be mad," I pleaded, sensing a chilliness in his voice. "The police think you killed someone, and you didn't. That's not right. I know you'd never ask me to look into it, so I was just trying to help."

"I have my people on it, Lola. Do you really think I'd just sit around and do nothing?"

"Well, how much do your people care?"

"Quite a lot," Dane said. "I'm paying them quite handsomely—I always have, I always will. If they know what's best for them, they'll care very, very much."

"About money," I said quietly. "But what about you?"

Dane blinked as if he didn't quite understand. He took his time to think, analyzing the look on my face and the words on my lips. "What does that have to do with anything?"

His question, though logical, surprised me. "Well," I began. "I'm not sure."

Dane perched against the edge of his desk, and I was temporarily distracted by the view. He looked handsome there, corporate and professional with an edge of something more. Something riveting that stole my attention and, if my suspicions were correct, wouldn't be letting go anytime soon.

"What I'm trying to say, Dane, is that I care more about you than some lawyer who's hanging around for a fat paycheck. Sorry—but it's true. I'm here because I like you. And that means I'm not going to give up. Ever."

"Neither are my lawyers."

I blew out a breath of exasperation. "I'm not telling you to take your lawyers or the police off the case. I'm just saying that I can't sit around and do nothing while you're falsely accused of murder."

"You're planning a party. That's something."

"False. I'm *trying* to plan a party. Every single venue worth booking is full for months. At this rate, we'll be having it in your backyard."

"No—nothing within Castlewood grounds."

"Unless you have other ideas..." I raised my hands. "I'm running out of options."

"What can I do?"

I shook my head. "I'll figure it out. Right now, though, I have to go."

"Where?"

"I'm meeting Babs."

"Does it have to do with Andrea?"

Pushing myself to stand, I dragged my gaze to meet his. "Yes."

"Lola—"

"Look—I *know* you would never hurt somebody. Do your lawyers know that like I do? Dane, I hate to say it, but the cops think you're guilty. What do your lawyers think?"

Dane's eyes watched me as I paced to the other side of the desk, squeezing between him and the edge of it. We were a breath apart.

"I'm not letting anything happen to you. I'm your *Personal Assistant*," I said with a smile. "And if you go to jail, I lose my job."

The corner of his mouth twitched up in a smile. "And you need money to finish Shades of Pink."

"Yes," I said. "That too."

Dane's hand came up to brush along my collar bone. The motion was surprisingly sensitive, and I shivered. His hand paused. "What's wrong?"

"Nothing." I hung my head, my hand coming up to rest over his. The beat of my heart pulsed underneath our fingers. "But I'm going to look into this one way or another. Whether you like it or not, I care about keeping you out of jail because I—" The forbidden four-letter word hung on the tip of my tongue, but I couldn't say it. "I like you. Which means you have two options: I sneak around in secret on my own time or—"

"I don't like that option."

"Then let me finish," I said with the start of a smile. "I keep you in the loop with where I'm going on my little investigation and what I'm doing. You don't have to like it, but you'll know where I am."

"What about a third option?"

"Which is?"

"You let me come with you."

"I'm sorry," I said. "That doesn't work. The cops think you're guilty. If you're wandering around town looking up Andrea's family and friends, that will be suspicious."

"But—"

"No," I said, returning Dane's hand to his side and straightening the collar of his shirt. "You have meetings, and so do I. Plus, I need to get Babs's advice on this whole party business."

"I can hire someone else to do it," Dane said. "A company or a venue. With enough money, anyone has an opening in their schedule."

"Absolutely not."

"You're stubborn."

"So they say." We shared a smile, but it left my face as I walked toward the door. "Give me until the end of the week. If I can't come up with anything suitable for your mother, I'll hand over the reins to whatever company you want."

He nodded, his eyes struggling to read mine. "Fine," he said. "And Lola?"

I turned at the doorway, raising an eyebrow. "Yes?"

"Thank you."

I nodded, then left Dane leaning against the edge of his desk. As I walked down the hallway, I could feel his eyes on my back. When I turned around before I started down the stairs, he raised a hand in a wave, a stiff wave that was now familiar.

I shook my head at him and laughed. Whatever weird, strange thing was happening between us didn't make the slightest bit of sense. All I knew was that I liked it.

# Chapter 8

"HOLD IT RIGHT THERE," Babs said, raising her cell phone. "I need to document this."

She snapped a picture, the flash so bright I blinked. "Stop it!" I said. "I don't want this moment documented."

"Say it," Babs said, grinning behind her office desk. "Say it loud enough for the receptionist to hear you."

I cleared my throat and glanced down at the two mugs in my hands. One of them had a smiling Santa's face on it, the other a gigantic pumpkin. "I stole your mugs."

"And?"

"And I promise I'll buy you a root beer float if you drive me to Glassrock."

Babs squealed and clapped her hands. "Hooray! Martie, we'll be right back! I have an errand to run with Lola."

"You have a client meeting at five," Martie said. "Be back before then. And have fun."

It took twenty minutes to get in the car, take the wrong exit three times, and purchase root beer floats from the longest line in fast food history.

"Now we're really on our way," Babs said, slurping on her beverage. "So, give me the scoop. Why'd you decide to come to Mama Babs for help?"

"I didn't feel like biking."

"Yeah, well, there's something else. You're stubborn enough to bike these roads."

I looked ahead at the winding, twisted rocky paths that seemed to hover in the air above a hundred yard drop straight to the ocean. No railings anywhere on these roads.

"Fine," I sighed. "There's one more thing. A party."

"*Ooh*! Did Dane ask you to go as his date?"

"No," I said. "The other way around. I'm planning it for his company. It's a charity gala in two weeks that's supposed to be this whole fancy shebang with almost two hundred people in attendance. Rich people who expect things like caviar and champagne or—well, I don't even know what they expect. I'm so out of my league, Babs!"

"Don't worry. We'll get it sorted out."

"Did you hear me? It's in two weeks."

"That's during the hubbub of the Sunshine Shore festival!" Babs's lips pinched together. "Nothing will be available then in terms of venues or caterers. Why the short notice?"

"Because Dane completely forgot about it. He's not interested in anything public. Parties, media, whatever else he's required to do, so it *slipped his mind*, and if his mother hadn't reminded us this morning, he would've never remembered."

"So, you saw his mom again?"

"Yes, and it sucked. She's not staying at the house anymore because she thinks it's a brothel. She and Mr. Clark went to stay with Dane's uncle."

Babs, in the middle of sipping her float through a straw, laughed so hard the drink bubbled at the surface. "Well, that's handy. Now you can sleep over."

"I'm not sleeping anywhere. I have this party to plan, a murder to look into..." I massaged my forehead. "I'm not cut out for a high intensity career."

"You're more cut out for it than anyone I know. Here, write this number down." Babs paused while I fished out a notebook and pencil from my purse. Once she'd spilled the digits, she reached over and tapped it with a manicured finger. "Make yourself an appointment to get your hair done."

"I don't have time—"

"Melinda, the best stylist in town, runs a wedding planning business on the side. She hates doing it though, so she refuses to plan a party for anyone but her family these days. But she is the *best*."

"I don't understand."

"Her first love is styling hair," Babs said. "Make yourself a long appointment—a perm or highlights or something—and get her talking. Mention you're struggling to plan an event and the suggestions will start flowing. She'll know where to look and what to book, I guarantee it."

"But I've looked into all the venues. They're booked."

"Not these." Babs shook her head. "She finds these unique, charming little places that nobody could ever imagine might be beautiful. Once she's got her hands on it though, the setting transforms like magic."

"That sounds a little too much like a fairytale to me."

"It *works*! I gave my aunt the same recommendation," Babs said. "She ended up dying her hair five different times in three months in Melinda's chair, but she had her entire wedding planned with her help. It was actually cheaper than hiring a wedding planner."

"Fine," I said. "I suppose it can't hurt, and I need a haircut."

"Dial." Babs held her phone out. "Now. She books up quickly, so let's see if anything's open."

I pressed the green call button despite all my doubts. If nothing else, I'd get a haircut out of the deal—and if I was running the social event of the season in less than two weeks, it couldn't hurt to spice things up.

"Hello?" I asked when a perky receptionist answered. "I'm looking for an appointment with Melinda tomorrow."

"Oh, I'm sorry. Melinda is full for weeks but let me double check." She paused and tapped on a few keys. "Actually, we have one appointment at nine that just opened due to a cancellation. Will that work? What service are you looking to have done?"

"That's perfect! Which service?" I glanced at Babs. "What are your longest appointments? Sure, a perm sounds great—see you tomorrow."

When I hung up and handed the phone back to Babs, she had a wide-eyed gaze fixed on me. "What the hell did you just do?"

"I made an appointment." I shrugged. "Just like you said."

"A *perm*?"

"It was the longest option, and I need a lot of advice."

"Perms are so nineties!"

I shifted under her look of horror. "I'll ask for a tame one."

"Fine," Babs said. "But when you come out looking like a poodle, don't blame me."

"A poodle?" I said faintly, but Babs had already parked the car and climbed out. "Hold on, a poodle? I can't look like a poodle. Should I cancel?"

"Nope," Babs said. "You need the advice."

"Well, what should I do?"

She scanned me up and down. "Pray to the curly gods that they take care of you tomorrow."

I stared open-mouthed after her as she marched into Glassrock, a community that had never been known for luxurious mansions or fancy beaches. Instead, as the name suggested, this city had been built on a large, barren rock, and the atmosphere reflected its origins.

The last time I'd been here, it was to face off with Graham Industries—a company that'd tried to ruin my boss's entire business, along with his reputation. Though they hadn't succeeded, it'd left me with a bitter taste in my mouth for the whole place.

This time, we stuck to the residential area and found most of the homes to be ramshackle little fixtures. Many people lived in clusters of trailers, their small, communal yards interspersed with clothing lines, bonfire pits, and random junk such as spare tires and halfway spray-painted bicycles. There wasn't even a hotel in town, since this wasn't a place where tourists stopped.

Crime rates had skyrocketed in this area of town, and I gave a nervous shiver as I stepped from Babs's vehicle, feeling glad I hadn't let my stubbornness win out—better I didn't bike around these parts. The only activity I could see from our place in the parking lot consisted of one or two women hanging clothes on the line. The rest of the community disappeared the second outsiders arrived. It was quiet here, too quiet.

"Babs," I whispered. "It doesn't feel right to be here."

Babs put a hand on her hip. "Maybe not, but if you want to meet Andrea's parents, you'll follow me to their trailer. Are you coming? I swear, Lola, if you made me drive all the way out here for nothing, you're buying me a burger and a milkshake on the way back."

I raised my eyes to the sky, shook my head, and followed her through a beaten-down gate that had *Beware of Dog* signs tacked on every square inch of space. "You drive a hard bargain."

"You're still buying me that burger," Babs said. "For the tip on Melinda."

"Sure, if we make it out of Glassrock alive."

Babs's eyes glittered with the thrill of it all. "In order to get out, we have to get *in*. Come on, I see their home."

I sent a prayer up to the curly gods and anyone else who was listening. And for the briefest moment, I debated following Dane's advice and letting the lawyers and cops handle everything.

Then I remembered the quiet smile to curve his lips, the softness hidden in his icy blue eyes, and the huge heart behind his cold exterior. With a shuddering breath, I stepped through the gates.

# Chapter 9

"I DON'T KNOW WHERE we went wrong," Amaliyah Ricker, Andrea's mother, informed us as she sat back on the couch. "But something went wrong between the time she was born, and the time she left us."

Amaliyah's husband, Bill, rested a hand on his wife's knee. "No clue," he said, exhaling a huge breath of smoke. "She used to be such a good girl."

"Really," I said, waving a hand in front of my face to clear the scent of illegal plants that were most definitely growing by the couple's window. "Tell me about those days. What was different? What made her go from being a good girl to... not being one?"

Amaliyah Ricker looked like a woman who'd experienced a good chunk of life's illegal offerings. Her skin was tanned and ragged, and even as we spoke she puffed on a substance that wasn't allowed in most states. Stringy hair framed her face, her eyes a dull shade of gray. "She got all C's in school. She was going someplace. Most kids around here don't even *go* to school, but not our girl—she showed up, *and* she tried."

"What did she want to do when she grew up?" Babs asked. "Did she ever say?"

"She wanted to be a star," her dad said. "She wanted to be rich and famous more than anything."

I nodded, scribbling a few things down on the notepad. "We're so sorry—again—for your loss. I can't imagine what you must be going through."

"Me neither," Amaliyah said. "It's like I'm in this haze. None of it seems real."

"I bet," Babs muttered for my ears only. "I think I'm in her haze too. The whole place is a hazy cloud."

"When you said she wanted to be rich, what did you mean?" I asked. "I think it's fair to say that most people want to be comfortable in their lifestyle."

Rick shook his head. "She hated our life. Hated everything about it. She couldn't get out of here fast enough. We couldn't afford college, but she went anyway and tried to pay on her own, even though we told her it wasn't worth it. One semester, and then she dropped out. What did she study? *Men*. Rich ones."

Her mother nodded. "We never heard why she dropped out. She'd cut ties with us by that point, but I always assumed she'd met some guy who'd be a doctor or a fancy-ass lawyer out for blood."

I hid a small smile as Babs frowned at Amaliyah's assessment of her career. "Yeah, those lawyer types are the worst," I said, hurrying to agree, even as Babs pinched the back of my arm. "Did you ever find out if she'd met someone?"

"I'm sure she did," Mrs. Ricker said. "But I don't know if it was before or after she left school."

"Why did Andrea cut ties in the first place?"

"She was embarrassed of us," Mr. Ricker said, so matter-of-factly it rang sad, but true. "We live a freestyle life. We go where the wind blows us and work when jobs speak to our souls. Sometimes, if there's no job speakin' to my heart, I don't work for a year, and Andrea—she didn't like having to go without."

I hurt inside, a rush of sympathy for both parties. My mom might not have been interested in sticking around for my life, but Dotty had been there—always. We never had a lot of money or all of the trendy things, but our lives had been full.

For the Rickers to lose their daughter, for Andrea to grow up with such want—the circumstances were devastating. I wasn't a psychologist, but it was pretty easy to see why Andrea sought the company of wealthy, respectable men with booming careers. I could hardly blame her.

"And then she met this someone," I prompted.

"He wasn't good for her," Amaliyah said, and her husband shook his head in agreement. "He wasn't good for anyone. Nothing but trouble."

"What sort of trouble?" I asked. "And apologies for asking, but could he have had a motive to kill your daughter?"

"Nobody had a motive to kill our daughter," Mr. Ricker said, his words twisted in anger. "She might not have liked us, but she was a good person. She had her issues—we all do—but she wouldn't have hurt anyone. Not on purpose. If you're looking for a reason someone would've wanted her dead, you won't find one."

"But the truth is that she was murdered," Babs said gently. "And that's a horrible, horrible thing. We're trying to find the person responsible for it, so any information you have might be helpful."

"Maybe she got mixed up in something. My husband is right. She is—" Amaliyah hesitated—"she *was* a nice girl. She wouldn't get in trouble on purpose. However, if a man with a pretty face and a fat wallet were involved, she might have let herself be influenced. She always did follow trends. She wanted to be *in* with the cool kids, and we could never provide that for her. She craved it all her life."

"Do you have a name?" I pressed. "Anything we might be able to identify him by?"

"Ryan Lexington," Mr. Ricker said, and his wife's face lit in surprise. "I remember it, though we met him only once. Andrea brought him around a few years back." He paused and did some mental calculations. "Andrea dropped out of school at nineteen, and it was right around then. She had just turned twenty-five, so that would've made it about five or six years ago."

"Why did they stop by?" I asked. "Just for a visit?"

"Oh, *no*," Amaliyah said with a ghosted smile. "She had this blanket she'd gotten some time before from her grandmother, my mother. Andrea always did love that thing."

"She stopped by to pick up a blanket?" Babs asked, raising an eyebrow. "Really?"

"You don't understand. My mother was everything that Andrea wanted to be. Wealthy, polished, a member of the highest of societies," Amaliyah said, a tornado of emotions in her eyes. "Andrea loved her dearly—she *idolized* her."

"Is she still a part of Andrea's life?" I asked. "Do you know where we could find her?"

"She passed away when Andrea was ten," Mrs. Ricker said. "Unfortunately, Andrea was old enough to remember the glamorous parts of her grandmother. But she was too young to remember the ugliness."

"She was a horrible woman," Mr. Ricker agreed. "I hate to speak ill of my mother-in-law, but she treated Amaliyah like dirt. Her own daughter was never good enough for her. I suspect that's a reason Andrea became so fascinated with wealth at a young age—she wanted to be her grandmother, while we wanted to put as much distance between ourselves and Amaliyah's mother as possible."

Mrs. Ricker nodded. "When my mother died, she left us a chunk of her money. Not much compared to her overall wealth, but enough. I didn't want it though, couldn't take it. We put a little aside for Andrea's funds and donated the rest to charity."

"Andrea resented us after that," Mr. Ricker continued. "Even though Andrea was too young to truly understand, she knew. Somehow, she knew we'd given away her chance at wealth, and I don't think she ever forgave us." Tears sparked in Mr. Ricker's eyes. "I wish things had been different, but they weren't. We made our choices, and Andrea didn't like them. So, she left."

"I'm sorry," I said, struggling not to cough in the increasing cloud of smoke. "I'm so sorry."

Amaliyah took a few puffs of her husband's cigarette. As she blew out a steady stream of smoke, she shook her head. "Ryan promised her wealth, but he wasn't rich like my mother. My mother had *old* wealth—the kind of money that was so deeply ingrained into her veins that it was a part of who she *was*."

"Ryan had new wealth." Mr. Ricker nodded as if it disgusted him. "Flashy cars, flighty attitude, the stuff that goes to a person's head. *That's* the sort of wealth Ryan had. Unfortunately, Andrea didn't realize that Ryan promised her the moon and gave her its shadow."

"She could have shot for the stars on her own," Mrs. Ricker said. "But instead she was an accessory to *him*. Ryan talked a big game, but he couldn't deliver on it. He'd never have been able to take care of Andrea like she wanted. It was doomed from the start. But he was handsome and confident, and that combination, with a bit of money, can be quite persuasive. Andrea fell for him, and she fell hard."

"What she didn't see coming was the possessiveness," Mr. Ricker said. "The bursts of anger. The kid had a hot head—rich and cocky—and that's what we saw. By the time Andrea figured it out, it was too late."

"Too late?" My blood chilled. "What do you mean, too late? I thought you didn't know much about him, but it sounds like you knew the situation fairly well."

"She called me once," Amaliyah said. "I wasn't home. She left a message crying, asking what she could do to leave. To get out of Ryan's life for good. The rest of the puzzle pieces we put together on our own."

Amaliyah lapsed into silence. Glancing at Babs, I waited, we both did, for Amaliyah to wipe her eyes with an old, frayed flannel blanket that hung over the edge of the couch.

"I was in the garden and missed it. I missed the last call my daughter made to me," she said. "By the time I called her back, she wanted nothing to do with me. She even sent me a letter saying that everything was sorted, and that she and Ryan had decided to get married—and not to wait for an invitation."

"That's when we knew it was over between her and us," Mr. Ricker said. "For good. We never heard from her again."

I sucked in a big gulp of air, the story beginning an ache in my soul. But I couldn't allow it to show on my face, not now. We needed to find a murderer, and Ryan was looking more and more likely a candidate by the second. "How long ago was the phone call?"

"A year ago," Mrs. Ricker said. "I don't know if they ever got married. From everything I could find, it doesn't appear they did. But what do I know?"

Babs and I shared a glance, and I knew we were thinking the same thing. What if Andrea had decided she wanted out of the relationship and Ryan hadn't been as enthusiastic about the idea? Would he have been upset enough to hurt her? Kill her, even? It still didn't explain the murder weapon, but a lot of pieces had yet to be connected.

"Do you know where he lives?" I asked Mrs. Ricker. "I think we'd like to pay Ryan a visit."

"You girls watch your step," Mr. Ricker said, a severe frown on his face. "That man is trouble. His temper is nothing to mess with."

"I understand," I said quietly. "Thank you for your help."

"He lives outside of the Sunshine Shore," Mrs. Ricker said. "That's all I know. I'm sorry I can't help you more."

On an impulse, I crossed the open space and gave Mrs. Ricker a hug. Despite the smoke hanging heavy in the air, she smelled like Dawn soap and fresh lemons. "I'm sorry for your loss. We'll find out what happened to her, I promise."

Amaliyah's eyes were damp as she pulled out of the hug and patted my cheek with a wrinkled hand. "Thank you."

After saying goodbye to the Rickers, Babs and I climbed back into her vehicle, pleased to see that it still had all of its wheels. In this neighborhood, one could never be certain.

"Well," Babs said. "Things don't look good for Ryan Lexington. I don't think I'm up for another emotional visit quite yet, though. I need my heart to stop pumping for a second. How about we grab burgers first? In fact, let's pick up enough for the construction crew and swing by your place with a meal for the boys?"

"You just want to stare at Johnny."

"Sue me. He's nice to look at and that meeting left me sad. I want to feel happy again and stare at biceps—is that *so* wrong?"

"The burgers are on you then," I said. "I'll trade you burgers for twenty minutes of uninterrupted stare-time."

Babs looked at her watch. "I've got time before my client meeting. Make it thirty minutes, and you've got a deal."

# Chapter 10

BABS CAME, SAW, AND left in a flurry of stubbed toes and flustered arm waving. Johnny and his crew showed their appreciation for the burgers with a huge round of man-hugs that sent Babs bumbling out the door, forgetting all about her promised thirty minutes of stare time at my construction crew.

"Your friend is hot," Johnny said, staring after Babs as she climbed into her car and drove off. "Seems funny, too. Is she single?"

"She's unattached," I confirmed, grinning through my teeth. "And she's super smart—a lawyer."

"No kidding." Johnny shook his head and let out a low whistle.

I shut the door. "Why don't you ask her out on a real date so she doesn't have to come over here and stare?"

"Is that what she was doing?" A cheesy grin turned Johnny's lips upward. "I think I might, if that's alright with you."

"Fine by me, but then again, you don't need my permission." I plopped down in the chair and rested my head in my hands. "Can you tell me one thing, Johnny? Why are men so confusing?"

"Did someone say something to you?" Johnny put down his hammer, his stare landing on me in a way that told me to say the word, and he'd pick that hammer right back up and use it on the guy who'd done me wrong. "Why you looking so blue, Pink?"

"It's nothing," I said, my mind flashing back to Dane Clark and his smoking hot kisses, his meaningful glances, and then his lack of follow up. "*Men.*"

"*We're* confusing?" Johnny thumbed at himself, then shook his head. "Nope. *Women* are confusing. We're just dumb."

"Maybe."

"Is this about that rich guy you're working for?"

My feathers ruffled some. "He's *way* more than rich, Johnny. Don't say stuff like that. He is brilliant. And he's handsome, and successful, and he's just..." I trailed off, realizing that I sounded like a high school girl on a crush. "He's perfect."

Johnny was staring at me with such a wide grin on his face that I stopped short.

"Miss Pink," he drawled. "I think you're in love."

"You're a nut, Johnny."

"Am I?"

I hesitated. "I don't know, maybe."

"Look, Lola—it might not be my place to comment, but obviously you wanted to talk about him, or you wouldn't have started up." Johnny picked up his hammer and turned toward the wall, examining where he'd left off. "The dude is *weird*. I've met him. And to me, it sounds like you love his weirdness more than his normalness—if that ain't love, I don't know what is."

"Holy guacamole." I threw myself across the room and landed in Dotty's chair in a heap. "I'm in *love*. Johnny, I can't be in love! He's still my boss. What do I do *now*?"

He shrugged, then let the hammer fly. It cracked loud against the wall. "I suppose you tell him."

"That's a horrible idea. He'll run away."

"If he's running away from you, babe, that's his problem." Johnny raised a shoulder. "A real man ain't afraid to say what's in his heart, and I'm sticking to it."

"You haven't told Babs how you feel."

"Lola, I just found out her name this morning. She's been showing up and staring at me for a few days, and that's the extent of our relationship." He laughed. "That ain't love. Not yet."

"Maybe someday?"

He raised the hammer and smacked the wall again. "I'm gonna ask her out on a date first, and we'll see how that goes."

"Men."

"What'd I do now?"

I was saved from responding by a knock on the door. Peeling my body off the chair, I made my way to the front entrance and yanked the handle to reveal none other than my former guest, Richard. He stood on my front steps holding a bouquet of roses. A very battered bouquet of roses.

"*She* did this! She did this to me, to the roses, and to my heart." Richard pushed his small figure into the storeroom—again without an invitation—and turned to face me. "She destroyed me. *Again.*"

"What'd *she* do?" I asked wearily. "And why do you smell like beer?"

"I'm Irish," he said. "I own a brewery. Don't worry though, I walked here. I just needed to have a beer to calm down after what happened with Stephanie."

Johnny made a noise of surprise, pausing with his hammer halfway to the nail.

"What are you looking at, man?" Richard looked at Johnny, who resumed whacking the wall with renewed force. "You don't have women problems?"

Johnny returned the hammer to the toolbox, gave me a look of sympathy, then muttered something about the bathroom. He disappeared to the rear of the house before Richard gathered his thoughts.

"What did Stephanie do this time?" I snapped my fingers to get Richard's attention since he was about as focused as a puppy on a sugar high. At the moment, he was busy shooting daggers with his eyes at Johnny's retreating back.

"Weren't you listening?" Richard held up the roses, the petals limp and falling to the ground with every motion. "First, she stomped on the roses, then she battered my heart."

"Is that the full story?"

"Yes," he said. "I showed up this morning with a plan. Just like you told me. I was gonna give her flowers and ask her out on a real date. I showed up, asked her out, and she shut the door in my face after stomping a few times on the flowers. I paid *six bucks* for these."

"You found roses for six bucks? That's cheap."

"I stole a few of them from Mrs. Fredericks's garden because she's got lots of them anyway, and she won't miss a few. Plus, it was for a good cause. The rest of them I found on sale."

"Okay," I said, noting the browned edges. "Well, I suppose the fact that you bought *some* of the flowers is a start. Tell me—what exactly did you say when you showed up?"

"I told her real respectfully that I loved her."

"Word for word, Richard. What did you say?"

"Okay, let me think." Richard squinted his eyes shut as his brain worked really, really hard. Then his eyes flashed open. "I walked up to the door, knocked, and she opened it. Then I says, *Hey woman, here are your damn roses.*"

It was my turn to close my eyes. "That'll do it, Richard."

"Oh, crap," Richard said, smacking a hand to his forehead. "You told me not to call her woman."

"That's right."

"I just don't get it!" He threw his hands in the air. "If you said to me, *hey, man, here are your flowers*, I'd be all like, *thank you, Lola.*"

"It doesn't work like that," I said sternly. "And if you come to me expecting advice, you have to listen. I'm going to stop helping you if you can't listen to the words I say."

Richard shook his head, an apologetic look crossing his face as his eyes narrowed in pain. "I'm so sorry. I screwed this one up bigtime. What can I do to fix it?"

"Don't call her *woman* and don't swear when you give her flowers. That would be the most basic of starting points."

"But those words just slip out. I'm fluent in profanity. At least, that's what my mom used to say to my teachers when I'd get sent to the principal's office. I can't help it!"

"Then write her a card," I said, "and leave it on the front porch with the flowers. Take some time to write down how you really feel. Using really nice, respectful words."

"Can you do it for me?"

"What, write the card?" I shook my head. "Nope. This is something you'll have to do on your own."

"I've got it!" Richard raised the roses above his head like the statue of liberty. "I'm going to write her a poem. I've always had a way with words. My mom said that too."

"Only if you can write a poem that speaks from your heart. I can see that you want to fight for her, Richard," I admitted, "but you'll have to allow her to see that, too. You have to tell her how you feel *inside*."

"You got it," Richard said with a salute. Then he extended the browning roses toward me and shoved them into my hands. "These are for you, Miss Pink. Thank you, thank you. I've gotta put my poet hat on."

"Good luck," I said weakly as Richard flew out the door. A movement from the corner caught my eye, and I turned to catch Johnny staring at me, hanging onto every word. "What are *you* looking at?"

"You are good at this love business," Johnny said. "Any advice for me?"

"You want to ask Babs out?" I narrowed my eyes at him. "You'd better treat her like a queen—and that's not advice, it's a threat."

"I'd never dream of treating her any other way."

I sized him up for a moment and determined he was telling the truth. "Then she's single and interested. And here's her cell phone number."

"I don't need the number from you." Johnny rose to his feet with a crooked smile. "What do you say about my taking a long lunch break, boss? I've gotta see a girl about a date."

"Sure." I threw my arms up. "Go ahead. It seems that everyone except the love guru can get a date around here."

Johnny walked over and rested a hand on my shoulder. "Your turn will come, Pink. And when it does, you just make sure he's worth it, okay? You deserve that much."

I nodded. "Go get her, Johnny."

I CRAWLED INTO BED early that night, having emailed Dane to let him know I'd be working from home the rest of the afternoon. It was nine o'clock before I'd exhausted my list of venues and catering places within fifty miles of the Sunshine Shore and once again, struck out on the list.

Not a single venue promised potential for the charity gala. It wasn't a matter of cost, either, it was a matter of availability. The festivities planned for the Sunshine Shore festival—fashion shows, carnivals, dinners and lunches and breakfasts and happy hours—had eaten up most available resources nearby. I was left scrambling with the crumbs.

The only catering company who'd volunteered to do the party on short notice was a sushi place that had a Grade B rating. One search on Google told me that the restaurant had sent ten people home with food poisoning in just the past month. I briefly wondered what Mrs. Clark would say if I booked them. The thought brought a brief smile to my face before it terrified me completely, and I shut down the computer.

In its place, I picked up my phone and dialed the castle. "Hi Dane," I said when he answered. "I am running out of options on the venue. I'm tearing my hair out over here. I really hate to admit it, but I thought I'd give you the heads up."

"Why didn't you come back this afternoon?" Dane asked. "I was surprised to receive your email. We missed you here."

"We?"

"Mrs. Dulcet, Gerard. The rest of the staff," he said. "Everyone loves you."

The sentiment was sweet, but it wasn't what I wanted to hear. "What about you?"

"Of course I missed you, too," he said. "And I would've helped with the venue list. Leave it alone, Lola—I'll hire a planner with connections, throw enough money at it, and the problem will go away."

"Nope," I said. "I only called to tell you I'd exhausted my current options, but I'm not done trying. I'm hopeful I'll have an update for you tomorrow."

"Fine, but that's not necessary."

"You gave me until the end of the week, did you not?"

"I did."

"Then give me until the end of the week," I said, smiling on my end of the phone. "Like I said, I have something lined up in the morning that might give me a lead. What's your schedule tomorrow afternoon?"

Dane hardly hesitated before responding. His schedule was as rigid as a cement sidewalk. "I have time set aside to eat from one to one thirty. Then I'll be making the rounds on the Warehouses until three. I have a conference call until four, then swimming until five. Stretching, weights, shower until six. Dinner at six thirty *sharp*."

I gasped. "You have half an hour unaccounted for at six! What will you do with all of your free time?"

He let an extended pause take over. Then, he gave a curious laugh. "Sarcasm?"

I laughed. "Yes. Any chance you could clear an hour for me to show you a few things?"

While he considered, I said a little prayer that Melinda would have recommendations like Babs had promised. If she did, there was no doubt we'd have to move on them soon. Plus, the idea of spending some time alone with Dane tomorrow sent a little sizzle of electric current down my spine.

Finally, he exhaled. "Two to four, I can be free."

"But your call—"

"I'll move it."

"You didn't even ask *why*!"

"You'll be there, right? That's why you're asking?"

"Well, yes," I said. "I want to go over a few things with you."

"Then it doesn't matter what we're doing. I'm happy to go anywhere with you."

Whatever feelings of frustration had cropped up earlier this afternoon in front of Johnny evaporated on the spot. Dane might have his own way of showing affection, but when he did, it was the best thing in the world.

"I'll see you tomorrow then," I said. "I'll meet you at the castle."

"Goodnight, Lola."

I sighed in relief, stretching out in bed with a grin on my face. Before I fell asleep, I sent off one more text to Annalise asking if she'd be up for a haircut tomorrow—aka a gossip buddy in the salon. Babs had already said she'd be busy all day at work. Plus, I'd bothered her enough.

Annalise responded quickly in agreement.

*Tomorrow is a new day*, I thought, shutting off the light. And I had a haircut scheduled, a lead on Andrea's murder, and two hours alone scheduled with my very attractive boss-slash-kissing buddy.

Life could definitely be worse.

# Chapter 11

"YOU'RE GETTING A WHAT?" Annalise stared open-mouthed at me. "Oh, Lola, you *can't* do that to yourself."

I left the smile frozen on my face. "What's wrong with a perm?"

"What made you think a perm was a great idea?"

"Um, lots of things," I said, glancing between Annalise and the front desk receptionist at Salon 68, Melinda's place of employment. "I like curls."

"Oh, Lola," Annalise said again. "I'll say no more—just remember, you got yourself into this."

"Shall I get you seated?" The receptionist glanced between us. "Melinda will be right out. She's getting things ready in the back."

"Great!" I chirped, trying to believe my head could handle a pile of springy curls. In reality, I'd never even considered a perm before yesterday. I mostly wore my hair in some version of a ponytail because styling it often felt like climbing Mount Everest. "I'm excited to try something new. *Experiment.*"

"I'm just getting a haircut," Annalise clarified to the receptionist. "No perms for me. Just a trim. One inch. Nothing drastic."

The receptionist nodded and led us back, getting me situated into a seat that felt a little bit like it an electric chair. Then again, my hair might look fried after whatever was happening on my head, so I held my breath and hoped for the best.

"I just love perms," a squat, jolly woman said emerging from the back room, her hands piled with styling tools. "Volume, *volume,* and more volume, I say!"

The reflection in the mirror told me that if this woman was Melinda, she had the dark hair and tanned skin of someone with

Latin roots. She spoke with the slightest accent that suggested English wasn't her first language.

"Um," I said, pasting a smile on my face as the first round of nerves tingled in my fingers. "How much volume are we talking about?"

"Don't be nervous," Melinda said. "I'll make you look like a star."

"I'm sort of reconsidering this whole perm thing," I admitted. "Is it too late for me to chicken out?"

"You could use some volume in this hair," Melinda said with a frown. "I promise it'll look good. Do you trust me?"

I'd barely exchanged two words with the woman, so I wasn't sure how to answer that. Instead, I dodged it. "Will I look like a poodle?"

She laughed. "Sit back and relax, honey. I'll keep things on the tame side. Just let Mama Melinda work her magic."

"Just a trim for me," Annalise said quickly. "One inch. I have to keep it the same length for the circus."

"Gabriella will be with you in a second," Melinda said to Annalise. Then she sized me up, made some noises with her mouth that suggested it'd been too long since I'd last seen a salon, and ended with a *cluck*. "Don't worry, dear, we'll get this mess mopped up in no time."

"Gee, I didn't know things were so horrible back there," I muttered to Annalise as Melinda left for more tools—presumably something stronger, like a hedge-trimmer.

"You think it's bad now?" Annalise asked. "Wait for the perm."

"You just watch," I said. "You'll be jealous."

Annalise raised her eyebrows, but she didn't have time before Melinda returned, set up her hair products like a tool belt, and launched into an attack on my head.

"Tell me all about yourself," Melinda said as she set to work. "You know, originally, I'm from Mexico. I moved here with my family when I was five, but I didn't make it to the Sunshine Shore until I was twenty-two and fresh out of hair school. I love it here, don't you?"

Melinda didn't give me time to respond, let alone tell her *all about myself*. Instead, she lodged right into a series of stories that explained every detail of her life from her first baby steps to what she'd eaten for breakfast yesterday morning.

"Oh, my, I can really talk when I get going," Melinda said with a laugh. "Can you believe how the time has flown? Time to move you under the dryer."

It'd been almost two hours of Melinda talking nonstop, and I was getting antsy. If I walked out of here with a frizzy head and no leads on a venue for the charity ball, I'd be quite upset.

Meanwhile, Annalise looked trimmed, proper, and pretty as she flipped through one magazine after the next up front. She'd been sending me half smiles all morning. Under normal circumstances, she would've left hours ago out of impatience. The fact that she'd stuck around was a testament to the horrors that would surely be the final product of my hair.

I glared at her as Melinda led me back to the chair and began unwinding my hair from the curlers. "So, do you know the Sunshine Shore well?" I asked, trying to gradually transition the subject to locations, or at a minimum, wedding planning. "It sounds like you've explored all there is to see around these parts."

"Oh, I have," she said. "In fact, when I read about that murder in the paper, I could picture the exact location with my eyes closed. Can you believe it?"

"The murder?" I played dumb, wanting to hear the details as interpreted by an unbiased third party. "Which one is that?"

"Which *one*?" She laughed. "It's not like we have a lot of them. Don't tell me you didn't hear about Andrea! That's old news by now. My goodness, if I'd have known you hadn't heard about that I would've told you hours ago."

"It vaguely rings a bell," I said. "But I've been so busy at work I haven't picked up a paper this week. I could hardly fit in my hair appointment."

"Tragic, isn't it?" She did the clucking noise with her tongue again. "Well, Andrea was a client here. A regular. She switched off between Gabriella and myself because she was in here so often. One person couldn't handle her."

"She was difficult?"

"No, but..." Melinda shook her head. "She loved beauty more than anyone I've ever known. Eyebrow wax, hair blowout, fingernails, toes, massage, Brazilians—you name it."

"Yikes. Well, I'm so sorry for your loss. She was a friend?"

"I suppose, just based on the sheer amount of time we spent together. She didn't talk much though. She preferred to look at her phone."

I briefly wondered if it was because Andrea had heard Melinda's life story three times over and had been trying to ward off additional commentary. "Do you know who killed her?"

"I haven't read anything about it in the papers, but I heard from someone that it was the man she was dating who offed her."

"Who was she dating?" My heart leapt as I waited to hear if she'd say Ryan's name, or if she knew the identity of a potential new boyfriend. "This was recent?"

"Recent, but not secret." Melinda dropped a few curlers onto my lap and walked over to grab a magazine. "I'm blanking on the name, but you'd know him. Lives up in Castlewood. There he is—right *there*."

My eyes followed her finger as she pointed to the *Technology* section in Glamoured magazine. There, in an issue from just last month, was a photo of Dane and Andrea arm in arm. Underneath the photo was a headline speculating: *New Squeeze for Tech Billionaire?*

The image stunned me silent for a long moment, though I'd seen the photo before. When I spoke, I could only manage a question. "You think Dane Clark killed her?"

She must have heard the gasp in my voice. "Do you know him?"

"I'm just surprised," I said, dodging her question. "Isn't he a billionaire? Why would he kill her?"

"A billionaire if not more. Have you seen that castle? I mean, the outside. Nobody gets on the inside. Except for Andrea, I suppose."

"Right," I agreed. "But just because they were dating doesn't mean he killed her, does it?"

"They're saying the murder weapon belonged to him," she said. "I don't think they wrote what it was though. A gun maybe? I don't know; I didn't read that far—or maybe they didn't say. I get mixed up between what I overhear in the salon and what I read in the news." Her voice quieted. "It's sad, you know. She'll never come in through those doors again."

"It is sad," I agreed, staring at Dane's photo. "I just can't believe it would be him."

"I hope she was dating that Clark guy," Melinda said, drawing me out of my thoughts. "He's gotta be better than the last one she was going with. He was a real dud."

"Ryan?" I said reflexively. "Wasn't that her last boyfriend?"

Melinda's hands froze in my hair. "I thought you didn't know anything about the situation?"

"Oh, no, I don't. Just a lucky guess."

"Wow, that's a good guess. Is it because you're Dotty Pink's grandkid? You know, Dotty came in here a lot. She told me a bunch of good things about my future. I loved that woman. You must've inherited a bit of her psychic powers, then."

"I guess so." I played with my fingers. "Why was Ryan so horrible for Andrea? He's not from the Sunshine Shore, right? I would've known him if he'd grown up here."

"He's from outside of the Shore in the burbs," Melinda said. "Last I remember Andrea told me that he'd moved into that new complex off Peach Street. She was thinking of moving in with him, but they were so hot and cold it was on one minute and off with his head the next."

"I know the one," I said. "Those condos are really nice. But they tore down a local grocery store, and I think I'd rather have the grocer."

"Me too," Melinda said. "But it's fitting for Ryan."

"What do you mean?"

"I mean that he came in here once or twice, and he thinks he is all that and a bag of hot Cheetos. And he is *not*, let me tell you."

"Do you think he had anything to do with Andrea's death?"

Melinda pursed her lips, sizing me up in the mirror as she unwound the last few curlers. "The way I see Ryan, it's like this: He's shiny and nice looking on the outside, just like the new condo he bought. But underneath, he doesn't care who gets hurt so long as he gets what he wants. He could care less whether he knocked a hundred local grocery stores out of business so long as he has some fancy new digs."

Annalise made her way to the back, her eyes on my hair as the last of the curlers came out.

Meanwhile, Melinda kept talking. "As to whether or not he killed her? I don't think so. If I'm continuing on with my analogy, he'd never do the dirty work—he'd never break ground or actually *build* those condos. Heck, he'd never have the guts to kick old Mr. Reynolds out of his store, but he'll most certainly plop himself into the buildings once they're all done. Nope—Ryan wouldn't do the dirty work. He doesn't have the guts to kill her."

"He sounds like a nice guy," Annalise muttered. "Poor Mr. Reynolds."

"Unless," Melinda said, ignoring Annalise. "It was an accident. Ryan Lexington has a temper on him, and boy does he unleash it when his buttons are pushed. Do I think he could've killed Andrea? No, not on purpose. In a blind rage? Now *that* I wouldn't doubt. Have you heard how she was killed?"

"Um, no," I said quickly. "Haven't heard."

But in the back of my mind, the blunt force trauma to the back of Andrea's head had my wheels spinning. I wondered if Melinda might have stumbled onto something without realizing it. Had Andrea tried to break up with him and he'd flown off the handle? Or had she secretly broken things off with him and started dating someone else? If he'd found out, he probably wouldn't have been happy. The question was, had it bothered him enough to have murdered her on accident and then struggled to cover it up and frame Dane Clark?

"Let me get you all fluffed and ready to go," Melinda said. "We're almost done here."

"I'm excited to see my hair," I lied. "I'm actually throwing this huge event for a charity, but it's a real *bear* to find a proper venue this close to the date—especially with things being all booked up for the festival."

Melinda shooed me toward the driers. "Is that right? What sort of party?"

"You know, ritzy investors, expensive food, delicate drinks," I said. "A real fancy thing. It's a shame *nobody* knows any good recommendations for location."

Melinda seemed intrigued by the challenge. "Well, that's not entirely true. I know a few places."

"Is that right?"

"There's the old bowling alley," Melinda said, stealing glances around the room to make sure everyone heard her advice. She glowed under being the center of attention. "It's out of use, but could be retro. There's the Reynolds family farmhouse—I love a nice wedding

there. Have you thought about the bluff? Or I hear tastings are
very in vogue these days. Maybe a nice, out of the way bar and grill
spruced up with some high-end decorations?"

"What about—" My words were cut off by the roar of the drier,
and by the time she pulled my head out from underneath it, I could
hardly speak—even to save Dane Clark's charity gala.

My hair. It wasn't *bad*.

"What do you think?" Melinda asked. "I gave you a real soft wave
that should just give you the slightest of boosts. Just use a little of
this, blow dry, then spray some of *that* and you'll have some real volume without the ringlets," she said as she handed me bottles of styling
products.

Annalise stepped behind the chair to get a better view. "Wow,"
she said with true amazement. "That is magnificent, Lola. Melinda—you are a *star*."

# Chapter 12

"I DIDN'T AGREE TO THIS." Annalise crossed her arms in the driver's seat of her car, refusing to turn the key. "I'm *not* bringing you to some woman's psycho ex-boyfriend's condo. Especially if he's a murder suspect!"

"But I paid for your hair," I wheedled. "Which looks fabulous by the way."

"Not as good as yours." Annalise glanced at my hair, which took a lot longer than normal because there was a lot more to look at. For once, it wasn't dead flat. "You asked for a *ride*."

"Exactly. My *ride* happens to be to the new condos where Mr. Reynold's grocery store used to be. You can just drop me off, I swear."

"I thought you wanted a ride back to the castle, or maybe to Babs's office. This is a life-threatening errand."

"You can stay in the car," I said. "In fact, that's a much better idea. Stay in the car and make sure I come out alive."

"Let you go in alone? No way."

"Annalise," I said, situating myself in the passenger seat to face her. "Look at it this way: if you do this for me, your good deed for the day will be done. See, I'm going there either way. You can either help me or ignore me."

"You're guilting me into helping you investigate a crime that's none of your business?"

"I paid over fifty bucks for you to get the ends straightened on your hair!"

"It does look good." Annalise eyed herself in the mirror. "Gabriella knows how to wield a comb."

"Please?"

"I can wait in the car?"

"I promise to only call you if I need help."

Annalise let out a sigh that shook her whole body. "I'm giving you five minutes before I bust through the door."

"Ten minutes—I'll need to *talk* to him."

"Five."

"Okay," I said with a smile. "Thank you."

We arrived at the complex, and as much as I hated to tie my new hairdo back, I slipped it into a low ponytail just in case things went south with Ryan. I couldn't have my new glamorous hair sticking to my Chapstick while it blew around like a L'Oréal commercial as I was running for my life. After I pulled myself together, I climbed out of the car, waved to Annalise, and headed for the building.

Annalise gripped her phone like a lifeline. She had three screens minimized—the dialer set to 911, speed dial to Babs, and a meditation app. "Five minutes," she called through the window, plugging in one earbud and tapping the screen to start her meditation. "Five minutes and I'm breaking the door down!"

I took an additional second to scan the parking lot, a twinge of sadness coursing through my veins as I realized that I stood on the very spot where Mr. Reynolds's family-owned store had stood not ten years before. It'd been here for nearly a hundred years.

Now the space was nothing more than a parking lot. Ahead of me stood the tallest building within an hour's drive of the Sunshine Shore. Though it stretched only four levels high, it was the closest thing to a skyscraper between us and the nearest metropolis. According to the address I'd finagled from Nicolas, Dane's Director of Operations for Clark Company, Ryan Lexington was on the second floor.

I buzzed myself in and waved at the doorman. Apparently both the buzzer and the doorman were a mere formality because I made it to the second floor with no problems. I located Ryan's apartment ten seconds later and knocked quickly before I could chicken out.

"Who is it?" A man's voice called from inside the thin walls.

I could hear his every footstep as he walked toward the door, and I heard when he stopped just on the other side of the peephole. Putting a smile on my face, I used the most chipper voice I could muster. "I'm Lola Pink."

Finally, the door opened after what I imagined was a thorough examination through the peephole. "Do I know you?" Ryan asked. "You said your name is Lola?"

"Um, I don't think you know me," I said, immediately averting my eyes from Ryan's mid-section. I guess the man didn't know how to use buttons. He had on jeans and a white shirt, but the shirt hung open to reveal an obviously fake-tanned stomach with a mediocre four-pack underneath. "I think we have a mutual friend."

Ryan studied me further, so I took the time to study him from the neck up. His hair was the sort of black that had me wondering if he added a little shoe polish to his shampoo, and his eyes were the sort of hazel that suggested he'd layered green contacts over brown eyes. Fake, just as Melinda had suggested.

At my extended silence, he raised his eyebrows. "Then may I ask what brings you here?"

"I am writing a story," I said. "And I was hoping to get a quote from you about something."

Immediately, his look of skepticism turned into a pleased expression, proving my theory right. If I flattered Ryan into thinking I'd sought him out because of *his* importance, maybe he'd jump on the opportunity to be quoted for my fake publication.

"Sure," he said. "Would you like to come inside for a moment? Unfortunately, I don't have long. I have a lunch meeting shortly."

I stepped into the apartment, my eyes scanning the place and catching sight of furniture that reminded me of IKEA. Perfectly respectable, nice-looking tables and chairs, but nothing that would last. Nothing unique or truly beautiful.

"What can I help you with?" he asked, buttoning his shirt as he spoke. "Sorry about my appearance. I wasn't expecting company."

"I'll keep this short," I said. "It's about Andrea."

At her name, Ryan froze. His fingers had pushed a button midway through the hole, and there it stayed as his gaze slowly raked up my body and landed on my face. The mixed color of his eyes was eerie now, and the black of his hair shone under the bright ceiling lights. "Andrea?"

I exhaled my nerves, quickly calculating how long it'd take me to leap out the door. Three seconds maybe? Then again, we were already four minutes into our meeting, and if Annalise's meditation session ran out, she might come looking for me at any time.

I couldn't decide if that would be good or bad. I didn't want her to get involved, but it would be nice to have company. The way Ryan was watching me for an answer sent shivers over my skin.

"I'm looking for quotes about her life," I said, scrambling. "A memorial article. Did you hear she passed away?"

Ryan turned back to the buttons on his shirt, his fingers shaking as he made his way up to the top, then back down to the bottom. Either he was truly shaken by Andrea's death, or he was a fabulous actor.

"I heard," he said carefully. "But we were no longer together. The relationship we had was a long time ago. How did you get my name?"

"How long?"

"Long enough that I shouldn't be the first person commenting on a story about her life. Who did you say we had as a mutual friend?"

"Who should be the person commenting?" I asked. "Was she close to somebody? A friend or a new boyfriend?"

"If she was," he said, his lips quirking into an eerie smile, "do you think she'd tell me about it?"

"When I spoke to her parents and friends, they mentioned that you were a big part of her life."

"If you've already talked to them, why are you coming to me? Surely they gave you plenty of quotes." Ryan took two steps toward me, and I moved backward simultaneously. I stopped when the back of my legs ran into the dining room table. "Unless you're here for another reason."

"No, I just thought—"

"What paper did you say you're with?"

"Tech..." I hesitated, trying to remember the magazine Melinda had pointed to during my perm. "Tech Industry Magazine Unlimited." I mostly spouted words until I ran out. Then I ran a hand through my hair, forgetting that it'd been tied back. My fingers got stuck as I tried to drag my hand out, and the whole moment turned into a huge mess. And worse, a dead giveaway that I was lying.

"You think I killed her," Ryan said, crossing his arms over his chest. He was taller than me by several inches, his posture clearly meant to intimidate. "I'll tell you what, *Lola*, I didn't. We were done. Over. *Finito*. I wouldn't risk going to prison over that bimbo."

"You asked her to marry you."

"And she didn't want to get married." Ryan's lips formed a thin line. "That's all there is to it. My friends said I dodged a bullet. I guess they were right."

"Do you have any idea who might have wanted her dead?"

Ryan ignored me, pulling out his phone. It hadn't rung, hadn't beeped. I waited, trying for patience as he flipped through a few search results on Google's front page. "What's the name of the magazine?"

I blanked. I completely blanked. "Uh-unlimited text—I mean, Tech Unlimited, uh..."

"Right." Ryan turned his phone off and put it in his pocket. "Forget about your acronyms; I know you're lying. Who are you working for?"

"What?"

"You're not a cop. I know how to smell a cop. You're not a friend of Andrea's—she prefers to hang out with women of her own..." he paused, giving a pointed look at my chest, "*caliber*."

I swallowed. "I worked with her, and she was a friend of a friend's. I saw her the morning of her death."

"More lies. Andrea didn't *work*."

"She modeled."

Ryan rolled his eyes. "Right. She modeled for creepy old dudes, at least until that jerk..." he trailed off, his breaths turning shallow, quick. His face darkened as the pieces clicked into place. "You work for *him*."

"Mr. Dane Clark," I said. "Yes, and Andrea—"

I stopped short, jumping to the side as Ryan's eyes flashed in anger. He leaned forward, and with a single swipe, he sent the vase in the middle of the table flying. It hurtled across the room, just barely missing my body as it sailed toward the entrance to his condo.

It was at that very moment that the door to Ryan's apartment opened and Annalise's head poked inside. Luckily, her training in the circus was grueling and intense—and had prepared her instincts to be lightning quick.

With one glance in our direction, her reflexes kicked in and she catapulted herself into a somersault, landing daintily across the room as the door shut behind her. The vase passed the exact spot Annalise's head had been moments before, smashing into the wall and shattering into a million pieces.

"That is a rude way to say hello!" Annalise pushed herself to her feet. "You almost killed me, *jerk*." Annalise must've been in shock. She'd been scared to walk through the door, but now she was marching toward Ryan with her finger extended. "I just got my hair cut, and you ruined Gabriella's style."

Ryan blinked in surprise, obviously unsettled at the small woman scolding him for bad behavior. "Sorry."

"Wait a minute," I said, waving Annalise off. "One last question, Ryan. What do you have against Mr. Clark? How do you know him?"

"I don't *know* him. All I know is that the second Andrea turned her sights on him, she decided I wasn't good enough for her." The frustration returned to his eyes, the twitchiness in his fingers making me nervous he'd start throwing plates next. "If you should be questioning anyone, it should be your own damn boss. Why don't you ask him who killed her? He's got to be mourning his *girlfriend*. Now get out and leave me alone before I call the police."

"ARE YOU SURE YOU'RE okay?" Annalise pulled up in front of the Clark estate after the short drive from Ryan's condo. "You're looking a little pale."

"I'm fine," I said, though we both knew that wasn't the truth. Between Ryan's vase throwing and his accusations against Dane, I was still shaken up. "I'm just thinking."

"But—"

"Really, I'm okay." I leaned over and hugged Annalise, giving her hair an affectionate pat. "I know you have to get back to practice. Thanks for all your help today. I already kept you too long."

Annalise glanced at the clock on the dashboard, her fingers tapping against the steering wheel. She was punctual to a tee, and her afternoon practices began in under ten minutes. "I'm already going to be late," she said finally. "So, if you need something, I can stay. I can call in sick. I haven't called in *once* this year, and the Bearded Lady has called in, like, five times this month."

"No, no—that wouldn't help anything. That's sweet of you to offer, but you should get going. I have to talk to Dane, anyway."

Relief flooded her face. "Okay," she said. "Then no offense, but can you hop out of the car? I might be able to make it on time if I drive creatively."

I laughed. "Live life on the edge, Annalise," I said, sliding out of the car, holding the door open for one last wink. "Be five minutes late."

She made a face at me and threw the car into gear before I could say goodbye. I shut the door, then made my way to the front of the house. However, it didn't take more than two steps before a flurry of activity drew my attention to the front door.

Dane appeared in the entryway, speaking in fast, clipped tones over his shoulder, his gaze focused on Mrs. Dulcet. He hadn't noticed me. "I'll be back in two hours. I'll take my conference call in the workout room later this evening."

Mrs. Dulcet saw me first, her hands flying toward Dane in a fluttering mess, trying to direct his attention toward me. He looked mildly annoyed as he continued talking, oblivious to me until his butler quite literally pushed him down the steps.

Recovering his balance, Dane finally sensed my presence. His gaze rose to meet mine, his eyes filled with a smile as he found me standing before him. "Right on time."

"Are you sure I'm not interrupting anything? You sound really busy, and this is my job, not yours. I can handle the event planning alone if you'd prefer."

"No," Dane said, his words measured. "I want to go. If I rescheduled other events, it's because I want to spend the time with you."

I watched Mrs. Dulcet's face brighten in relief at Dane's explanation. My heart matched her face. "Are you sure?"

"Lola, I have many flaws, and one of them is my brutal honesty." Dane gave a lopsided smile. He took careful steps toward me, looking beautiful in a bright blue shirt underneath a well-tailored suit. His features were enhanced with a uniqueness that made him even more alluring. "I want to spend time with you, and I'd prefer not to spend the time discussing whether I want to be here."

Since I couldn't find an argument to top his, I shrugged. "Shall we take one of your cars, or my bicycle?"

His bark of laughter surprised me. Behind him, Mrs. Dulcet snickered as well, unsuccessful at hiding her lurking presence. She stepped into the light, giving a shake of her head as her eyes gleamed. "You'll *never* get Dane Clark on a bicycle. I'll eat my hat if you do."

"Why not?"

"He's terrified of bicycles," Mrs. Dulcet replied. "Took a horrible spill once when he was five, never got back on it."

I narrowed my eyes at Dane. "Seriously?"

"Must you?" Dane turned to face his housekeeper, his obvious adoration of her clouded with a tinge of annoyance. "Can't you keep *any* family secrets?"

"He has three motorcycles!" Mrs. Dulcet quipped, covering her mouth as she giggled and tried to stifle it. "But he wouldn't get on a bicycle if it'd save his life."

Gerard saved Dane in that moment, pulling up the driveway in a beautiful old Aston Martin *a la* James Bond. Gerard climbed from the car and gave it a look of pure love before holding open the door and passing the reins to Mr. Clark with a toss of the keys.

"She's just out of the shop," Gerard said gently. "She'll purr like a kitten. Enjoy yourself, kids."

"The car is too much, Dane," I said as I climbed inside. "What if I spill coffee or wine or pasta sauce, or—"

"We'll clean the car," he said with a quick smile. "Or you can leave the pasta sauce and wine for later, and we'll stop for a nice cup of coffee between errands. You won't win this argument, Lola."

"Well," I said, slipping into the pristine interior. "In that case, let's go, Mr. Clark."

# Chapter 13

"THIS IS YOUR EVENT coordinator's *final* suggestion?" Dane looked across the center console to where I squirmed uncomfortably in the passenger's seat of his beautiful vehicle. We'd already visited the bowling alley along with Melinda's other suggestions, but none of them had worked out. "How did you say you found her? Are you sure she's planned events before?"

I fidgeted with the binder holding my crazy hair in place. "Well, she's not a *planner*, per se. She does all sorts of things: perms, highlights, waxing."

"What?"

"Nothing," I said, waving a hand toward the small house in front of us. "Stop here. Melinda said Mr. Reynolds's family has a nice spot out back for weddings. An old barn, very rustic and quaint."

"Old barn?" Dane murmured. "Interesting."

"Look, I know it's not what your mother is probably used to with her charity galas, but it might be fun to switch things up. Instead of a glamorous venue, maybe we can show the rich folks another side of the town. Retro is in these days, you know."

"The rich folks—that's what you think of me?"

"Not *you*," I said. "You're not stuffy like the rest of them."

"That's good to know. Then what am I?"

He parked the car and turned his attention toward me. Crystalline eyes scanned my face, his expression one of amusement as a smile played at his lips. *Sexy.* That's what he was, but I couldn't find my voice to say it aloud.

I also couldn't tell him that he was handsome or intelligent or adorable in his quirkiness. I couldn't bring myself to show him how I felt by running my hands over his broad shoulders, down his arms to the gentle fingers that so often found themselves on my lower back.

"You're...*ah,* you're very nice," I said, my face heating due to the noticeably long silence in which I'd thoroughly analyzed his features.

"That's all I ever wanted to be when I grew up," he said, a deep laugh warming the temperature in the car. "*Nice.*"

"Let's go," I muttered, before I landed myself in more hot water. "I didn't tell Mr. Reynolds we'd be coming, but after his grocery store was torn down, he took to gardening and watching TV. He should be around."

Dane followed me out of the car, and to my pleasant surprise, his fingers found themselves on my lower back. Together we approached the small, single story home set in a cul-de-sac with four other similar houses, all owned by one sibling or another of the Reynolds family.

Behind his house was a large, shared garden and the barn. The barn was set far enough behind the house that it couldn't be seen from the road, but I knew it was there, just behind the layer of trees that gave it a nice, secluded shield and a layer of privacy for custom events.

I walked up to Mr. Reynolds's house and knocked on the door. He'd been a regular at Dotty's hut, and I knew him well. When he didn't answer after the first few knocks, I tried again, then explained to Dane, "He's practically deaf." I turned the handle and pushed the door open.

Dane rested a hand on my wrist. "What are you doing? You can't just walk into someone's house."

"Everyone walks into Mr. Reynolds's house. I'm checking on him—I'm doing the neighborhood a favor." Before Dane could scold me further, I called Mr. Reynolds's name loud enough for the dead to hear.

"Who's that?" he asked. "Annie, is that you? Or Mary, did you forget something?"

Dane raised his eyebrows at me.

"I *told* you he gets a lot of visitors. He's a popular guy." Raising my voice, I stepped into the living room and waved. "Hey, Mr. Reynolds, it's me—Lola. How are you?"

Mr. Reynolds was a rumpled old man, his glasses as thick as the table next to him. He had a scruffy mustache and hair poking out of his ears, and when he smiled, his whole face lit up. "Is that you, Pink? Dotty's granddaughter?"

"It's me." I grinned, crossing the room to give Mr. Reynolds a hug while Dane stood stock still behind us. "I have a favor to ask you. The barn out back—are you still renting it out for events?"

"For you?" His soft gray eyes melted, his thick wrinkles forming a quirky, lovable face that turned to look briefly over my shoulder. "Is it a *wedding*?"

My face turned back to a shade of red I wasn't proud to display. "No, no—not a wedding. Charity event."

"I rent it out for weddings," he said, shaking a finger at me. "*Your* wedding. Dotty would've loved it. That Dotty, she made for a great friend."

I nodded, sinking into the familiar feeling of listening to stories about Dotty. The beautiful thing about having a grandmother who'd been so loved by everyone was that she never truly felt gone. Her stories, her memories were preserved in the hearts and souls of everyone on the Sunshine Shore.

"I used to go to her every year to find out my Christmas presents," Mr. Reynolds confided in me. "I started meeting with her back in eighty-four and went every year until she passed."

I blinked, taking a long breath before allowing the smile to form on my lips. It got easier and easier to listen to stories about my grandmother, but when someone as sweet as Mr. Reynolds lamented her absence, it was still hard. "She was an incredible woman."

"I hear you're taking over the shop. You'll be the new Psychic in Pink?" he asked. "The town needs one."

"I'm not very good at seeing the future," I said. "I'm more of a hindsight sort of girl. I'm renovating the shop though, turning it into a sunglasses hut. We'll have a coffee bar, keep some of Dotty's furniture—it'll be nice."

Mr. Reynolds reached out and clasped my hands, his gray eyes watering as he looked into mine. "Whatever you turn that place into, you keep the spirit of your grandmother alive, understand?"

"Yes," I murmured. "I'll try my best."

"Her spirit's there, in every breath of that wood, every curve of that fat red chair. You leave that porch light on through the night—rain or shine—and if someone comes to you for help, don't turn your back on them," he said. "That's what Dotty Pink brought to this town, and it's in you, too." He nodded, pointing toward my chest. "You've got that same bright spirit, girl. Let it shine."

I swallowed, the lump in my throat preventing me from commenting.

"Now, you might not be psychic, and I'm not either, but I can see the two of you have a future together." He pointed between me and Dane. "When you get married, I'll lend you my barn. It's a real beauty. Rachel just used it last week for her ceremony."

"Rachel..." I hesitated. I knew almost everyone on the Sunshine Shore, but there were no Rachel's with wedding announcements in recent history. "Rachel who?"

"Harrington. Todd, that was the groom's name," Mr. Reynolds said. "Todd and Rachel got married there last week."

My spine went rigid. "Mr. Reynolds, Todd and Rachel Harrington have been married for nearly ten years."

"No." He shook his head. "I decorated the place myself just last week. I think they'll have some firecracker children though, what with his red hair and her temper."

He was right; they would have feisty kids. In fact, Rachel and Todd had three feisty kids aged six, four, and two. They lived down the street from Mrs. Fredericks, and we often had to fight them over the cookie jar. And by fight, of course I meant share.

"So, can we look over the barn?" I asked him. "Do I need a key? If the space works, of course we'll pay."

"We'll pay very well," Mr. Clark said. "You have my word."

"Go on and look, no keys necessary. I left the door unlocked when I milked the cows," he said, waving a hand. "I have to get back to my show, now." Mr. Reynolds turned to the infomercial blaring on the television, dismissing us with a flick of his wrist.

"Cows?" Dane asked. "At a charity gala?"

"There haven't been cows here since I was twelve years old," I said with a sigh. I stood up, squeezing Mr. Reynolds on the shoulder. He barely moved, focused on the flexing biceps in the infomercial on screen. "Let's go," I said to Dane. "It's worth a look while we're here."

"Is he going to be okay?" Dane asked. "Should I call someone to care for him? I don't like leaving him here alone."

I already had my phone out and pulled up the number for Anita Reynolds. "I'll call his daughter," I said quietly. "She lives across the street."

After a brief conversation in which Anita thanked me, then agreed to come right over, I glanced up at Dane. While I had Anita on the phone, I asked her about the barn.

"My dad is right about one thing," Anita said, "the door is unlocked. Though it hasn't been in use for over a year, so it's probably a bit of a mess. If you want it, you can use the space for your event—we don't even need a fee. You'll just want to fix it up a bit, and that'll be payment enough."

"Thanks so much, Anita," I said. "We'll let you know."

"I'll be at my dad's—you know where to reach me if you have any questions. And Lola, is it a wedding we should be expecting?"

"No," I said, my voice catching as I glanced at Dane. "A charity event. Thanks again, Anita." When I hung up the phone, I smiled at Dane. "Ready?"

He slipped his fingers through mine, wordlessly giving my hand a squeeze as we made our way through the pastures behind the house and toward the ancient barn. Seeing as we'd already exhausted the rest of Melinda's suggestions, if this one didn't work, we'd be in serious trouble.

"OH, *no*," I said, once we'd pried the huge, dusty doors back from the front of the barn. "No, no, *no*! Everything is wrong!"

"It's not *wrong*," Dane said sounding unconvinced. "It's just not *right*."

Before us sat an open space the size of a ballroom. The size of it, however, was the only thing that worked. A mouse, and then something larger, skittered across the floor at the beam of light. The floor was pure dirt—dusty, uneven piles of the stuff with tufts of grass poking out from every available crack and crevice. The roof undoubtedly leaked when it rained. Even now, in the daylight, sun dripped through tiny fissures where the rafters didn't quite meet.

"It's got a nice..." Dane trailed off. Apparently, he couldn't find any redeeming qualities either. And he was too honest to lie. So, he just stood there in silence, not saying anything at all.

I patted him on the shoulder. "Thank you for trying to make this work, but you can be honest. It's a mess."

There were enough cobwebs around us to stuff a pillowcase full of them, and I dared not imagine what sort of creatures and critters hid in the darkest corners. Maybe ten years ago this place had been beautiful. If I wasn't mistaken, an old strand of lights hung from the rafters, and I could imagine a glittering ballroom floor where now there were only ruins. I suspected that even the slightest whiff of electricity through these wires would send the place up in flames.

I had nothing left to say. I turned to Dane, refusing to cry. I'd failed, and it would be best for all of us if I gave up on my stubbornness and let a professional with real connections—not just a hairdresser who gave surprisingly delicious perms—sort out the details for the charity gala. But I couldn't say the words yet, so I let my head fall to Dane's chest—his solid, perfect chest—and let the frustration wash over me.

Clearly Dane wasn't used to girls collapsing on his chest, so he just stood there, hands at his sides, expression straight forward. His breathing moved to an erratic sort of pace, and I could sense his nervousness and discomfort at the whole situation.

"Dane," I instructed. "I need a hug."

When he didn't move, I helped him out. I lifted one of his hands and guided it behind my back, then the other. He kept his hands situated there as I rested my head against his chest.

"Good," I said. "Now squeeze, and don't let go. Don't stop until I tell you to stop."

Dane did as he was told, bringing me into a warm embrace. With each passing second, he loosened up somewhat, and by the time a full minute had passed, we stood in a real, true squeeze.

"I'm sorry," he whispered against my hair. "I'm sorry things didn't work out, but it's not your fault. I can hire someone."

"Maybe," I said on a sigh. "I'm not cut out for the job. I hate to disappoint—"

"Lola!" His shout interrupted my apology as a resounding *crack* sounded over us—a rafter collapsing in two, probably shaken from its perilous position above us by the footsteps below.

As I looked upward, the wooden plank began a downward trajectory that promised to flatten us both. I froze, unable to move as the thick piece of wood hurtled straight at my head—I couldn't scream, couldn't cry, couldn't move.

Until I let out an *oomph*, my breath leaving me in a whoosh as Dane dove with me, pushing my body toward the floor while circling his arms around my torso. He rolled away just as the log crashed to the ground next to us with a resounding thud that shook the very foundations of the barn.

The silence that followed was deafening.

"Dane," I whispered a second later. "Dane!"

He lay on top of my body, squishing me in a most delicious sort of way, the scent of his crisp, pine-scented cologne mixing with the dusty layers of the outdoors.

However, he didn't respond. "Dane," I said, my voice turning panicky. "Mr. Dane Clark, are you okay?"

"Fine," he grunted a second later, but it was then that I caught sight of him hunched in pain as he struggled to lift himself off me. He grasped his shoulder, and it was only once we were sitting up and I'd peeled back the layers of his shirt that I realized what had happened.

"It hit you," I said. "The beam clipped your shoulder as it fell."

"I'm fine," he said, holding his arm across his body. "But I vote *no* on this place."

I stifled a laugh. "Of all times to start joking, you pick this one?"

"I learn from the best," he said with a pain-riddled smile. "What do you say we head home?"

"I'm so sorry," I said, resting a hand on his good shoulder as I struggled to figure out how to help him stand. "I shouldn't have brought you here. If I was a professional, I wouldn't have—"

"Lola, stop," he said, his voice a thin line of concentrated effort. "This has been the best afternoon I've had in a long while. I *enjoy* spending time with you. Next time, let's avoid dilapidated buildings."

He leaned forward, a soft hiss as he adjusted his arm and then pressed his lips to mine. There was more emotion in this one kiss than in all the kisses added up over my lifetime. Hot, needy, and a bit possessive, it consumed us. I sank into him, my arms slipping around his neck until he recoiled with a hint of pain on his face.

"I'd love to continue," he said, gritting his teeth. "But my arm is killing me. Rain check?"

I swallowed, dazed from the lingering effects of his lips on mine. "Oh, of course. Yes. Um, let's go."

He took my hand, and we carefully picked our way over the fallen rafter and across the broken floor. As we moved, I glanced over at Dane, hating to ask my next questions, but knowing they'd come up sooner or later. If not for me, then from the police. While I'd hesitated to ruin a nice afternoon together with talk of Andrea's murder, the tone had already shifted with our own near brush with death, so I dove right in.

"I hate to change the subject, but I might have an update on Andrea's murder investigation," I said, striving for casual as we freed ourselves from the shadows of the barn. "Earlier today I spoke with Andrea's ex-boyfriend. He seemed to think she was dating someone at the castle."

"Really? Who? She didn't come around except for our business activities. At least, not that I knew of."

I looked carefully at him. "He seemed to think the man was you."

Dane shook his head. "Lola, I told you. We were nothing except acquaintances. I swear to you."

"I know, I believe you—it's just...I wonder why he'd think that." I frowned deeper. "Did he really fall for the pictures in the media? If not, do you think it's possible she actually *was* interested in someone at the mansion? If *so,* that someone might have had access to your paperweight!"

"I don't know." Dane's mouth turned into a grim line. "Tomorrow is Andrea's funeral. Come with me. I think it might be interesting to see who shows up."

"Who are you expecting to show up?"

"I am not sure," he said, his eyes falling icy on mine. "But if someone loved Andrea—don't you think they'd want to say goodbye?"

# Chapter 14

"COME HELP, IT'S AN emergency." Richard's voice rolled like a clap of thunder through my cell phone, and I had to pull it back from my ear to avoid damage to my brain tissue. "Lola, *please*. I need to talk to you in person."

"What's this about?"

"What's everything about?" he asked. "*Love*."

I glanced over at Dane, who after spending the last hour and a half convincing me that he had recovered from his near-death experience with the fallen beam had tuned into a conference call back at the castle. "You have a *love* emergency?"

"You could say that. Please. Meet me at The Lost Leprechaun—food and drinks on me. It's urgent."

"I'll see what I can do."

"You're an angel, Lola."

I had to admit that after a very long day of doing nothing but failing: failing to choose a venue for the charity ball, failing to keep Annalise out of harm's way, failing as a friend and co-worker to Dane Clark, it was nice to hear from someone convinced I had advice left to offer.

"Feel free to leave—I can handle the rest of the evening on my own," Dane said, putting the phone on mute while a clipped English accent continued speaking in the background. "I'll see you in the morning. If you need a ride, get Semi or Gerard."

I nodded, waved, and shut the door behind me before sneaking downstairs to see if Mrs. Dulcet had any leftover food I could snag for dinner. Thankfully she did, and I stashed the leftovers in my purse before hopping into the back of Semi's SUV and giving him GPS directions to the family owned Irish pub on the Sunshine Shore. He promised to wait outside while I made quick work of my meeting at The Lost Leprechaun.

"You made it!" Richard said as I pushed open the door. "I thought you'd never come. I called you *ages* ago."

He'd called me no more than twenty minutes before, but I didn't correct him. I was too busy taking in the rich mahogany wood that covered every surface of this place. Oak barrels provided the base for quaint cocktail tables in the center of the room, while stools made from deep colored wood sat behind a slab of thick stone that served as the bar.

Behind the counter were several taps, a variety of fancy mugs, and a window through to a small kitchen in the back. When I looked the other way, I found long picnic-style tables in a room the size of Mr. Reynolds's barn.

A few people mingled at the tables, hopping from one to the next and chatting within groups as a series of small tasting glasses were placed before them. By the time I turned back to the bar, Richard had poured three small glasses of beer.

"No, thanks," I said, pushing the flight away and sliding onto a stool. "I really can't stay long. What's the emergency?"

"I need to run something by you," he said. "Do you remember how I told you I'm versed in profanity?"

"Too clearly."

"Well, I think I did it. I wrote a poem for my Stephanie, and I even cut out all of the bad words. Every damn one of them."

"Really?"

He nodded, a proud expression on his face. "I'd like to read it to you. I've gotta test it on you before I give it to Stephanie to make sure it's respectful enough."

"*This* is your emergency? Why didn't you read it to me over the phone?"

Richard scratched his head, wrinkled his nose, and then shrugged. "I guess that would have made sense. You should've told me that before—it's a little late to change plans now, ain't it?"

I rolled my eyes, then gestured for him to get moving. I waited as he pulled a wrinkled sheet of paper from his shirt pocket. With a colossal clearing of his throat, Richard put one leg onto the step behind the bar, braced himself, and began with gusto.

*Dear Stephanie.*

*I love to see—*
*When you look at me.*
*You look so cute in your blue hat,*
*and I don't think that you are fat.*
*I love you with all my heart,*
*I'll buy you a ring from Kmart.*
*If you want—*

"Halt!" I said before he could continue. Then without explanation I reached over, grabbed his note, and ripped it in half. I gave him the top half and then crumpled up the bottom half, popped it in one of the spare glasses of water, and then swirled it around. "You can't say the word *fat* in a love poem."

"I thought it was endearing," he said. "I was going for cute."

"The first part is sort of cute, but that's about it."

"I'm not going to lie, I think this is going to work." Richard trembled with excitement as he viewed the half sheet of paper. "I feel like I'm on top of the world. I'm going to break into her house and leave this on her pillow."

"Nope—try again."

"I'm going to break into her house and leave this on her kitchen table."

"Try again."

"I'm going to break into her—"

"Try *again*."

"Oh!" It finally dawned on Richard. "I'm going to *knock* on her front door and not break into her house."

"Ding, ding, ding."

"You're the best," he said. "Are you sure I can't tempt you into having a beer on the house? My dad wouldn't be happy if I didn't offer a friend of mine a free sampler."

"Does your dad own this place?"

He nodded. "I'm technically Richard Junior. My dad is Richard Senior. He goes by Dick or Big Richard."

"So, ah, Richard Junior," I hesitated. "Does Big Richard ever host events in here?"

"Oh sure. We watch soccer matches and serve beer, we host bachelorette parties and serve beer, we host Bingo and serve beer—we can do whatever you want."

"With a side of beer."

"You catch on, lady."

"What about a charity event?"

"I don't need *charity*," Richard said. "I might not have as much money as Donald Trump, but I'm doing okay."

"What if I paid you good money to rent this place for...let's call it a big party. A very *classy* party."

"Let me talk to Big Richard," he said. "My dad's away on business, but he'll be back tomorrow."

"Great," I said. "You know where to find me."

"You haven't tasted the beer yet," he said, gesturing to the flight before me. "Take a sip."

I leaned in, took the smallest of gulps, and gave a nod of approval. "Perfect."

"Stephanie's *perfect*," Richard said dreamily. "And I'm going to tell her how I feel with this poem tonight. I owe you, Lola. I owe you big time. Anything I can do for you, just let me know."

"Okay, sure thing, Richard."

It'd been a long day, and I needed time to think after hearing Richard's poem. The evening had turned into a beautiful one, so I told Semi to head back to the castle. I wanted to walk.

I took the beach path and made my way toward Psychic in Pink, and I was so wrapped up in my own head that I didn't hear Babs approach from behind. I jumped as she called out *hello*.

"Sorry," she said, catching up to me. "You seem on edge. How are you doing? What happened today? Annalise didn't get around to filling me in and, oh, *Lola*—you got the perm. It looks incredible! How did that happen? Your hair actually has some bounce to it!"

I grinned, then filled Babs in on my day as we walked. "I don't know what part of the day ranks worse: Ryan almost clocking Annalise in the head with the vase or Dane getting hit with the rafter."

"Well, it sure wasn't the perm," Babs said, toying with the ends of my hair. "Melinda did a great job."

"Hold on, where are *you* coming from?" I asked, suddenly noticing Bab's extra red lipstick and extra-dark eye liner. "You did your makeup differently."

"I got asked on a date last minute, so I had to spruce up with whatever I had in my purse," she said, puckering her lips. "Johnny and I grabbed coffee. He found me at the office working late and bought me a cappuccino from Dungeons and Donuts. He's fantastic—he asked me out on an *official* date tomorrow." She clapped her hands, twirled, and stared at the sky before coming back to earth. "What about you? Any word from Dane on the love life?"

"Yeah," I said. "He asked me on a date to a funeral."

"You're kidding me."

"Okay, he didn't *ask me out* to a funeral. But we are going to Andrea's ceremony in the morning," I said with a sigh. "I mean, I suppose I'd like to ask him where things are headed between the two of us—romantically—but it's too weird this close to Andrea's death. I need to give some time for things to settle."

"I suppose," Babs said with a frown. "So about this funeral—you didn't know Andrea at all, did you?"

"I met her once," I said defensively. Babs wasn't convinced, so I continued, "Yes, we're worried her killer might be there. If it was an act of passion, maybe her killer is feeling remorse and will have come to say their goodbyes."

"Well, I guess I should say my goodbyes, too."

"You never met her."

"Nope, but if there's a chance of drama, I want a front row seat." Babs leaned in and kissed my cheek. "Goodnight, Lo. I'll see you in the morning."

# Chapter 15

THE NEXT MORNING DAWNED sunny and bright.

And completely *wrong*.

Everything was wrong about it, but it took me a long while to put my finger on what exactly was off. That's when I realized it wasn't something additional making the morning feel weird, it was the *lack* of everything else.

Nobody named Richard pounded at my door, nobody named Babs whirled in unannounced, and nobody named Johnny swung a sledgehammer or fired up an electric drill. The place was *silent*. It'd been so long since I'd sat alone in my own house that it felt downright eerie.

I glanced at the clock, surprised to find the sunlight already in my eyes. Where was Johnny and crew? Usually they arrived before...*Oh, no!* The sunlight! I flew out of bed and rubbed my eyes as I stared closer at the clock.

"Oh, *crap!*"

Thankfully, I wasn't scheduled to be at the castle for my usual nine a.m. start time this morning. Instead, I'd planned to head straight to the church for Andrea's funeral ceremony at ten thirty. According to my clock, it was already ten, and I wasn't dressed, washed, or fed. Surely the rest of Clark Company would already be heading toward the funeral, wondering what was so important that the personal assistant to the boss had to miss the ceremony.

Scrounging in my closet I pulled out the same black dress that I usually saved for first dates, slipped into it and added a shawl. A pair of low black heels topped off the outfit and as for my bright pink purse—it was staying. There was no time to transfer everything over to a more subdued shade—I'd just have to tuck it under my shawl when I entered the church. I slipped my new pair of Angelo sunglasses onto my head and took the stairs two at a time.

I skipped coffee and breakfast, tossed a tic tac container in my purse for nourishment, and called my morning routine good. Since everyone I knew was either at work or en route to the funeral, I was left with my bike for transportation. Toting my bright pink purse, I hopped aboard and began a vicious pedal toward the largest church on the Sunshine Shore.

Fifteen minutes later I screeched to a halt. The church loomed before me, a gorgeous structure on a cliff overlooking the ocean. Everyone said it was a beautiful backdrop for wedding photos and baptisms, and it appeared to be just as beautiful for a funeral. However, the cliffs looked sharper, the water crisper, the ocean more dangerous than usual.

As I surveyed the view, a honk from behind startled me, and I hauled my bike up the hill and locked it against a sign post just as an expensive Jaguar pulled to a stop. To my surprise, I recognized the faces as they stepped from the car: Dane's parents, and another man similar in age. Probably Randall's brother, Anders Clark.

The Clark clan didn't see me right away, so I ducked my head and tried to vanish before they could witness my vehicle of choice. However, I stopped mid-spin as I caught sight of an expensive new Tesla arriving. I recognized the faces in that car, as well: Andrea's parents. It startled me to see the hippie-ish pair owning such a spendy new vehicle. It jarred with the personalities I'd seen when Babs and I had visited.

"*Lola*, is that you?" Amanda Clark's clipped voice rang in my ears, freezing me in place.

With one hand on my bike seat, I turned and forced a smile back at Dane's parents. "Mrs. Clark. How are you?"

"I'm well." She hesitated, taking a moment to scan my dress. "You *do* know that this is a funeral and not a speed dating event?"

I glanced down, patting the fabric against my legs. The dress almost reached my knees while the arms were outfitted with long, lace sleeves. A modest V-neck crossed my chest and allowed room for a small silver necklace.

"Hi there, I'm Anders." The third person from the Clark's vehicle held out a hand and gave a smile. "You must be one of Dane's staff?"

"*Yes*," Amanda said quickly. "She's his personal assistant."

"It's a pleasure to meet you." I accepted Anders's proffered hand and gave it a shake. "You're Mr. Clark's brother?"

"Guilty as charged." With salt and pepper hair, a warm smile, and eyes the color of blueberries, he seemed the softer, friendlier version of Randall Clark. He winked. "For what it's worth, I think you look lovely today."

Amanda rolled her eyes. "Come on, Randall. Let's find our seats before the church is full—we're already running late."

"Don't let her ruin your fun," Anders said with a laugh as his brother and sister-in-law disappeared. "So, you must be the one he's been talking about."

I glanced over my shoulder. "Who?"

"Dane. Not that he talks all that much, as I'm sure you know, but last week we *did* have a conference call, and he mentioned he had hired a new personal assistant a while back which, in itself, was unusual. Dane doesn't bother himself with trivial things."

"Oh. Trivial things, of course."

"No, you're not a trivial thing! That's my point. People come and go in the business, and he's so busy brokering deals for millions and inventing the next new gadget that he doesn't have time for anything else—including *fun*, no matter how much I've tried to convince him otherwise. When he talked about you, though, he sounded different. Happier, I'd venture."

"Oh, I wouldn't go that far."

"Do you love him?"

"Mr. Clark..." I trailed off, feeling the intense pressure of the infamous Clark gaze. I sensed he'd know if I lied, so instead, I opted for silence.

"I see," he said quietly. "Well, I'll let you go inside. Sorry for your loss. I had never met the woman, but it's a tragedy she's gone so soon."

"It is." I glanced down at my hands which were giving away my nerves, twisting and turning in front of my body. When I glanced up, Anders had already returned to the driver's side door of his vehicle. "Oh, and Mr. Clark?"

He looked over the car. "Yes?"

"Please don't say anything to him—or his parents. I don't think they like me much."

"Of course not." He grinned again as he began to slip inside. "I suppose I'll see you around then."

I smiled back. "I suppose so."

I slipped into the church. At the lectern, a man in a suit was speaking to a crowd dressed in black. I spotted the Clark family at a pew in the middle of church. Moving off to the side, I took a long minute debating whether I should wait out the ceremony back here, alone, or chance a walk down the aisle to join Mrs. Dulcet in the row behind the Clarks.

Dane turned mid-debate, his eyes searching through the crowd, his height giving him an advantage over ninety percent of the mourners. His gaze sailed over my head and, for a moment, my heart stopped as he missed me.

*Screw it,* I decided in a sudden burst of confidence. I wanted to sit next to Dane. He was clearly looking for me. Was I going to let a little thing like his mother's disapproval stop me from standing beside the man I loved?

I stepped deliberately into the aisle, passing by a row of cops intermingled with the mourners, and marched—very quietly—down the red carpeting until I arrived next to Dane. I watched his face for a reaction as I brushed my hand against his shoulder, my heart thudding as a look of surprise hit him first. Then slowly, it morphed into one of delight, and he quickly shuffled deeper into the pew to allow space for me.

"I saved you a seat," he whispered, easing an arm behind my back and pulling me to his side. "I'm glad you made it. Is everything okay?"

I nodded. With those simple words, my worries disappeared. And when Mrs. Clark stared right past me, I barely noticed. Because Dane pressed a kiss to my forehead, grasped my hand, and for the rest of the ceremony, he never let go.

# Chapter 16

"IRONICALLY, SHE WOULD have liked this funeral, don't you think?" A woman standing around next to me clucked and shook her head as she spoke in low tones.

I turned to reply before realizing that she was speaking to a man on her other side, and the conversation clearly wasn't meant for my ears. The woman who'd spoken was dressed in a fashionable business suit, trendy jewelry, and had a pair of sunglasses in hand that drew my eye even in this time of sadness.

"Her death is unfortunate," the man agreed. His bright blond hair stuck straight up in a way that was probably meant to be all the rage. He held a cigarette in one hand, and judging by the thin, almost-emaciated build of his body, he puffed on that thing more than he ate junk food and was dying to get outside and light it. Just a hint of a lisp escaped as he spoke again. "But what are you going to do about it?"

"There's nothing more to do." The woman sighed, more out of weariness than sadness. "I already have Leslie lined up for the show. She offered to step up of course, but everything will be all wrong. The colors won't match Leslie like they did Andrea—I specifically accessorized to bring out that gorgeous color of her hair."

The man next to her tsked as if it were all Andrea's fault for having such an unfortunate time of death. I rocked back and forth on my heels, sidling closer to the group as I searched for a way to enter the conversation without seeming nosy.

"Hi there—I'm sorry to interrupt," I said, taking the leap as I turned toward the female next to me. "But I was admiring your sunglasses. Are those the new Chanel? I didn't think they were even on shelves yet. Where on earth did you find a pair?" When in doubt, always go for the compliment, I figured—and this time, I didn't have to work hard to find one. Nor was I disappointed with the results.

The woman offered a bland smile at first, then did a double take with keen interest spreading across her face. "Hey, I know you."

"I've lived here most of my life," I offered. "My name is—"

"Lola Pink?!" The man next to her squeaked with excitement. "Regina, that's Lola Pink."

The woman named Regina nodded, her lips curving into a more real smile as she extended a hand for a shake, moving the sunglasses easily to the other hand as I met her halfway. "It's a pleasure to meet you," she said. "I'm a huge fan."

"A huge fan?" I wrinkled my nose. "Of what?"

"Your collection!"

"Collection?"

"Your vintage collection!" Regina grinned broader now, amused. "I read the article on you."

I flushed, having completely forgotten about any such article. Before Dotty's death, we'd been a little short on cash, so I'd submitted photos of my vintage sunglasses collection along with a short article describing them to the local newspaper. They'd paid me a couple hundred bucks and run the article in the Sunshine Times. Dotty framed it, and it still hung on the wall in her office.

"I'd totally forgotten about that," I told her. "Sorry, but I'm not familiar with your name. Are you from around here?"

"I'm from the city," she said. "I don't get down to the Sunshine Shore much, but with the events approaching and this tragic accident—"

"Regina Fullerton," the male said, leaning over her shoulder. "And I'm Marcus Hewitt. I'm Miss Fullerton's assistant, and she is one of the hottest up and upcoming designers!"

"Up and coming?" Regina frowned. "I've already arrived, and I'm already at the top, Marcus."

"Of course, of course," he said quickly, the lisp more pronounced. "She's supplying most of the designs during the fashion show."

"Oh, wow. A real celebrity." I beamed at her, pushing hard for the flattery. "How did you know Andrea?"

"She was going to be the lead model in Regina's show," Marcus said. "Until she wound up dead, of course. A real shame, seeing as Regina had completely refashioned some of her designs to go with that red hair. That was the entire focus of the line. A disaster now, of course."

"A disaster that Andrea's dead, of course," Regina said, looking irritated with her assistant for his lack of sympathy, and probably worse, his lack of filter. "She was the muse for most of this line, and it's not as simple as just finding another red-haired model for the show like everyone tells me. Andrea *was* the line—sassy, understated, a fresh face. She'd even gotten new breasts for the occasion. It's not an easy process to find the perfect muse, let me tell you."

"I'm sure," I said dryly. "And I'm sorry Andrea's death is such an inconvenience for you."

Regina's eyes flashed to mine. "I'm sorry for your loss—did you know her well?"

I gave a shrug, not wanting to lie. "I guess I didn't know her as well as I thought. She hadn't mentioned anything about the show."

"Of course not. Because I made her sign an NDA."

"NDA." I nodded, smiling proudly. I'd signed one of my own recently, and although I still couldn't remember exactly what the letters meant, I did understand them. "I see. That explains it. I'm sure she was looking forward to the show." I hesitated and glanced toward the front of the church as I prepared my next question. "Do you have someone taking over for her now that she's...gone?"

"Yes." Regina sighed. "Although not ideal, the show must go on. I don't mean that harshly, I just mean..."

"I understand," I said. "You have to do your job despite the unfortunate circumstances."

She nodded, biting her lip as she turned toward the front of the church as well. "I suppose we should be going."

"Who did you say is taking her spot?" I asked. When Regina shot me a sharp look, I shrugged. "Just curious. Forget I asked."

A frown tugged her lips downward. "I suppose it'll be public soon enough. Leslie Gray will be stepping in. She'll do a fabulous job, I'm sure."

Marcus, too, looked disappointed. "But she's no Andrea." He gave a fake sniff and wipe of his eyes. "Andrea really embodied the whole line."

"We should be going. I have arrangements to make." Regina turned to leave, and I followed along with Marcus.

The rest of the crowd, including Dane and his entourage of employees, had begun filing to the church basement after the service ended for refreshments and small talk. However, it appeared the fashionista and her friend weren't planning to stick around, and my curiosity got the better of me. As they pushed through the front doors, I tagged along behind them.

As we stepped into the sunlight, I slipped on my Angelo shades. I'd ended up getting them for a steal on eBay. These babies were one of the kind, and even a funeral hadn't stopped the sun from shining on the Shore. A woman needed to protect her eyes.

Regina started to tell me goodbye, but the word froze on her lips as her eyes landed on my face. "Are those an original pair of Angelo sunnies?"

I nodded, proud and—I hated to admit it—pleased that someone had recognized my sunglasses for the beauties they were. "I snagged them for twenty bucks! Someone clearly didn't know what they were giving away."

Regina inhaled quickly. "You're kidding."

I shook my head and rested my fingers lovingly on the frames. "Nope. They just arrived this week."

"They're perfect." Regina's hands crossed over her heart. "May I hold them?"

"Try them on," I said feeling downright giddy at being able to share the excitement with someone other than myself. Babs did appreciate a nice set of shades now and again, but she was focused on the looks. She didn't appreciate the style—not like Regina. "Enjoy. They're beautiful."

"They are." Regina's breath came out in a soft hiss as I handed the frames over. She placed them gently over her nose, then waved mysterious hand signals to Marcus that apparently meant for him to pull a compact out of her purse and hold it up. "Simply gorgeous. How much do you want for them?"

My hand crept out and my smile disappeared. "They're not for sale."

"I figured." To my relief, Regina removed the sunglasses, though she held them back for a moment as she eyed me up and down, a gleam there that told me she had a plan. "How much to rent your collection?"

"Excuse me?"

"Vintage is all the rage these days. In fact, my line with Andrea was inspired by the fifties. Hence the reason she was the perfect model: that vibrant red hair, the curvy figure. She had the look of a fifties housewife meets pin-up girl. Not like the uber slender models that are so in vogue in Paris."

"That's on the way out," Marcus said. "Vintage is on the way in."

"Oh, I don't know," I said. "I really like my collection. I was planning to display them at my store, Shades of Pink, once I get it up and running."

"I've seen your store," Regina said, a calculated gaze on her face. "Or rather, the...bones of it."

I wrinkled my nose. "Construction is a lengthy process."

"And costly." She smiled, knowing she had me by a tender thread. "What if we paid you enough to create a special little case for your collection—a gorgeous display? Hell, what do I care? Take the money and your honey to Bermuda. We won't short you on the funds. As an insurance policy on their safe return, I'll sign a document that says I will pay double what anything is worth in the event something gets broken. You'll be praying we break things."

"I suppose," I said. "You'd just need them for the day?"

She nodded. "One day. Practice in the early afternoon, show late in the evening."

"That's feasible," I said, still seeing blinking dollar signs that could lead to additional construction money. Even with the help of Dane Clark's hefty salary paid to my account, cash seemed to disappear faster than I could earn it. "Sure, that's fine. Let's do it—I shouldn't keep a collection this beautiful hiding in my closet, anyway."

"There's the spirit," Regina said. "We'll take precious care of your babies. What if you swing by my office this week? I'm down near the pier in rented space next to Dungeons and Donuts—and bring a few of your favorite pairs. We have to choose a headliner of course."

"Sure. Any in particular?"

Regina winked. "I trust your judgement. Drop by with a selection and we'll choose together. I'll have all the paperwork ready for you to sign and half the money as a down payment. We can negotiate there."

I raised a hand and stuck it toward her. "Sounds great."

We shook, wrapping up quickly as we both broke into fake coughing fits when a group of mourners flowed from the building, one of the women crying freely.

"Oh, don't feel so bad," Marcus said with a pleased smile. "Andrea would have loved that a gathering in her honor brought new friends together over fashion."

In a strange way, he had a point—but the moment was gone. Regina signaled goodbye, then gestured for Marcus to accompany her from the building. He scurried after her like a quick rabbit, unlocking the door to a sleek black rental car parked illegally in a handicapped spot.

As they drove away, a hand came to rest on my shoulder, startling me. Shortly after, the familiar, spicy scent of Dane Clark hit me with a wave of recognition, and I sunk instinctively closer to his touch. By the time I turned to face him, my lips held a hint of a smile.

"Are you doing okay?" he asked gently. "You disappeared after the funeral."

"I'm fine. I met someone who recognized my sunglasses and we got to talking." I shrugged. "By the way, did you know Andrea was going to be the lead model in the biggest fashion show of the Sunshine Shore festival? I was just recruited to help supply the shades for the event."

Dane frowned at my question. "No, I didn't. I told you, Lola—we didn't talk for enjoyment, not really. If we did, it was Andrea speaking to me, and..."

His face colored red.

"And you tuned it out?" I offered. "It's okay, I understand."

He looked down at his feet. I rested a hand on his shoulder. "It's okay. Look, Dane—the ceremony was really beautiful. I think, in a strange way, Andrea would have really liked it. Come on—I can't keep you all to myself out here. Let's head downstairs for some refreshments; I'm sure there's a queue of people waiting to talk to you."

I WASN'T WRONG. THE second we left the sunny outdoors and descended to the basement level, eyes tilted toward Dane and whispers followed wherever we moved. I tried to stay chipper and positive and ignore the stares.

"It looks beautiful down here," I said, gesturing to the gorgeous displays of flowers, wreaths, and photos lining the walls.

The food was a magnificent display in itself—piles of fruit set in fantastic shapes and designs, more desserts than I could ever finish in my life, and enough main courses to please even the pickiest of eaters.

"Wait a minute, isn't that Mrs. Dulcet?" I pointed behind the buffet tables. "I recognize the guy next to her, too. He works in the kitchens at the castle, unless I'm mistaken."

Dane sipped from his lowball glass containing a serving of top shelf whiskey. "Yes."

"You donated your kitchen staff to the event?" When he didn't seem inclined to answer, the rest of the equation dawned on me. "You fronted the money for this whole thing. The flowers, the decorations, everything."

"It was the least I could do."

"Did you get them the car too?"

His somewhat sullen expression snapped into business mode. "A car? What are you talking about?"

"The Tesla. I didn't see the Ricker's as the type to go for a new vehicle, but I guess if it came free..."

"What are you talking about?"

"Andrea's parents. I thought it was weird they bought a new car the week of their daughter's funeral, but—"

"Gerard." Dane interrupted me by calling over the caretaker of his cars. "Can you find the Rickers's new Tesla and give me some details on it? It should be parked in the lot."

Gerard nodded, apparently used to unusual and vague requests. As he turned on a heel and left, I glanced around at the rapidly convening crowd of mourners swarming toward Dane.

"I'm, ah—I'm going to go with Gerard to keep him company," I said softly. "Why don't you catch up with a few guests, and I'll meet you back here in a bit?"

Dane gave a distracted nod as three guests began speaking to him at once. He didn't make it out of the castle much, and when he did, it was a spectacle in and of itself.

I scurried along the path Gerard had taken, catching up with him outside in the parking lot. He located the Tesla quickly and peeked through the windshield, his face frowning with whatever he'd found.

Finally, my curiosity got the best of me. "What is it?"

"This car is new; it's only been driven thirty miles. If I had to guess, the owners purchased it this week."

"No plates yet," I said, pointing to the dealer's name plastered across the front and back of the vehicle. "Definitely new."

"I know the head salesman there." Gerard pulled out his phone, put it on speaker, and dialed. "Brett, help me out. Which one of you sold the latest Tesla to some locals recently?"

"I made that sale," Brett said, a hint of pride in his voice. "You're talking about those hippies? They paid cash."

Gerard met my gaze over the phone. "Those are the ones. Say, did they mention anything about why the sudden purchase?"

"Not really," Brett said. "It seemed like they just decided to come out one day and blow through a wad of dough. I don't ask too many questions if the paperwork goes through. And they paid cash, so...*aww*, man. Don't tell me there's something fishy about their money."

"As far as I know, it's all good," Gerard said. "Look buddy, don't worry. I just wanted to confirm you'd sold the vehicle, that's all."

"It was me," he said. "They seemed excited, if that means anything to you. The woman said something about how they'd waited too long to have it, but I didn't catch the rest of it."

Gerard said goodbye, hung up, and looked to me. "Any reason Andrea's parents might have experienced a sudden windfall of money? Enough that they didn't mind dropping close to six figures on a brand-new car?"

I shook my head, mystified. "No clue. They told me they donated a bunch of money to charity when Andrea's grandma died. Like I said, they don't seem like the *flashy new car* type of people."

"Grief? People react in different ways."

"I suppose it's possible."

"Um, Lola?" Gerard's sudden change of tone had my hands turning clammy. "I think there's someone here to see you."

I turned, feeling eyes on the back of my head, to find none other than Andrea's ex-boyfriend standing at the door of the church with a glass of wine in his hand. "Ryan? What are you doing here?"

Ryan stood flanked by thin rays of sunshine. His eyes were red-rimmed, and upon closer inspection, I realized the wine glass he held was actually filled with a darker liquid. Whiskey, if I had to guess.

He raised a shaky hand and pointed at me while using his other shoulder to balance against the wall. "You. We need to talk."

# Chapter 17

I EXCUSED MYSELF FROM Gerard, who waited reluctantly near the doorway, watching as I guided Ryan over to a low brick wall that ran the length of the parking lot. I sat him on it, and then stood before him.

Undoubtedly drunk, Ryan swirled his empty glass over and over again, trying to inhale the last few droplets of alcohol as his eyes crossed. "She's *dead*."

"Lola..." Gerard returned to my side. "I think you should leave him alone. He's unstable."

"It's fine! We're in broad daylight. People are all over the place." I gestured to the steady stream of mourners exiting the church, some of them returning to their cars while others mingled in small groups. "He's more likely to fall asleep than he is to do anything stupid. Anyway, Mr. Clark will be waiting for you. Why don't you let him know what you found out about the Tesla."

Gerard shook his head. "Lola—"

"I'm just going to sit here while he sobers up for a few minutes and make sure he doesn't drive," I explained patiently. "Send Dane outside if that'll make you feel better."

Gerard looked across the parking lot, probably judging how long it'd take to rush back should something go wrong. But he must've come to the same conclusion that I had—in bright daylight, in the middle of a church parking lot, there wasn't much risk for something to go wrong. Especially now that Ryan had kicked his feet up and was wobbling into a sleeping position on the wall.

Finally, Gerard sighed, then made his way back into the church, glancing over his shoulder once more before he disappeared inside.

I knew I didn't have long before Gerard or Dane returned, so I gave Ryan a light tap with my toe. "Hey, *you*. What are you doing here? What did you need to talk about?"

Ryan mumbled something that made zero sense, coughed, then burped.

"Ryan!" I stepped backward. "Why did you come to Andrea's funeral? Did her parents invite you?"

"Small town," he slurred. "I know things."

"What sort of things do you know?"

"Andrea was going to turn thirty next week; I knew that. I got her a card. I told you that our relationship was a long time ago, but I lied. Sometimes, we still went out. I was her backup plan, you know. I loved her."

"I'm so sorry, Ryan. This must be horrible for you."

"It's right here." Ryan dug in his pockets, but the motion was too much and he tumbled off the ledge and collapsed in a heap on the ground. "*Herrr-umph.*"

He'd gone off the far side of the wall, so I approached the bricks with caution. Peeking over the side, I found Ryan in a dead slumber, snoring almost loud enough to be heard from the church.

"Ryan?" I reached out and poked his shoulder.

No response. Unsurprising, judging by the potent scent coming off of him.

Crumpled in his outstretched hand was the birthday card. I retrieved it and stood with a hip resting against the ledge, examining the front page. It was simple, a silver rose engrained in expensive material. The edges of the card were frayed, however, and a stain that looked like coffee took up the lower left corner. Judging by the state of the paper, Ryan had carried this card around for some time.

Another loud snore wracked his body. I felt a little bad snooping while he was out cold, but since he'd been about to show me the card anyway, I cracked it open.

There, written in surprisingly straight handwriting, was a message that read: *Happy Birthday, Andrea. I love you.*

The simplicity of the message brought a wave of sadness over me, despite the circumstances. I'd hardly known Andrea, and here was Ryan—a guy who'd almost taken my best friend's head off with a vase—in a stupor on the ground. The whole thing seemed senseless. Andrea had only been twenty-nine—too young to go, despite her flaws.

"Why didn't she love me?" Ryan shifted on the ground, then looked up at me with a surprisingly clear gaze. "What did I do wrong?"

I shook my head. "I don't know, Ryan."

"I loved her. She was perfect—the perfect woman for me." He kept his eyes fixed on me. "Why didn't she love me back?"

"I'm sorry," I said. "I don't know."

"There was someone *else*," Ryan said. "There must have been. *He* killed her, but why? How could anyone kill Andrea? She was perfect."

"Do you have *any* idea who else it might have been?"

"*Him.* There." Ryan pointed over my shoulder. "It must be him."

I looked over my shoulder to find Dane striding toward us, looking none too pleased about the situation. The clock ticked away from me, and I hurriedly shook my head.

"It wasn't Dane," I said. "I am positive it wasn't him, Ryan. You have to trust me on this. Andrea worked for Mr. Clark, and that's it."

"Then why'd she go to the castle at night?" Ryan blinked in confusion. "I followed her there once. When I asked her later if she'd had a shoot, she said *no*. She was hiding something."

"When was this?"

"Last week. I wanted to give her the card." He stared at the note in my hand. "I hadn't figured out what else to write in there. I needed to hand deliver it to her so I could tell her how I felt with my words."

"I know, I know," I said, handing the card back over as he slurred a thank-you. "I'm really sorry about this, Ryan, but she's gone. I hate to ask you this now, but where were you on the evening she was murdered?"

He turned a blank expression on me. "I just told you I loved her. I wouldn't kill her."

"But she'd chosen someone else. Didn't that upset you? Maybe a heated argument, or a fight or—"

I couldn't complete the question because two things happened at once. Ryan shook off his stupor and climbed to his feet, reaching for me, his hands grasping at my throat. Surprised, I moved back from the ledge, but he was stronger than me, and I couldn't pull away from him. I coughed, spluttered, and yanked at his hands, but he wouldn't budge. His hands clung to me, choking me, stealing my breath as I stumbled backward.

At the same time, Dane must have sensed something was about to happen because he propelled himself across the last bit of parking lot in seconds. He pulled Ryan off me in a single motion, threw him against the ground, and knelt with one knee on Ryan's chest. "Keep your hands off of her, understand?"

Ryan couldn't suck in enough air to breathe, let alone speak.

"Dane, let him go. It's my fault, I provoked him."

"I don't care." Dane spoke in a rumble that registered deep in my stomach. "There's never a reason to lay a hand on a woman."

Ryan made a gurgling sound in his throat as Dane sunk his knee into the other man's chest, all those hours of swimming and lifting weights combining to form an intimidating creature—a man who moved with grace and strength, with unrivaled intelligence.

Dane was completely in control, which made him all the more scary. He watched, eyes alert, as Ryan's face began to turn shades of blue and purple that couldn't be healthy. My body remained frozen in place until Ryan's eyes widened.

Lunging for Dane, I tugged and tugged, but he didn't budge. It wasn't until I accidentally brushed against the place on his shoulder that was bruised from the falling rafter that he finally reacted and flinched.

"Dane, please," I begged. "Let him go. He's drunk and emotional, and you're already in trouble. Stop this before you make everything worse."

Finally, Dane stood of his own accord and backed away. He turned to me, his eyes flashing with anger as he glanced at my neck. My hands raised there, and I flinched as my fingers made contact. Surely there were red marks, if not bruises. My skin felt tender to the touch. Meanwhile, Ryan inhaled deep breaths on the ground.

"What's going on here?" A deep, male voice spoke from behind us. It was Mr. Clark Sr. flanked by his wife, Amanda, and a small group of mourners dressed in black.

"Dane?" Amanda said in her clipped voice. "What are you doing?!"

Dane brushed his hands off on his clothes, then ignored his parents and reached over to help Ryan to his feet. The latter didn't want anything to do with Dane. Ryan crab-walked backward, his eyes livid, spitting as he spoke.

"*He's* the one who killed her," Ryan snapped, raising a trembling finger to Dane. "He killed her, and he just about killed me. Arrest him before he hurts anyone else."

"You were choking me," I said, stepping between Dane and Ryan. "You were trying to kill *me*."

Ryan stood up, wiped a hand across his mouth. "Whatever you say," he said, his eyes flicking toward the entrance of the church. The cops that had taken one of the back pews were filtering out, slowly registering the disturbance. "He knows the truth," Ryan said to the growing crowd. Swiveling his gaze back to Dane, he yelled, "You stole Andrea away from me!"

"Is this true?" Amanda asked her son as the cops convened on us. "Were you dating that girl?"

"Let's go," Dane said to me. Resting a hand on my back, he led me away, back to the church where he spoke in low tones with Gerard and Mrs. Dulcet while the police began asking questions to anyone in the immediate vicinity. When he finished, he turned back to me. "Are you ready to go home?"

"My bike," I squeaked. "It's locked out front."

"Make sure it gets home," Dane instructed Gerard. "You're coming with me, Lola."

# Chapter 18

"PLEASE PASS THE BUTTER." Amanda spoke to the table and looked at the wall, but I had a feeling the request was pointed at me. "And the salt."

I handed over the plate of butter to where she sat at the head of the dining room table, and then I did the same with the salt. Amanda's husband sat across from her, Dane across from me. Dinner was a tense event, and I didn't blame Mrs. Dulcet for staying tucked away in the kitchen as much as possible.

We ate the roast in silence for a few long minutes. "It was a lovely ceremony today," I offered. "That was very generous of the Clark family to prepare it and help with costs."

"It was a lovely ceremony until my son decided to fight a drunkard like a lunatic." Mrs. Clark daintily cut a pea in two slices. "Then it turned into a PR *nightmare*. The police will probably want to take you in for questioning again Dane, if not worse. Don't even get me *started* on the media circus outside the gates of Castlewood."

"It's not Dane's fault," I said without thinking. "He was sticking up for me."

She fixed a stare on me, her eyes a different shade of blue than her son's. While Dane's eyes held a piercing intensity that spoke of intelligence and even humor, hers were dull, almost gray, and empty. "It's his fault for getting involved with a woman like you in the first place."

"Mother!" Dane warned. "We'll not discuss this over dinner."

"I told him this was all a bad idea to begin with," she continued. "Sleeping with the staff is never a good idea. Don't you agree, Randall?"

Her husband's face turned a slightly uncomfortable shade of red. "Yes, of course, dear."

Dane's eyes narrowed to glittering pieces of diamonds. "You may leave if you're not happy here, mother."

"*What* did you say?" Her voice was a harsh whisper.

"You're no longer welcome to dine with us," Dane said, "if you cannot treat my guests or my staff with respect."

"Dane," I said with a slight shake of my head. "It's okay, I'll get going. It's late anyway, and—"

"Don't move, Lola." Dane's voice came as a command, and there was no arguing with the stony expression on his face. "What will it be, mother? Apologize to Lola, or this dinner is finished."

Mrs. Clark dropped her fork. It clattered onto the plate before her, and when a single pea rolled onto the tablecloth, she didn't even seem to notice. Nor did she notice when one of the young, bright-faced members of the kitchen staff came to clear it away.

"Get out of here," she snapped, shooing away the overzealous new staff member. "Dane Clark, you will never speak to your mother like that again."

"Amanda," Randall said, a hint of pleading in his voice. "Please just apologize. It doesn't matter, anyway. She's just *staff*. She'll be gone next month."

I blinked, looked down at my plate, and tried to pretend I didn't exist.

"I don't see how I can apologize when I didn't do anything wrong." A steely silence met Amanda's declaration. She looked from one of us to the next, skipping over my face in exchange for her husband's. "I'm just being honest, Randall."

"Mrs. Dulcet, please bring my mother's coat," Dane said. "Call Uncle Anders and let him know my parents will be returning soon."

Amanda's mouth cracked open as scurrying sounds from one room over filtered back to us. "Dane *Clark*!"

"Amanda, *apologize* for crying out loud!" Randall's voice boomed. "I want to stay in my son's house and eat a damn meal instead of running over to Anders's every time the two of you argue. Why does it matter who he sleeps with? He's not going to *marry* the girl."

Amanda took one look at Randall, then scanned across the table. Either her husband's logic made sense, or the tone of his voice had instructed her not to push him further. "I'm sorry if I've offended you," she said briskly toward me. "But I'm just looking out for the well-being of my son."

I nodded, looking down at my plate. It wasn't that I loved the way Mrs. Clark treated me, but in a way, I could understand. She was a woman from a certain level of society, and she wanted the best for her son. Growing up with a mother who couldn't have cared less if I'd dated a convicted murderer or the President of the United States, a part of me wished that she had cared enough to at least *meet* my boyfriends—not that there had been many of them.

Randall clapped his hands. "Now that *that's* settled, Mrs. Dulcet—cancel the car and serve dessert, will you?"

For the rest of the evening, Dane's gaze didn't once land on his mother. Her gaze didn't land on me. Randall's gaze didn't veer from the warm brownies he shoved into his mouth along with the bits of melting vanilla ice cream on the side. Only when coffee was served did Mrs. Clark break the silence.

"Why was *he* even there?" Amanda asked suddenly, frowning at the extra scoop of ice cream on my plate. "The ex-boyfriend. Isn't it strange that he showed up at that woman's funeral?"

Dane spoke to his plate. "I'm sure he wanted to pay his respects to the dead."

"But their relationship was over," she said. "Clearly the girl didn't love him, or she would have been with him."

"I was in attendance." Dane's voice was liquid silver in the murky silence. "And I'm the one suspected of murdering her. I think that's far stranger, don't you?"

That caused Mrs. Clark to freeze, but only for a moment.

"We all know you didn't kill her—the accusations are a clerical error," Randall said. "Of course you should have been at the funeral. You did the right thing, son, paying the expenses. The Clark Company takes care of their employees—after all, that's the only way to maintain loyalty and control. It would be incredibly rude to not pay your respects because of a clerical error. It's about the strategy, Dane—this will help company morale."

"The accusations aren't a *clerical error*," Dane said through gritted teeth. "The murder weapon was a paperweight from *my* desk. Someone was setting me up."

"But it's an obvious set up," Amanda said. "Nobody thinks you had a hand in her death. What I *can't* believe is the way that woman's parents were flaunting their money around."

"Money?" I asked.

"Yes, the thing that you use to buy goods and services," Amanda quipped. "If you're not familiar with it, you should try to acquire some."

"*Mother!*" Dane rose to his feet, but his father interrupted first, catching my eye and speaking directly to me.

"Andrea's parents have come into an extreme amount of wealth with Andrea's passing. My wife is merely trying to say that it's considered rude to arrive at their daughter's funeral in a new car purchased with money they received due to their daughter's untimely passing."

"Money they received?" I looked to Dane. "Did you know about this?"

"Of course not," Amanda said. "We know people. Amaliyah Ricker's mother was a client of our accountant's firm. She happened to have created a trust for her granddaughter, Andrea, before her death. Now, that was years ago, but Amaliyah came in the office a few weeks ago causing quite the scene. Fortunately, I happened to have an appointment that day and overheard a few things. Marie, our accountant's wife, filled me in on the rest of the details."

Dane turned to his mother with newfound curiosity. "What details?"

Amanda gave a smug smile. "As it turns out, Andrea's grandmother left all of her money in a trust fund to be delivered to Andrea on her thirtieth birthday."

"What?" I gaped, my reaction a reflex. "That is *not* the story I heard."

"Well, you didn't know the accountant who handled their trust," Amanda said. "So, I'm not sure where you heard anything at all."

"I talked to Amaliyah. She said her mother left money for them when she passed, and Amaliyah and her husband gave it all away because they didn't want it," I said. "It was a pain point between Andrea and her mother—Andrea wanted the money, but Amaliyah wanted nothing to do with it."

"Andrea liked money, sure," Amanda said. "But only because she didn't have any of it. Andrea was dirt poor and so were her parents. If they told you anything different, it's a lie. They've never given money away."

"But—"

"Amaliyah wanted her mother's money. Her mother didn't give it to her. *That* was the pain point," Mrs. Clark said. "The reason Andrea sought financial wealth later in life is because she grew up with nothing. Nobody likes to have nothing now, do they?"

Amanda looked all too pointedly at me, and I found myself nodding along.

"So," I said, puzzling through this new information, "the only way Amaliyah would've inherited her mother's money is if Andrea passed away before her thirtieth birthday—*then* the money would have gone to her instead of Andrea."

Mrs. Clark nodded. "Now tell me how the police still believe my son is a suspect when Andrea's own parents have a motive to the tune of one point two million dollars," Amanda said, waving a hand in disgust. "What motive did Dane have to hurt Andrea—*nothing*! The girl was nothing to him except for a pretty face on a magazine cover. You didn't love her, did you, Dane?"

Dane cleared his throat. "Andrea and I were business acquaintances and nothing more. I wouldn't even classify us as friends."

"And," I said, gaining momentum as pieces clicked into place. "According to Ryan, Andrea was turning thirty next week. This would have been the Rickers's last chance at the money. I assume the trust went to them in the case of Andrea's untimely death?"

"If that's not motive, then I don't know what is. And she wouldn't have given them a dime after the way they raised her," Mrs. Clark said. "People like Andrea don't know how to manage that amount of money. She would have blown it on plastic surgery and a monstrosity of a new house, *if* she could manage that much."

"But Andrea was their daughter," Dane said in a sole defensive argument that completed our conversation. "How could someone kill their own daughter? And more, I hadn't ever heard of these people. How could they have gotten inside the castle and stolen the paperweight?"

# Chapter 19

I SAT UP IN A BURST of adrenaline sometime after midnight.

I'd tucked into my bedroom above Psychic in Pink shortly after dinner and drifted into a restless sleep sometime later. It was impossible to say if I'd jolted awake due to one of my pulse pounding nightmares, or if the shot of fear was due to something in reality.

I hesitated, listening—and then I heard it. *I hadn't dreamt the noise.* A whisper of movement flickered from downstairs, someone picking their way across the living room floor.

*Someone had broken into my home.*

There was no time to change into real clothes, so I threw on the bright pink robe as I climbed out of bed and made my way toward the top of the staircase. The Sunshine Shore was a safe town, save for the latest fiasco with Andrea's murder. Dotty and I had never had so much as a robbery in all of our years here; in fact, I'd only begun locking the door recently. Something about being alone in the house had me taking the extra precaution.

A muffled crash alerted me to the intruder's position. My visitor must have stubbed a toe on the kitchen table. Judging by the low curse word mumbled afterward, it was a man.

I held my cell phone in my hand and pressed the 911 button. I'd already hesitated too long, frozen partly by fear and partly by curiosity. The phone rang once.

"I'm calling the police," I yelled downstairs. "They're on their way. Leave me alone!"

The intruder paused, all floor squeaks coming to a halt. "Lola, is that you?"

I couldn't see the man's face in the dark, but I sensed his presence. I knew that voice. "Richard?"

"911, what is—"

"Oh, I'm so sorry." I brought the phone back to my mouth. "It was a terrible misunderstanding. I'm okay—I thought someone had broken into my home, but it's just a friend of mine. I'm so sorry to have wasted your time."

After disconnecting with 911, I flicked on the lights and found Richard squinting in the brightness.

"Howdy, Lola. I needed your help."

"What were you *thinking*? You have got to stop letting yourself in here uninvited." I wrapped my robe tighter around my body. "You don't ever need my help after midnight unless you're deathly ill. Understood? And in that case, you're better off calling an ambulance."

"But—"

"Understood? We need boundaries, Richard."

"Fine." He glanced down at a huge moving box in his arms full of what looked like junk. "I couldn't sleep."

"Well, I could, and you disrupted me." I sat down on the staircase. "And I'm not happy about it."

His shoulders slumped. "I'm sorry. Would it help if I told you I talked to Big Richard, and he's all for renting out The Lost Leprechaun to you for that fancy schmancy gala you've got planned?"

"That does help some," I admitted, perking up slightly. "We'd need it on the last Saturday of the Sunshine Shore festival—rented exclusively for the evening. Would that work?"

"Two grand food and drink minimum, and we'll let you have the venue for free," he said. "You can do whatever you want to it, so long as all decorations are taken down by noon the next day."

I felt a smile growing over my face. "You've got a deal. Do we need to sign a contract?"

He extended my hand. "We do things the old-fashioned way. I know you're not a gentleman, but how do you feel about shaking on it and calling the red tape good?"

"Fine by me." I returned the handshake, my mind already scrolling through the invite list. If I got RSVPs out immediately, that would still give people a week to clear their evenings. It wasn't ideal, but it was better than nothing.

After we shook on the arrangement, I was feeling marginally less annoyed that Richard had broken into my house. I was even feeling charitable at the deal he'd garnered for us with his father.

"Alright," I agreed. "Tell me what's on your mind. I'm already up, anyway."

"*Great*. I need some help because I have a date today with Stephanie." His shoulders went from slumped to straight in a second, and his eyes widened with excitement. "The poem *worked*. She loved it."

"That's great!"

"Now I need help making it perfect. Every detail has to work—it's my only chance to get her back." His arms were trembling with excitement as he set the box down on the stairs. "Since you're a psychic and everything, I figured I would get your read on my plan before I screwed everything up again."

"Why the box?" I couldn't help my curiosity. I was nearly certain I saw a feather duster in there. "And why is it *here* with you?"

Richard began taking items out one by one, displaying each like a proud cat who'd brought back trophy mice. "I have handcuffs, perfume, cologne, two golf clubs—in case she's picked up mini golf since she dumped me—a baseball glove, a hockey stick, a beach towel, a sexy French maid costume—"

"Let's start at the beginning," I said. "*Handcuffs?*"

"I'm trying to think of every possible item we might need. See, she told me that she just wanted to get coffee. No strings attached, just to talk. I don't know what that *means*, so I'm trying to be prepared for any possible outcome."

"Let me repeat. *Handcuffs?*"

"I figure it might go like this: we start at Dungeons and Donuts. I buy her the biggest cappuccino in town. We have a great time—I have a list of jokes to make her laugh for starters. Then, after she's primed and in a great mood, I take her out to my car where I have this box of wonders in my trunk."

"Do go on," I said. "I can't imagine what happens next."

"I'm going to give her *options.* She used to say I never liked to trying anything new, but I'm going to show her that's all *wrong.*" He grinned. "We can try mini golf. Then, I figure we'll play catch at the park. I have a ball in here somewhere, I think. Maybe kick around a soccer ball. I have beach towels in here for us to lay out after, and I think I even have some non-expired sunscreen..."

As Richard rifled through his box, I struggled with advice. He was trying, I had to give him that. "Handcuffs?" I asked again. "Please explain how meeting for coffee to *talk* requires handcuffs."

A larger grin spread across his face. "Just in case she wants to try something new after our dinner. I made *real* romantic reservations at Nancy's new place, see. They use real wine glasses and you have to order from a laminated menu. If she's feeling romantic, maybe she'll enjoy the French maid costume." He held up a feather duster, tickled his own nose, and sneezed. "Or not. I won't be offended if it's too wild for her."

I let out a longer sigh, wishing it was a little later in the morning so I could justify making coffee. "Let me get one thing straight. Stephanie said she just wanted to meet for coffee."

"Yeah, and to talk."

I ran a hand over my forehead, stood up, and dragged myself downstairs. Resting a hand on Richard's shoulder, I simply shook my head. "It's too much. Your idea is, ah, good in theory, but all of *this* is overwhelming."

"But—"

"You trusted me with the poem and it worked, right?"

He nodded.

"Well, this is the same thing," I said. "*Trust me*. Leave this box of stuff here for now and pick it up later so you won't be tempted to use any of it. It'll just push her away, I promise you."

"I can keep it in my trunk, just in case."

"That won't lead to anything good," I said. "She just wants to talk. If you bombard her with everything at once, she'll push you away faster than you can say *hello*."

"Then how am I supposed to win her back? I'm not good at *talking*."

"Hey, you wrote that poem, didn't you?" I spread my hands wide and raised my eyebrows. "That came from inside your heart, and she must have noticed. Latch onto whatever it is that made you write those words—the part of you that loves Stephanie more than everything else—and use it. Don't scare her away or pressure her into a relationship. Just be yourself, and that's all you have to do."

"Be myself minus the curse words?"

"Yeah, that's a better way to say it."

"What if I take along the golf clubs just in case..." He stopped speaking at my stern expression. "Fine. I'll leave everything here."

I gave him a nod of confirmation. "You've got this, Richard. I'm rooting for you."

"Thanks, Lola. I don't know what I'd have done without you."

To my surprise, I found that the weasley little red head *did* have me rooting for him. Something in his persistence had suckered me into caring about how things ended between him and Stephanie. He was rough around the edges, but his intentions were good.

"Oh, one more thing," I said as I walked him to the door. "That list of jokes you wrote out to use when you see her?"

His hand went protectively to his pocket. "What about it?"

I wiggled my fingers in a *gimme* sort of motion. "Fork it over."

"But—"

"*Now.*"

With a final heave of his chest, Richard handed over the jokes. "Don't use them," he warned. "They're mine. I've copyrighted them. I want them back with the rest of my things."

I took once glance at the jokes and made the easiest promise of my life. "I'd never dream of using these."

"Hey, Lola," he asked tentatively as he spun to face me on the front steps, "can I call you later to analyze how it went?"

"You can call, but you can't break into my house."

"We have a deal."

# Chapter 20

BY THE TIME I'D OFFICIALLY returned to the waking world, I'd grabbed a few more hours of sleep—but still not enough. I'd tossed and turned after Richard's visit, finally giving in to the pull of coffee just after six. I was dressed and ready for work by seven—entirely too early to do much of anything except putter around the place.

Johnny showed up to work just after seven, and I'd annoyed him with my questions by quarter after. I left the house around seven thirty and rode my bike over to Babs's office. As I suspected, she'd arrived early and was already there when I parked outside and stole a cup of coffee from her machine.

"You're not hanging out here for an hour." Babs pushed a pair of no-nonsense glasses up onto her nose. She barely qualified for a prescription, but she liked to keep a pair of specs on hand just in case she needed to look 'more like a lawyer'—her words, not mine. "You're driving me crazy pacing around here like that."

I sat, sighed, and studied Babs. She was the curviest, most stylish lawyer I'd ever seen, and her specs made her look more like a sexy librarian than they did a lawyer—but I wouldn't tell her that. I watched her work for a few minutes, tapping my fingers against the edge of the mug, still agitated.

"I wish I had a car," I said. "Not that I actually want one, but—"

Babs held up her keys. "Get out of here. Sorry I can't join you. I've got a meeting at nine, and I can't be late."

"Thank you, thank you!" I leapt up, snatched the keys from her hand, and hustled outside after a quick refill of stolen coffee.

Holding the mug in one hand, I slipped behind the wheel of Babs's car and clocked in a now-familiar address on my phone's GPS.

Then I turned the car toward a place I didn't have a strong desire to go. But I needed some answers, and my questions wouldn't ask themselves.

My trip to Glassrock was precarious at best. I was an out-of-practice driver on a good day, and today wasn't a good day. I had the added challenge of attempting to operate the vehicle with only one hand, due to the coffee mug I held in my other, and its inability to fit in the stupid cup holder.

After enduring a snail's paced drive and the honks from frustrated drivers behind me, I pulled into the rundown parking lot outside of the Rickers's ramshackle home, pulling Babs's car up behind the brand-new Tesla I'd seen debuted at their daughter's funeral.

As I stepped from my car, I frowned at the sight of boxes on top of boxes stacked outside on the small patch of grass that counted as a lawn. Someone was on their way out of here, and that someone was moving quickly.

"Hello?" I picked my way over a box of pots and pans and stepped around a tattered armchair with a sign on it that said TAKE ME. "Hello, Mr. and Mrs. Ricker?"

Mrs. Ricker stuck her head out from the front door, her eyes widening as she recognized me. She stood, wiped her hands against the threadbare apron she wore, and leaned against the doorframe. "Can I help you? Again?"

I offered a smile and aimed for politeness. "Hi Amaliyah, you might remember me from the other day—I came to visit with a friend of mine. Or," I said, dodging something strewn across the grass that looked like an old batch of stew. "You might remember me from yesterday at your daughter's funeral."

Amaliyah's eyes hardened. "I remember you—the nosy one. What are you doing here?"

"Are you and your husband moving?" I asked. "You didn't mention anything the other day. Where are you headed?"

"The nosy one," she repeated, her jaw tightening. "What can I help you with?"

"I was hoping you could clarify something for me." I stopped my forward progression a few feet away from the front steps leading to their home. To meet Amaliyah's eyes, I had to look up at her perched above me, and it made me uncomfortable to see the large block of knives sitting on the counter behind her. "I'm sorry about being nosy. If you'll remember, I'm looking into your daughter's murder."

"You're not a cop."

"No, but I care about what happened to your daughter."

"It doesn't seem like you knew her all that well."

"I didn't, but I know my boss, and he's being framed for her murder. He didn't do it."

She tilted her nose upward. "How can you be so sure about that?"

"I know him." I swallowed hard. "He wouldn't do that."

"You're in love with him," Amaliyah said in a moment of stark clarity. "I can hear it in your voice. Love blinds, you know. Remember that. Are you sure you know him as well as you think?"

I pushed past the flickering doubts about Dane Clark—the reality that he kept a barrel of secrets I knew nothing about, and probably other barrels of secrets that I didn't even know existed. "This is about Andrea, not me—not even Dane. Unless...there's a reason you don't want me to find out what happened to her?"

The edge on my words set something off in Mrs. Ricker. She threw the door open, letting it bang freely against the wall behind her before she took the steps down one huff at a time. She moved right into my space bubble and held a finger just under my nose. "I understand when I'm being threatened, missy, and I don't like what you're insinuating."

"I'm not insinuating anything—I'm just asking questions and trying to do a good job."

"Well it's *not* your job, so maybe you should let sleeping dogs lie. We've put Andrea to rest. We've come to peace with her being gone, now let us move on. Do you have children?"

At the abrupt change of subject, I shook my head.

"Then don't talk to me as if you know what it's like to lose a child." There was a pinch of venom in her voice, though whether it was directed at me or reminiscent of something deeper, something darker in her, I couldn't say. "You come here hinting that I might have something to do with my daughter's death? I should have you arrested or thrown out of here. You're not the cops, and I'm not required to talk to you, so get off my property."

With a sinking feeling, I realized I'd gone at this all wrong. I'd let my suspicions get the best of me and jumped to conclusions. Even worse, she was completely right. I was a nobody—not the police, not a PI, nothing. And I'd all but accused a woman of having something to do with her daughter's death.

It still didn't add up for me: the money, the new car, the moving. I hesitated, weighing the pros and cons of disappearing like I should at this moment or pressing just a hint further. If I could find her pressure point and lean on it just a bit—not to make her pain worse, but for Andrea's sake. To find the person who'd ended her life all too soon.

With that shred of conviction holding me in place, I pressed just a little bit harder. "I see you have a new car."

My words all but stunned Mrs. Ricker. Her hands froze in the middle of toying with her apron and the fabric bunched beneath it. By the time she unfroze, I realized I'd hit a nerve.

"Why are you leaving, Mrs. Ricker?" I asked softly, aiming for a new approach. "I am truly sorry if I came off accusatory. I don't think you had anything to do with your daughter's murder, but I also feel strongly that my boss—my friend—is innocent too. And yesterday, seeing Andrea's photos at the ceremony..." A very real lump grew in my throat. "It's not fair that her murderer is going unpunished. I know I'm not the police. I don't have a license to be here, and you don't owe me anything. I'm just trying to find out what happened to your daughter."

The bit of poison that'd hardened in Mrs. Ricker's eyes broke. It vanished like a cloud of smoke and disappeared on the next breeze. Her hands unfroze, the apron falling in wrinkles against her lap as she eased onto the edge of the TAKE ME armchair.

"Mrs. Ricker?" I glanced at the ground, found a patch of clean grass, and rested a knee there. "Are you okay? Did I say something?"

"We're fools," she said. "Fools."

"What do you mean?"

"The money. I knew we shouldn't have touched it, but we didn't know what to do."

"What money? What are you talking about?"

"There is—was—a trust fund set up in Andrea's name," Amaliyah said after a pause. "Last time you were here, I lied to you."

"Why did you lie?"

"Not for the reasons you think." Tears pooled in Amaliyah's eyes, and she hugged herself close, looking suddenly thin and tired. "Because I wanted my daughter to love us for...us."

I shook my head, not understanding.

"Ever since she was a young girl, Andrea had been excited by the idea of money. Wealth and fashion and fame and glitz. Nothing we could give her at the time." Amaliyah didn't seem to notice as the first tear fell and skidded across her cheek. "The bits about her grandmother—most of that wasn't a lie. Andrea always did want to be like her grandmother. She told us she wanted to live with her ever since she understood how to talk."

"Most people love their grandmothers," I said, my mind flicking to Dotty Pink. "I loved mine more than anything. She raised me; I didn't have a mother around."

"But Andrea did. I wanted her to love me, to want to be with me, even if she didn't want to be *like* me." Amaliyah shook her head. "But there was no convincing her. My husband and I tried, but no matter what, we couldn't seem to get Andrea to see our point of view. She insisted on wanting name brand things, items we couldn't afford, things we just couldn't buy. We struggled for money, and my mother didn't offer us anything to help—not that we wanted help."

I nodded, listening.

"We were never enough." Amaliyah shook her head, lost in her own daydreams. "When my mother passed away, she did leave us money as I told you, but it didn't come to us, and we didn't give it away to charity. In fact, I assume the reason my mother *didn't* give it to us is because she didn't want to see money "squandered" to a charity. She didn't believe in such things."

"She put the money in Andrea's name—a trust that wouldn't release funds until Andrea turned thirty."

Amaliyah nodded miserably. "She found out. The time she visited us, she confronted us about it. I tried to explain—to let her know that we had every intention of letting her take the money freely when she turned thirty—but she didn't want to hear it."

"Why lie to her in the first place?" I asked. "If the money was in Andrea's name all along, would it really have mattered?"

"I didn't want money to be the reason for Andrea to like us—her parents. We are her parents, Lola. She should have loved us for that reason alone and because we loved her back, not because we were the avenue to a large inheritance. If she knew about the money, she would have held on until she got it—and then left."

"And in not telling her, you just pushed her away sooner," I said, puzzling it out as I spoke. "I don't see—"

"Of course you don't see! You don't have a child. You don't know what it's like for them to dislike you because you're not enough. Because you can't provide everything they want and desire."

I had a fleeting glimpse of my own mother pawning me off to Dotty, and I wondered—hoped, even—that she'd felt some of the same things. It felt easier to me to understand why she'd left me on Dotty's doorstep this way. The only other alternative was that I just hadn't been wanted—for no reason at all. And that didn't feel great.

"Maybe I don't know what that's like, and I can't imagine the hurt you're feeling," I said. "Even if you kept the money from her—why are you spending it now? The Tesla, the move."

"What's left?" She shrugged, helpless. "My daughter is dead. My parents are gone. It's just my husband and myself now, and for the first time, we have more money than we know what to do with." She gave a wry smile. "Andrea would've loved to see the money used."

"I'm really sorry, Mrs. Ricker, and I mean that. I can't imagine what it's like to lose a daughter."

"No, you can't," she said shortly, broken from her reverie. "I lied to you, but only because I was ashamed of the truth. My daughter didn't love me because I was her mother, and I kept the money from her in hopes that would change. It never did, and when she found out about her trust, things only deteriorated. I haven't spoken to my daughter in years, Miss Pink, though I never stopped loving her. And I most certainly did *not* have anything to do with her murder."

I nodded, offered another quiet apology, and backed away from her. I still wanted to ask where she was going, what they planned to do, what her husband thought of all this—but I sensed the conversation was over.

"Thank you," I said again as she climbed the front steps. "If I find out who was responsible for this, would you like to know?"

Mrs. Ricker's face crumpled into weariness, as if my question brought back the reality of it all. A reality she'd temporarily pushed away as she focused on memories from the past.

Then she looked up, shook her head once. "No," she said firmly. "It won't bring her back. Goodbye, Miss Pink."

I sincerely hoped this was goodbye. I hoped that she was as innocent as she claimed to be—as innocent as I believed her to be. I hoped that where she and her husband were headed, they could find a peaceful existence. The hole where Andrea had been would always exist.

I knew this because even though I hadn't seen my mother in over twenty years, there was a part of me that wondered, that worried, that loved and longed. I only hoped the Rickers could find a happiness like I had. Because even though my life wasn't traditional, and I hadn't been raised in a typical home, my life was full. My friends were wonderful, my grandmother had been a beacon of love and hope, and my new employer...

I hesitated. I hesitated on the word love, on the word employer, and on the word friend. I still hadn't classified Dane Clark in his entirety, but I had hope. And hope is exactly what I wished for the Rickers.

# Chapter 21

THE ENTIRE DRIVE, VISIT, and return to and from Glassrock took under an hour, which meant I still had half an hour before I had to be at work. It would be pushing it, but while I had Babs's car, I figured it wouldn't hurt to stop home and grab a few of my favorite sunglasses and pay a quick visit to Regina down by the pier.

Not only would I get my visit with her out of the way, but I wouldn't have to pack the sunglasses into cases and shove them into my backpack, praying they didn't break as I pedaled my tush across the Shore.

Best of all, I could pick up a doughnut at the coffee shop before going to Dane's. I had a theory he'd instructed Mrs. Dulcet to tone down her baking since I'd been spending more time at the castle, and it hadn't gone unnoticed.

I stopped home, grabbed an array of styles, and packed them lovingly into the trunk. Then I drove right up to the office where Regina had told me she'd rented space and climbed from the car as I hit speed dial on Dane's number.

"Hello?" he answered on the first ring with a hint of worry. "Is everything okay? Lola, where are you?"

"I'm fine. I'm down by the pier," I said, breezing past his concern and tucking the warmth of it away to savor for later. "I happened to get up early today and thought I'd run a few errands, but I got carried away. I'm really sorry, but I might be a few minutes late coming to work."

Dane hesitated a beat. My stomach sunk. I'd momentarily blanked out how much Dane hated tardiness. His schedule was meticulous, and I'd probably just thrown a wrench in a year's worth of activities.

"I'm sorry, it was stupid of me to think I could get everything done in an hour," I said, easing back onto the driver's seat of the car. "I'm going to head to the office now—I'll see you in ten minutes."

"What are you doing?"

I turned his question over for a second. "Right now? Or on my errands, or what?"

"Does this have anything to do with Andrea?"

I squinted, my face scrunching as I debated which version of my story to tell. The one where I told the whole truth, or the one where I told him about the fashion show portion and left the rest out.

"Lola..."

"Yes," I said on a sigh. "A little bit. I went to visit Andrea's parents this morning. After finding out about the trust fund in Andrea's name yesterday, I wanted to see for myself how the Rickers reacted when I confronted them about it. They lied to me the other day, and I needed to see if they'd admit to the truth."

"And?"

"They're moving. Mrs. Ricker admitted to getting the trust fund money when Andrea died. I'm still not convinced she had a role in her daughter's death. Amaliyah seemed genuinely upset about Andrea being gone. I don't think she would've killed her own daughter for a financial payout."

I could practically hear Dane's gigantic brain churning through information. My own brain had flicked through a hundred new thoughts by the time he finally spoke.

"You don't think they're responsible for her murder?" he asked again. "Are you sure?"

I surprised myself by not having to think too hard. "I'm not positive, but my gut tells me they're innocent. Mrs. Ricker seemed really sad. She's dealing with things in an odd way, but I think that's due to shock and grief more than anything else."

"And Mr. Ricker?"

"I didn't speak to him. I don't know, I suppose he could be involved, but I don't have any evidence for it. They seemed like parents who loved their daughter. They didn't make the right choices, but then again—who makes all of the right decisions?"

"Me," Dane said simply. Then he offered a quiet laugh. "That's a joke, Lola."

I couldn't keep back a smile. "I know, Dane. You do a pretty good job—unlike me. Anyway, I swung by the pier afterward because I have Babs's car, and I want to talk to Regina about the fashion show. I'll fill you in on it when I get to the castle, okay?"

"Okay. Thank you, Lola—for caring enough to keep looking. I just wish you'd taken Semi with you."

"Like I said, I'm not known for making all the right choices."

"You make plenty of right decisions. And it would be a tragedy if you made *all* the smart choices. If you did, I wouldn't have met you."

I thought back to the way I'd impatiently signed the initial contract to work for Dane with relish, and I had to give him the point. "True enough."

"Lola..." It seemed there was something more he wanted to say, and I held my breath as he struggled to find the right words. "Drive safely."

My breath exhaled in a whoosh. "Thanks, bye."

I hung up sounding shorter than I would've liked. Had I really expected the man to say that he loved me over the phone? Even if that's what I wanted to hear?

I climbed out of the car again and slammed the door with a little more gusto than necessary. My fingers tugged in an angry motion through my new hairstyle as I popped the trunk open. I was too frustrated to appreciate the new levels of volume in my hair, which was a true shame.

I calmed slightly as I reached for the box of sunglasses, gently cradling it against my body as I made my way up the steps to the office.

"Oh, there you are—lovely to see you so soon." Regina greeted me a hair's breadth before I reached the door. "Prompt and earlier than I expected, just as I like."

I nodded, not really in the mood for small talk. She led me through the front door into an office area that looked significantly bigger on the inside than it did from the outside. One big open space took up the front half of the building, and a polished, thin receptionist twiddled a pencil behind a huge desk. A few small coffee tables and couches were scattered in a half moon around her, while a variety of offices sat behind closed doors, except for one.

"This way," Regina said, leading the way to her office—the only open door in the facility. "I guess it's a slow time of year because the largest office was available for rent."

I closed the door behind me and set the box on the desk between us. The room had a modern, sterile sort of feel to it, which made sense. It wasn't Regina's office—it was a rented space. One day soon she'd pack up and leave, and the next guest would breeze in to take her place, and then the cycle would repeat.

"I got a little carried away choosing my favorites," I said, cracking open the trunk and removing the smaller, sturdier cases one by one. I rested them in a neat row across her desk, relieved that Regina showed the patience and restraint to leave them untouched while I continued to unpack.

"No such thing as overboard," Regina said once I'd finished laying out nearly thirty different cases on the desk. "May I?"

I nodded, watching intently as she began cracking the boxes open one by one. Ironically, I'd never intended to start a sunglasses collection—nor had I intended to hunt and cherish vintage finds. But my tastes were just a bit quirky, and I happened to like the unique, hard to find shapes and the little-bit-wild frames. Over time, I'd accumulated enough for it to be considered a collection.

"Oh, these are gorgeous." Regina properly oohed and ahhed as she opened the containers one by one. "I don't know how I'll ever choose."

As she'd predicted, Regina had a difficult time choosing which shades to use for the show. I sat back in my chair, feeling the boredom set in now that I was no longer worried about her mishandling my glasses—she touched them like a scientist preserving dinosaur bones—and I glanced at my watch. Already ten after nine—good thing I'd called Dane, or else he'd have sent out a patrol, or worse, to find me.

"Sorry, sorry," Regina murmured, more to herself than to me. "I'll make my choices. It's just that they're all so fabulous."

"Why don't you hang onto them for a bit? I can come back and—"

Loud voices from the reception area drove me to lose track of what I was saying. I watched as Regina's eyes flicked up, her shoulders tense.

"That'll be Leslie Gray," she said, sounding none too happy about it. "I asked her to come here for some fittings. In fact, you might as well meet her now. Maybe we can try a few on and see what fits Leslie's face the best. Once we choose a headlining pair, the rest will be easy to slot in behind."

"Sure," I said, none too thrilled with the idea. The way Regina shied away from her, I couldn't imagine that was a good thing, seeing as Regina seemed unintimidated by most men, women, and children. "I have a few more minutes before I have to get back to work."

"Work—right. You work for Dane Clark, don't you? That billionaire?" Regina glanced up at me, interested. "Do you know him well? They're saying he killed Andrea, you know. Are you sure it's safe to go back to work?"

"I'm sure," I said firmly, and I left the rest of her questions untouched.

"I'm just saying that I wouldn't feel comfortable going back until all of this was cleared up. But then again..." she trailed off. "Let me get Leslie her coffee and then bring her in here."

I watched through the open doorway as a leggy strawberry-blonde woman leaned against the receptionist's desk. She wore skin tight jeans, a cropped leather jacket that was entirely unnecessary in these temperatures, and the latest Gucci sunglasses that were entirely unoriginal.

I couldn't help a hint of distaste even as I studied her, though I had no reason to think such thoughts aside from her taste in clothes. Regina scurried for the coffee while Leslie watched, and once she'd gathered it in a Styrofoam cup, she handed it over and welcomed Leslie with a smile and a gesture toward her office.

Leslie didn't bother to thank Regina for the coffee, nor did she offer a greeting as she strode into the room. I stood, offered a hand for her to shake, but when Leslie wrinkled her nose and showed her two full hands—coffee and a slim wristlet—I retracted it.

"That's my seat," she said, and then plopped in the chair I'd vacated seconds before. "Who are you?"

"That's Lola. I told you about her—Lola Pink, she's the sunglasses stylist for the show," Regina said in a soothing voice. She offered me a second chair with an apologetic smile before sliding around to her side of the desk. "Lola swung by this morning with a variety to choose from, and I was thinking the three of us could look them over together."

Leslie's gaze flicked to me, and then toward the desk. She appeared unimpressed with my selections. "They're so old," she said, gesturing to a particularly cute pair of pink shades with a hint of the cat-eye style frame. "And these are so round. That was so last year."

"Most of these are vintage," Regina offered. "That's the look we're going for. Now, I'd like to have you try a few on to see what frames your face best. You have such lovely cheekbones."

Flattery worked well with Leslie, and as Regina expertly guided her through the styling process, I sat back and watched, unable to keep from wondering if this woman wasn't only rude, but a cold-blooded killer. The thought hadn't truly seemed realistic in my head, but now that I'd seen Leslie in person, it made a girl wonder.

"So, is this show supposed to be big?" I asked. "I'm pretty clueless when it comes to fashion. Except for sunglasses."

Leslie looked like she begged to differ about my taste in sunglasses fashion, but Regina swooped in to appease us both. "It will be the West Coast show of the year. Of course, New York is probably a tad bigger—but only because there's so much space and so many local designers there. We're sure to make papers, news, and magazines across the country. It'll be great exposure for Leslie."

Leslie looked unsurprised by this, which led me to believe she'd known it'd benefit her career to be the headliner. She picked up a pair of blue, odd-shaped aviators, and folded the arms back and forth.

"Um..." I reached out, rested a hand on her wrist. "Please don't do that. Those are really fragile, and I've already had to replace one screw."

Regina's jaw tightened as she watched me face off with her top model. She couldn't afford to lose either one of us, it seemed, yet she wasn't exactly maintaining control of her show.

Leslie shot me an icy cool glare that sent shivers up and down my spine, and when she spoke, her voice was as frosty as the arctic. "Fine. Choose whatever you want, Regina. I think they're all stupid."

Leslie stood and let herself out, the coffee left behind to cool on Regina's desk. I waited in silence as Regina's hands, shaking, pulled the cup toward her and gestured toward the open chair. "Sorry about that. She can be difficult. Models, you know."

"Andrea wasn't like her." I didn't move from my seat in case Leslie came back. I wasn't here to play musical chairs. "Andrea was...warmer."

Regina's eyes gave me a knowing look. "She was the muse. This show is all warm colors, old fashions, curvy women—it's fun, and it's retro."

"So why get Leslie to fill in?"

"She was already in the show's number two slot. She knows the routines, and I've worked with her before." Regina gave herself a little shake, as if convincing herself more than me. "I can handle her. It just takes some getting used to."

"Did she know that she'd get the number one position if Andrea couldn't be in the show?"

Regina looked up at my question, taking a minute to digest the insinuation behind it. "If you think she had anything to do with Andrea's death, you're wrong. Leslie is high maintenance, but she's not a murderer."

"Do you have the paperwork for me?" I stood, figuring my work here was done, and this conversation was over. Not to mention, I was running almost an hour late to the castle. "I'll leave these here and pick them up later. Please take good care of them."

"I had my lawyer draw up a contract. Look over the proposed average price per pair and let me know if I appraised everything correctly—it's a guesstimate, but I rounded up. We can adjust the specifics after making the selection. There's a clause on that, too."

I took a quick scan of the paperwork, knowing I should probably hand it over to Babs, but the language was clear and concise, and the values she promised if something was broken were more than generous. I almost wouldn't mind if one of my lesser favorite pairs broke, and I got the insurance on it. I'd be able to nab six pairs for the price of one payout.

The receptionist sat sulking behind the desk as we entered the lobby. "Leslie went to get a real coffee," she said sounding snappish. "Apparently the stuff I make isn't good enough for her."

Regina barely acknowledged the receptionist as she walked me to the door. With an apologetic smile, she shook my hand. "I'm sorry about today, but we all appreciate you doing business with us. And Lola—"

I froze, watching her raised eyebrows.

"Take care of yourself, okay?" Regina gave a flimsy smile. "Be careful."

I nodded, still puzzled as I retreated down the front steps. The door closed behind me, and I fell into my own little world as I headed toward the doughnut shop to grab some breakfast and a coffee. A quick glance at my watch told me Dane would be through eating at the castle, and I didn't want to bother Mrs. Dulcet for leftovers.

I had barely turned the corner onto the path that snaked along the Sunshine Shore when I ran smack into Leslie Gray. We collided, and a bit of coffee splashed over her shirt and down her front.

She cursed, first at the coffee, then at me. I was surprised to see her, and by the time I apologized, she was already furious.

"I'm sorry," I said. "I'm sure Regina has a bunch of clothes you can change into while you're there. She said she wanted to do some stylings on you, anyway."

"Yes, but this is brand new Ralph Lauren! Do you even know how much clothes cost?"

I looked down, noting that I was, indeed, fully clothed, and nodded. "I'm sorry," I repeated again, though the collision was both of our faults. If anything, she'd been the one texting as we'd come around the blind corner. I'd tried to dodge, but she hadn't even seen me until it was too late. "Actually, though, I was looking for you."

"Why? To ruin the rest of my clothes?"

She made no sense, so I moved right along with my questions, hoping her agitation would make for looser lips than a more composed version of Leslie Gray.

"Did you know Andrea Ricker well?" I asked. "She was scheduled to be the headliner for the show before you."

The model considered me more seriously for a moment, seeming to forget all about the coffee stain on her blouse. "Of course I knew her. We weren't friends, but I knew of her."

"Did you like her?"

The flash in her eyes was answer enough, though Leslie downplayed it with a snort. "Most women don't like me. I have it all, and they don't like it."

"I'm sure that's it," I said tersely. "Did you know you'd be next in line if Andrea couldn't be part of the show?"

"Duh," she said. "I even tried to talk Regina out of hiring that floozy. The only modeling experience she had was pretending to be the fake girlfriend of that idiot billionaire."

My eyebrows flew up. "Idiot billionaire? Dane Clark has been called many things, but never an idiot."

"His PR team hired a girl to be on the cover of a magazine with him. How lame is that? He should be able to get any chick he wants. Instead, he uses a model."

"Do you know Dane?"

"No." She glanced down at her fingernails. "Andrea talked about him a lot. She once tried to get me to believe that they were really dating, but I saw right through it."

"They weren't?"

"She wishes." Leslie rolled her eyes. "Dane didn't pay any more attention to her than he might the shoes he was wearing. She was just an accessory the PR team dressed him with like anything else. Picked off the rack like a tie."

I hated to admit this confession was a relief. I trusted Dane and took him at his word, but the continued reassurance wasn't unwelcome. After all, she'd said one thing I knew to be a fact: Dane could have just about any woman he wanted. He had it all—looks, smarts, money—and most women would be happy enough with that, despite his inability to function normally in social situations. Why he'd chosen me to take a chance on, I'd never truly know.

I exhaled and focused on the problem at hand. "I hate to ask you this, Leslie, but where were you on the night Andrea was killed?"

Her mouth parted into a round 'O'. She truly hadn't realized where I was going with my line of questioning, and that, in and of itself, had me wondering if she could've planned a ruthless murder from start to finish. I could see her temper getting out of control possibly, and it being an accident, but there was no way she could've moved a body on her own. She was just too small, too thin, and too dainty.

"I did not kill Andrea." She hissed at me, her long eyelashes pinching together as she leaned closer. "I can't believe you're even asking me that. I'm Leslie Gray—supermodel. You think I'd throw it all away for her?"

"It's looking pretty good for your career—headlining this event."

"The only reason I tried to convince Regina to hire me instead of that bimbo was because I deserved it. My face is known; my name is known. I'm a supermodel, and I draw crowds. Andrea? She's a fat old chick who stumbled into a cushy job as a Barbie for Mr. Clark."

"You didn't answer my question."

"I was at my boyfriend's house," she snarled, her eyebrows knotting in fury. "This is over. I'm not discussing any more with you, and you can't make me. You're not a cop."

I let her go, watching as she climbed the stairs and threw the door open. She began barking orders the second she stepped inside, and I felt a rush of sympathy for Regina and the receptionist.

I hurried into the car without my coffee, without breakfast, and with a severe streak of hunger gnawing at my stomach. I drove the short distance to Babs's office and left her car in the lot, carrying my borrowed mug inside and popping it straight into the dishwasher. Babs was on a phone call, so I dropped the keys on her desk and waved goodbye to Martie, her receptionist.

Still wondering if Leslie Gray had it in her to kill another woman, I climbed onto my bike and pedaled up the hill to Castlewood. By the time I arrived at the front gates, I'd come to one streamlined conclusion: Leslie Gray didn't commit cold blooded murder. If she had a hand in Andrea's demise, it was accidental, or she had an accomplice. Or more likely, both.

Mrs. Dulcet let me into the castle with a demure smile and greeting, and though I returned her words robotically, I was preoccupied with my thoughts. I wondered if Regina would know the name of Leslie's boyfriend, and if so, if he would corroborate her alibi.

"Dane's in the dining room," Mrs. Dulcet said after I snapped to attention. "I think he's waiting for you."

"Oh, of course. Probably needs to go over the updated schedule."

Mrs. Dulcet gave a tilt of her head, then gestured for me to lead the way. When I reached the dining room, I found Dane sitting alone at his side of the table, a pot of coffee before him and two full place settings. He looked up, his eyes brightening when he saw me standing in the doorway.

"I hope you're hungry," he said, his lips turning to a genuine smile. "I waited to have breakfast with you."

"Oh, Dane. Why did you do that?"

"I missed you," he said simply. "It was no trouble at all. I'm glad you're here."

Everything else—the puzzle, the wondering, the despair—disappeared. The weight lifted from my shoulders, or at least lightened. I strode across the room and pulled Dane into a huge, awkward hug before he had time to stand.

It took him a moment to react, but when he did, he rested his hands on my shoulders and pushed me back a step. Then he stood, rising to his full, intimidating height, and pressed me hard against his chest. His arms wrapped around my back and I sunk into him, inhaling his spicy scent, feeling the hard, lean lines of his muscles.

"Thank you," I whispered against his chest. "I needed that."

"Needed what?"

I squeezed him tighter. "You."

# Chapter 22

BREAKFAST PASSED RAPIDLY. Too quickly, in my opinion, and after light chit chat and pleasant conversation, we found ourselves inevitably winding back around to discussing work.

"Sorry again about throwing off your schedule." I glanced down at the newly printed and revised itinerary. "I can take care of everything you've requested here by mid-afternoon. Once I finish, I need to follow up on plans for the charity gala if that's okay with you."

"Lola." His voice came out harsh. "Of course you may. You don't have to ask permission like a child."

"I didn't mean to ask, I was just—"

"I wish you wouldn't work for me any longer."

I froze at his words, my heart thumping so harshly against my chest I could barely stay still. "What did you say?"

"I said I wish you wouldn't work for me any longer."

"But Dane, I love working for you. I have friends at the castle, and you are the best boss I've ever had." I didn't add that he was my only real boss other than Dotty Pink, but this was one of those moments where I didn't need to see the grass on the other side—I just knew it wasn't greener anywhere else. "I'm sorry if I've done anything to upset you. Is my work not good enough? No, you know what?" I stood up, my fingers gripping the table as I looked across at Dane. "I'm sorry, but I'm sick of apologizing."

"Lola—"

"I work really hard here, Dane," I said, my voice wavering ever so slightly. I hated that it wasn't steady, but now that I'd gotten up on my high horse, I couldn't seem to let myself get down. "I know I make mistakes, and I'm not a quarter—not even a fraction of a quarter as smart as you. I know that, you know that—we all know that. But I promise you, Dane, I care about you. Please don't fire me."

"Fire you? No, Lola—I would never." Dane swooped up from the table and crossed the room in two seconds. He took my shaking hands in his and grasped them, firm and hard, as he sat me back down in the chair.

"But you just said you wished I wouldn't work here any longer." I pressed trembling fingers to my forehead. "I will go if you want. I understand if my work isn't good enough for you, or maybe it's because I screwed up this stupid charity gala—"

Dane interrupted me with a laugh. The sound was so real, so genuine and surprising, that it sent a bolt of anger through me for no reason at all.

"Do you think this is funny?" I asked. "I just poured my heart out to you. I thought we had a special connection, and then you just go and fire me over croissants. It's not fair!"

"I'm not firing you, Lola." Dane knelt before me, and for a moment, my heart stopped thumping entirely. He was on one knee, taking my hands in his, holding them to his chest. "I only said that because your working here complicates things."

"What things?" My heartbeat was back, reluctant and strong, pitter pattering as if it was unsure whether to stop or go, like one giant game of Simon Says in my heart cavity.

"You must know what I mean, Lola—don't you?" He pulled me closer until our foreheads touched. His icicle eyes bore holes through to the back of my skull, but in a meaningful way—as if he needed me to understand. "What you and I have here—it's hardly a normal working relationship."

I cleared my throat, bobbing my head back and forth in agreement.

"Things are hard enough for me as it is. I can't seem to get a read on you, and it's driving me crazy. Anytime you walk into the room,

I want to do this." Dane let go of one of my hands, reached for my chin, and tilted it forward. His lips met mine with an incredible softness.

My free hand reached for the back of his head, my fingers finding thick, silky locks as I pulled him closer to me. He deepened the kiss, sighing with a hint of longing that sent my heart back to the races. If I didn't get a handle on my emotions, I'd be in the cardiac ward before long.

"Then, I have to do this." Dane dropped his hand and retreated, standing before me. He pointed a finger to the schedule on the table. "We talk about business. We pretend there's nothing between us. I have to introduce you to my parents as an assistant when you're so much more than that."

My chest constricted, and I found it harder and harder to breathe. "What are you suggesting, Dane?"

"I'm not firing you; I don't even want you to quit—you're the best personal assistant I've ever had, and not just because you make me laugh, or because you entertain me, or because you care about me more than any normal person should." Dane's lips curved into a tender smile. "I'm just explaining that I wish things weren't like this—that I didn't have to separate our time between business and...whatever else we are."

"What are we, Dane? What do you want us to be?"

"I'm in love with you, Lola. I don't know what that makes us, but I know it's true. Before, I didn't understand the word. I didn't know what it meant, and I didn't expect I'd feel it for anyone at all, let alone this soon."

"I love you, Dane." I felt my eyes tear up as I stood and moved closer to him. "I love you, Dane—I really do. But I don't know where to go from here."

"Will you be mine, Lola?" Dane held my hand in his. "I'll marry you, if that's what this all means."

"We've only known each other a few months. We can't get married yet."

"Why not?"

"Because—" I stopped, unsure of the correct response. "Because we're still getting to know one another."

"But I want to spend my life getting to know you." Dane's hand came up and pushed my hair back from my face. "You're so wonderfully unique that I don't think a hundred years of being with you will allow me to learn everything about you. I don't want to wait any longer."

"But it's not practical. I'm—I'm your assistant, and we're in the middle of this murder investigation, and—"

"You're fired, and you know I'm innocent."

"True, but..." I hesitated. "Hold on a second, did you just fire me?"

"Isn't that what you want? Don't you want to be with me?"

I stood, the smallest fingers of despair threatening to shred my hope, my love for this man, to ribbons. "I'm not wealthy. I'm not well-off naturally, and I have a house I'm trying to fix up, and I need to eat food, and—"

"Move in with me. Be my wife, and you won't need to work. I have enough money to last us forever."

"I-I can't do that."

"You don't want to marry me?"

"It's not that simple. I enjoy working. I don't want to get married just to become a housewife—not that there's anything wrong with being one, but it's not my dream. I enjoy working with you."

"Then that's settled. You'll work with me, not for me."

"I don't understand."

"If you marry me, the Clark Company will be ours. You won't need a salary, and we won't need to tiptoe around business because everything will be shared."

"You can't possibly want to give up that much control. You barely know me. Don't get me wrong—I love you, and I care about you, but what would your parents think?"

Dane considered this for a long moment. He took a step back from the table and turned to face the window, beginning a stare that lasted for quite some time. When he finally turned back around, his face was passive.

"Lola Pink—in all my years on this planet, I never thought I'd find someone I wanted to share my life with." He held up a hand as I started to interrupt. "I'm not good with feelings and emotions, or knowing the right thing to say at any given time—especially in front of women."

I inched forward, the desire to reach for him almost too great. However, I knew he needed space.

"You came into my life, and I frankly don't even recognize it any-more sometimes. I haven't had a proper schedule since I met you, and somehow, it's the best schedule I could ask for. Where I'm order, you're chaos, and—I need you. A completely ordered life is boring."

"And complete chaos is overwhelming," I whispered. "I need you, too, Dane."

"You don't have to answer me now, but I want you to think about it." Thankfully, Dane closed the gap between us. He pulled a chair next to mine, and we sat close, his hand skimming my thigh. "I love you, Lola. I am ready to be married to you, if you'll have me. You already know what people say about me—that I'm cold, or ruthless, or—"

My hand on his cheek silenced him. "You're not any of those things. Not with me, and not in here." My hand skimmed down his face and landed on his chest. "Let's think about this, okay? I don't want you to make this decision and then regret it. Because it's one you're stuck with for the rest of your life."

"It'd be an honor to be stuck with you for the rest of my life." He held my hand over his chest, stuttering to a complete stop when he realized what he'd said. "I mean—I didn't mean stuck with you, I meant—"

"I know." I laughed, leaned in, and pressed a kiss against his cheek. "About that schedule—do you have some wiggle room on there?"

Dane lifted the sheet of paper and tore it in half. "Mrs. Dulcet—have Nick handle my calls and cancel all of my meetings for the day. Including urgent matters."

"Mr. Clark, is everything okay?" Mrs. Dulcet stepped into the dining room to find Dane and I standing, hand in hand, flushed cheeks glowing brightly. "Oh, yes, dear—I see. I'll take care of it."

Dane led me through the castle until he reached the common area in the living quarters. Staff rooms lined one hall along with several guest bedrooms, and the Clark quarters lined the other hall. Instead of taking the usual route to my sometimes-bedroom with the space shower, Dane gripped my hand harder and pulled me toward his.

When we reached the door to what I could only assume was were Dane's private quarters, he pulled me tight against him, our bodies perfectly aligned. My hands wound around his neck, and as he began to speak, I interrupted him with a light kiss.

He looped his arms around my waist, his fingers settling on my skin there—any awkwardness or uncertainty between us long gone. He held me tight, possessive against him, and when he broke our kiss to look into my eyes, there was a darkness in those irises that signaled a hunger for more.

"Are you sure you want to do this?" Dane asked. "You can say no, and I'll try to let things go back to normal."

"Dane, stop." I pressed a finger to his lips. "I quit."

"What?"

"I can't do this anymore. You can't either. I quit."

"But you wanted to work—"

"You fired me already, so my quitting is just a formality," I said with a smile. "We can figure out the rest later. For now..."

Dane rested his hand on the knob and turned. "I love you, Lola Pink. I don't know what I did to deserve a chance with you, but I'm the luckiest man in the world."

"My, you've become suave, Mr. Clark," I said, leaning playfully into his arms as my eyes raked over a bedroom fit for royalty. "You have made falling in love with you very, very fun."

"I hope things are about to get better, Miss Pink." Dane Clark closed the door, then turned the lock. "I'm going to ask one more time if you're sure before—"

I took two quick steps toward him, my arms coming around him the second our bodies touched. My words were a breath across his cheek. "I'm sure."

# Chapter 23

"HAVE YOU EVER DONE this before?" I rolled over in bed and faced Dane, watching as his eyebrow crept upward into a cute arch over his blue eyes. My cheeks grew hot. "Not *that*. I'm talking about blowing off your schedule to do nothing."

Dane's hand trailed over the bare skin of my back as he pulled me closer to him. "I wouldn't exactly call that doing *nothing*."

"Dane!"

"No," he said with a light laugh. "Then again, there are plenty of things I'd never done before you entered my life."

I inhaled a fake gasp. "Have I corrupted you, Mr. Clark?"

"Feel free to corrupt me all over again if you like."

I laughed and curled against him, savoring the warmth as his arms tightened around me and held me close. With his semi-marriage proposal, it wasn't all that difficult to imagine spending our nights like this—wrapped in one another's embrace, surrounded by sheets softer than clouds and beneath a comforter as delicate as a sigh.

We faced the window, watching fat clouds drift by to a backdrop of pale skies with the slightest hint of mountains in the background. Treetops glistened at the lower edge of the window, and my mind went to the heavy forest that surrounded the castle beyond the snow-globe-esque setup of the Clark Company.

"If we were to get married," I began, the moment feeling dreamy and surreal, "would we still have secrets?"

I could almost feel Dane frown, though my back was to his chest. "What sort of secrets?"

"There's so much I don't know about you."

"Well, what do you want to know?"

"I know everything I need to know." I took a step backward as I recalculated. "I just mean—the extras. I don't know exactly what it is that you do here, for example. Then again, I probably wouldn't understand even if you told me. You have the uber-mysterious Warehouse 11. Heck, I'm sure there are things I don't *know* that I don't know about you."

"That's very deep and broad, Miss Pink," Dane said. "I will explain everything you'd like to know. As for the business, I don't think it's possible to keep you posted on everything that goes on around here on a daily basis as that's a full-time job for more than one person. Even I have to let go of that control."

"Yeah, right."

"It's true. Most of the Warehouses are contained. As for your question to Warehouse 11, that is my...personal project. A passion project, pet project, whatever you want to call it."

Something about the almost defensive way Dane spoke of it raised a tiny hint of alarm. "It's legal, isn't it?"

"Very much so."

"It's not creepy?"

"Is that what you think of me?" Dane's breath trailed across my neck as his fingers ran in thin lines through my hair. "That I have a personal 'creepy' space for my hobbies?"

"No, but—" I stopped talking, forced a glance over my shoulder, and was rewarded with a brief kiss from Dane's lips. "Mmmm."

"But?"

"But nobody around here seems to know what's inside of it. It's just—odd."

"Don't you have anything in your life that's just yours? That is nobody else's but your own, even if it's nothing but a book, or a place you go to think, or a memory?"

I flicked through my memories of Dotty Pink and realized there were a few I held onto with a ferocity that was mine alone. Memories

I couldn't—or rather wouldn't—share with anyone. Except maybe Dane when the timing was right.

"Yes," I answered quietly. "I suppose you're right. I'm sorry to pry."

"You're not prying, Lola—you're curious. And that's one of the many qualities I love about you." Dane leaned in and pressed a kiss to the back of my head as his arm snaked over my stomach to reel me in even closer. "If I seem evasive, I don't mean to be. I'd just prefer to show you rather than explain, if you don't mind."

"You don't have to do that. I really was just curious—I trust you, Dane."

"I know, and that's why I'd like to show you. When the time is right."

I rolled over to face him, my head resting on the pillow at the perfect vantage point to stare into his eyes, my hair spread wildly across the sheets after he'd pulled out my hairband. He said he liked it that way.

I meant to thank him, but the flash of vulnerability in his eyes required so much more. Instead, I leaned in toward him, my lips coming to rest against his cheek, then his forehead, then finally I pulled back and pressed my lips to his.

He sighed, closing his eyes. I realized that, for the first time, he looked relaxed. Calm almost, peaceful—despite the fire burning behind those brilliant eyes and the urgent way his hands gripped me close. He'd always been a beautiful man—confident and proud, brilliant and surefooted. He was even more beautiful like this: vulnerable, open, and warm.

I felt a prick in my eyes at the thought that he'd let down his guard for me. I recognized how difficult the risk must be for him. To see him here—bare-chested, hard-muscled, soft-spoken—before me, giving up a day to be with me when he had a billion things to do and not enough time to do them, made me sigh.

"I really love you, Dane."

My mind worked faster than my words, and I was already reconsidering his offer of marriage. After a broken childhood home, a part of me longed for the stability of a family. Of a husband who not only could, but who wanted to provide for me, who supported my dreams, who treated me like I walked on clouds no matter how much I'd eaten for breakfast.

Dotty Pink had provided me with all the love in the world I'd needed, but it didn't mean I hadn't wondered about the alternative. About what a home with two happy parents might look like, a home with a house and a yard and a dog, or maybe a few siblings.

The idea took me by surprise. I'd never much considered marriage or kids—I'd been too busy stumbling about my twenties and adjusting to the working world, paying my bills, and navigating the ugly waters of dating in the twenty-first century. All of those worries would cease to exist with one single word.

"Dane," I hesitated, the moment of certainty gone with the first break in silence. "Do you remember earlier this morning when we were talking about the possibility of us...being together?"

He gave a single nod.

"And I said there were other things to figure out?" I waited for a second nod. When it came, I took a shuddering breath and continued. "What do you say we figure out a few of those things?"

"Are you saying—"

"Do you want kids?" I blurted. "What about my job working for you? What about Dotty's place—er, my place? What about my friends? Your parents? Where would we live?"

"Shall I answer your questions in the order they were asked, or in reverse order, or shortest answer to longest, or—"

"Dane, I'm panicking. Help me out a little. Just answer any damn thing."

He looked a little surprised, but before he spoke, he studied my face for a long moment, as if he were tucking away the expression on my face and cataloguing it for later. So that he'd know the next time I looked like this—my eyes probably wild and my voice a little scratchy—it was panic he was facing.

"I've never thought about kids much until you asked. As you wish."

"As I wish?" I pushed myself up in bed. "What does that mean? I'm not having kids with a guy who doesn't care one way or another. I'm not doing that, Dane. My mom decided about five years too late that she didn't want a kid, and I'm not doing that to my own children. I refuse."

He held up a hand, and when I calmed, he rested it on my thigh. His eyes flicked up to mine. "I'd love to have children, and I'd never dream of abandoning them. But you are my first priority, Lola. If you want children, then we'll have them. If you don't, we won't. I'll love you either way, and if we decide to have them—I'll love them fiercely."

I didn't doubt a word he said, and my hand came to rest on his in a quiet apology. "You mean that?"

"Of course. I probably wouldn't make for much of a father." He winced. "But then again, I'm sure you already know that. Not that it would stop me from trying, from loving them."

"Oh, Dane." My hand came to rest on his cheek. "You're rarely wrong, but you are so horribly wrong about that."

"As for the rest of your questions—I assumed we'd live here, but I suppose if you like your grandmother's place we could try staying there..." He looked completely unsure and wildly out of his element. "We would need to get you a car, however, because I'll not have you going back and forth on that bicycle of yours."

I threw my head back and laughed. "We could live here—it only makes sense. But what about Dotty's place? The shop? *My* dreams?"

"Getting married shouldn't be the end of your dreams, Lola. It should be the start." Dane tugged my hand, pulling me down to lie next to him again. "If you want to keep it and run your business, I'll help you any way I can. If you decide you don't want to, or you want to hire it out, we'll do that too. It's up to you, and you don't have to decide now."

I played out that scenario in my mind. Marrying Dane, moving in to the castle, no longer working as his personal assistant but as a team player in the business while running Shades of Pink as my own project. The picture was a pleasant one, and I told him so.

Dane smiled at the image and clasped my hand tighter. "As to the question about your friends—I don't understand it. What about them?"

"Can they come visit?"

Dane blinked. "This isn't a prison sentence."

I gave a weak smile. "Okay, that was more of a panic question. Plus, if Annalise and Semi stay together, I might see even more of her around here."

"I'm not sure how much more of them I can see," Dane said with a twinge of discomfort. "They're not subtle with their affection."

"I think I'm just surprised by all this," I said, settling deeper into the soft embrace of the bed. "You're always so calculated and sure—and logical. A marriage proposal feels out of left field. Your parents certainly won't approve."

"My parents will like you when—if—they give you a chance. And if they don't, it's their loss. I won't let them ruin my happiness. As for the proposal, it doesn't feel fast to me. In an odd way, it seems right."

"I understand," I murmured. "Or rather, I don't understand how it does, but I know what you mean. I feel it too."

"Being hauled to the police station and accused of murder is one way to open a person's eyes," Dane said lightly, though there was a darker edge to his words. "No matter how much of my life I try to manage, there will always be elements out of my control. I had to learn that the hard way—I probably still haven't learned."

"You threw out today's schedule real fast."

He kissed my neck in a spot that made me giggle. "I had a very good reason," he said in a low, husky voice. "And I'm trying to learn how to follow my...would you call it, intuition?"

"You could call it that."

"I don't know if I believe in soulmates, Lola. I can say I certainly didn't believe in them a year ago. Today..." He trailed off, his mind spinning as he twirled a piece of my hair lazily between his fingers. "I'm not so sure. And now that I have you in my arms, I'm realizing that I don't want to let you go—ever. It's as sure to me as anything else that I know."

"Let's do it. Let's get married."

He blinked, as if the weight of my words hadn't sunk in yet.

"Er—if you still want to," I said, retracing my steps. "I mean, it will take a little while to get everything ready, and if you decide you want to back out—"

"I won't. I won't ever back away from you. When I decide I want something, Lola, I go after it as if the world is ending." His lips pressed gently against my forehead. "And I want you more than anything in the world."

My sigh contained everything left in me. My last bits of logic, my last bits of self-control, the last bits of doubt about this being too fast, too illogical, too wild. As I exhaled, I let it all go. And when I sucked in my next breath, it was full of confidence. "I love you, Dane Clark. I want—"

A knock interrupted my proclamation. Dane's eyebrows inched up, and he looked positively livid. If his eyes could shoot knives, the door would've been impaled with one glance.

"I'm sorry, truly sorry," Mrs. Dulcet called through the door in a sweet, uncertain voice. "I know you said even urgent matters can wait, Dane, but this one is out of my control."

Dane sat up in bed, and I followed suit, dragging the sheet up and around me. His arm snaked over my shoulders and pulled me to his chest, even as his eyes flashed back to business mode and his voice lost all traces of softness. "What is it?"

"The police are here," she said. "They need to speak to you. I don't think they'll leave without talking to you. I'm sorry."

After a long pause, Dane gave the slightest shake of his head. "Fine. I'll be right with them." As Mrs. Dulcet's footsteps retreated down the hallway, Dane turned to me. "You can stay here, Lola. I'll be as quick as I can and return to you."

Despite his confidence, his face had gone as pale as the sheets, and his lips were pressed into a tight line. He moved to stand, but I gripped his hand tight and held on.

"No," I said firmly. "If it's alright with you, I'd like to come with you."

"Why?"

"I want to be there next to you," I said calmly. "If you'd like that. Otherwise..."

Dane's smile was forced, and it didn't meet his eyes, but his voice dripped with gratefulness. "I'd like that."

# Chapter 24

WE DRESSED QUICKLY, silently, as my mind flicked through variations on the scene. Most of the possibilities weren't good ones: either the police had uncovered more information that painted Dane in a bad light, or they needed to follow up on earlier questions. Unless it was something we hadn't yet predicted.

"I didn't do it," Dane said, adjusting his tie in the mirror as his eyes met mine in the reflection. "You look concerned."

"I know you didn't do it," I said, approaching him and taking the tie from his trembling hands as I straightened it. "I love you. I'm just wondering why they're here."

"I suppose we'll find out." Dane took a deep breath, settled the unease, and with a calm, cool expression pasted over his displeasure at the interruption, he reached for my hand.

I managed a nod as I gripped his hand tightly and followed him through the hallways. Mrs. Dulcet had shown two cops into a formal sitting room near the dining area, and Dane proceeded into it without introduction. We settled next to each other on a loveseat across from the two detectives—each one taking an armchair across from us.

Both detectives eyed me with a hint of surprise and a bit of wariness. They looked stiff and out of place in this room, and I wondered if Dane and Mrs. Dulcet hadn't planned things that way to keep them out of their element.

Between the four of us sat a tray of exquisite cheese and crackers, fruits and nuts, dainty pastries and tender slices of meat. A small silver coffee pot sat next to the platter along with cups thin enough to crack if held wrong.

"Gentlemen," Dane said, shaking each of their hands with a firm, hard shake. "Help yourselves to a bite to eat while I have my butler call my lawyers."

One of the men—the larger of the two—eyed the plate with distinct want. But the other, taller and with a lean runner's build, gave a slight shake of his head. "We're okay, thank you. I'm Detective Plane, and this is Detective Ross. I don't think it'll be necessary to call your lawyers, Mr. Clark. We just have a few follow up questions for you. We'll be brief and straightforward."

Dane considered this for a long moment. Finally, he gave a succinct nod.

Detective Ross, the hungry-looking cop, forced his eyes from the platter of food in grudging agreement. "Who are you?"

I'd been reaching for the coffee when he asked. Glancing up in surprise, I looked to Dane for assistance.

"This is my girlfriend, Lola Pink." He said this with practiced ease, as if we'd been a true couple for years instead of hours.

"You didn't mention a girlfriend when we questioned you before," Detective Plane, the athletic looking detective, said. "I believe we asked specifically."

"I didn't mention one because I didn't have one." Dane gave a polite smile. "In fact, we just became 'official' as one might call it right before you arrived."

Detective Ross's face colored at the implication. "How did the two of you meet?"

"I believe I mentioned I had a personal assistant," Dane said. "You'll recognize her as my former assistant. She no longer works for me."

The two detectives exchanged an interested glance. "Curious time for you to be soliciting your female employees," Detective Plane said. "You're aware that you're still the prime suspect in a murder investigation?"

"Okay, hold on a second." I held up a finger. "He's not soliciting anything from me, and he never has. For your information, our first kiss was months ago. We've been kissing on and off ever since—so it's not quite as new as you might think." My face colored at the exposition of our personal business, but if it'd help clear Dane's name, or at least remove unwarranted suspicion, I'd happily embarrass myself. "Andrea's death is really sad, and we want to find out who killed her as much as anyone. But my relationship with Dane is a completely separate matter. He's innocent—he'd never harm a soul."

"And you can say that because of your long relationship?" Detective Plane said sarcastically. "Years of experience, hmm?"

"I know you're mocking me," I said, trying not to let the coffee cup rattle in my hands as I took a sip. "But it's the truth."

Detective Ross turned the gleam in his eyes from the platter of food onto me. "What about you, Miss Pink? Interesting timing on your part. The woman last associated with Mr. Clark—romantically—is now dead."

"I've explained to you there was nothing romantic between Miss Ricker and myself," Dane said, danger lacing his words. "We had a business relationship and numerous witnesses and contracts to back up my statement. Surely you've looked into that by now if you're even semi-interested in being thorough."

Dane's chastisement went far enough to put a sheepish look on Detective Ross's face, though it didn't change Detective Plane's in the slightest. If anything, Plane looked egged on by Dane's obvious frustrations.

"Fine," Plane said, sparing me a glance before looking to Dane. "Have you and Miss Pink talked marriage despite your short...shall we say, engagement?"

Dane sat up straight, a visceral reaction that was a dead giveaway. "How is that any of your business?"

"Whether your relationship with Andrea was business-only or *not*," Detective Plane leaned on the *not* part of the sentence, showing his clear skepticism, "to others, it looked entirely real."

"Sure. To anyone who reads a magazine and believes the words printed on its page, then fine." Dane spoke flatly, as if these people were uninteresting to him. "It's for those exact people that my PR team insists I keep up a certain image."

"Let's say, for instance, a woman had her sights set on you, but she thought you might otherwise be taken," Detective Plane suggested. "Maybe she suspected things were getting serious, seeing as you've appeared with Andrea at several events over the past few months and have been photographed widely with her on your arm."

"What of it?" Dane's voice was terse. "I've explained why that is already. Numerous times. Perhaps you should consider taking notes when I speak."

Undeterred, Detective Plane continued. "Let's say this woman—hypothetically—got the idea in her head that the two of you might be together someday. Romantically. Wouldn't you think she'd want your current squeeze out of the way?"

"Andrea was not anything to me aside from a contract," Dane said. "I don't know how—"

"They think I did it." The words came softly from my lips, but sure. "They're talking about me, Dane. They think I murdered Andrea in cold blood so that I could be with you."

Detective Plane widened his hands, his eyes focused on Dane instead of me. "I'm just throwing out scenarios. Your sudden relationship seems odd to me. Did you even know Miss Pink when you started seeing Andrea?"

"Get out of my house." Dane stood. "This is over. You came here to talk to me, and now you're accusing Lola? No. We're done."

"Just a moment, Mr. Clark. We got an anonymous tip earlier today from someone claiming to place you at the scene of the crime," Plane said. "Hence our return visit."

"Right," Dane said, exasperated. "And it didn't cross your minds that this might be the same person who stole my paperweight and is trying to frame me for murder?"

"We can do this here, or you can come with us to the station again," the detective said, foregoing all niceties. "I'm sure that would reflect wonderfully on your company."

"I didn't—" Dane fumed, but I interrupted.

He didn't hear me the first few times I said his name, but when I rested my hand on his wrist and repeated his name for a third time, he registered the sound. "Sit down," I said gently, guiding him back to his chair. "I can handle this. Don't make a fuss over me."

"They cannot come into my home and accuse my fiancée—" Dane began.

The word sent me for a start, and I wasn't the only one who noticed.

"Now you're engaged?" Detective Plane said, glancing at my bare finger with amusement. "Interesting choice of a ring for someone with your level of wealth."

"Listen." I could sense Dane's frustration and the ensuing confusion. He wasn't used to being off balance, wasn't used to speaking and not being heard. I was plenty used to being confused, so I handled the moment with ease. "Dane and I are innocent. We'll cooperate, but you need to give us a minute—it's a lot to handle at once."

Detective Plane finally looked at me with a semblance of understanding. His gaze flicked between us as if things suddenly made sense.

"I started working for Dane Clark a few months ago," I said. "We—or at least I—developed feelings for him quite quickly. Based on our mutual relationship, I'd say he felt the same."

A quick nod came from Dane, and I squeezed his hand in approval. His face remained stony.

"We kissed not long after we met. Shortly after that...well, I'm sure you know about the incident with Luke Daniels, my former contractor who's now in prison."

The detectives nodded. The Sunshine Shore was a small town, and word traveled quickly.

"After that mess was cleaned up, I continued working for Dane both because I liked him as a person and because I enjoyed my job." I took a deep breath, forcing my voice to remain even.

"When did you become aware of Andrea?" Detective Plane asked. "Did you know Dane was working with her?"

"I knew the PR team used models for the photoshoots. I was not aware of the details."

"When did you become aware that Dane's relationship with Andrea wasn't over?" Detective Ross asked pointedly.

"It wasn't a relationship—" Dane growled, but he was cut off by the detective.

"Their business relationship, then," Ross continued. "Did you meet her in person ever?"

"Yes." I cleared my throat, wishing I could avoid what I had to say next. The situation almost implicated me on its own. "I met her the morning she was killed."

Detective Plane sat back in his chair, the look on his face one of satisfaction. As if that was the end of the story. "Give me a second, Lola." He ran a hand over his face, as if deep in thought. It was clearly an act. "You get hired on at Clark Company. You develop feelings for Dane, which may or may not be reciprocated."

"They are reciprocated in full," Dane said through his teeth. "There was never any question about my feelings for Lola or my lack of feelings for Andrea."

"Then out of the blue, you discover that Dane is still seeing Andrea for whatever purpose," Plane continued without pause. "And your world spins a little out of control. We know she was here for a photoshoot the morning of her murder and stuck around afterward to look at the photos."

Dane nodded in confirmation to the latter.

"Did Andrea perhaps wander upstairs after?" Detective Plane asked, theorizing more than asking. "Did you get a little out of control seeing Andrea with 'your man'?"

I could feel my blood pressure skyrocket at the air quotes the detective used, and I could sense the rush of blood through Dane's veins, the wild pounding of his heart, though I couldn't hear it over my own.

"No," I said tersely. "That's not at all what happened. You're completely wrong."

"Maybe you didn't mean to do it," Detective Plane said. "It could have been an accident, Lola. We've seen that before. We understand crimes of passion—they're just that. Filled with passion."

"I had no more passion toward Andrea than I do to the cracker on that plate," I said, nodding toward it. "She meant nothing to me or Dane."

"But getting her out of the way could only help matters, right?" Detective Plane pressed. "Speed the marriage process along? I'm curious to know if you wanted to be Mrs. Clark first and foremost, or whether you are after Dane's money. Would you have eventually killed him too? Another blow to the head, or maybe this time you'd have gone with a simpler way?"

"Did Dane help you move the body, Lola?" Detective Ross asked. "Dane, if she coerced you into helping her, this doesn't have to end you. We can cut you a deal and—"

"Get out of my house." Dane stood. "You came here on a bullshit tip. You have nothing on us. Unless you're planning to arrest us—and if you do, my lawyers will shred your theories to bits—you'll leave. And while you're at it, I would highly recommend checking into the Rickers's finances while you're on the subject of inheriting money. It seems they've had quite a windfall since their daughter's demise."

Detective Plane was much better at hiding his surprise than Detective Ross. The latter's mouth parted and he looked dumbfounded at his partner. Plane frowned and moved along quickly.

"One last question." Plane held up a finger and looked, for the first time, directly into my eyes. "Where were you on the night of Andrea Ricker's murder, Miss Pink?"

I remembered with vague horror the ding of the microwave as my stupid burrito spun to a stop. "I was at home," I said, struggling to speak clearly. "Alone."

AFTER MRS. DULCET SHOWED the detectives out and slammed the door behind them, Dane wrapped me in his arms, holding me to his chest in a breath-stealing squeeze.

"I am so sorry, Lola." He murmured soothing words against my hair, his fingers pressing hard against me. "If I'd never shown up at your doorstep, you wouldn't be in this situation at all."

"Dane..." I pulled back slightly, having taken a few moments to gather my breath, the shattered pieces of my confidence, and pull together one last march. "Wait. There's something I need to know."

He looked at me, his gaze rightfully curious. "Yes. Anything."

"You haven't yet asked me if I did it," I said, my voice hoarse. I hated to even speak in such a way, but it needed to be said. "For all you know, I could have. I was home alone. You had to know I was a little jealous of her."

"I didn't pick up on that until you told me. I explained you had no reason to be jealous, and I thought you believed me."

"I do believe you, but I did have strong feelings for you, and I still do. Why didn't you ask me if I murdered her, or even killed her on accident?"

"Because..." Dane stopped, considering. He bit his lip in thought, taking a long moment to consider my question. Then a light behind his eyes flicked on, one that lightened the dead stare the detectives had brought out in him. "Because," he said gently. "I just know. I know you, Lola—and just like you believe in me, I believe in you. I know you would never hurt a butterfly, let alone a human being."

"And the stuff he said about the two of us—" I cleared my throat—"the two of us getting married? You believe that I don't want to be with you for your money?"

"Oh, Lola." He pushed the hair back from my face, and to my surprise, an amused smile appeared on his lips. "There are far easier ways to become rich than marrying me."

I couldn't help it; I let my head fall forward against his chest, relief flooding out of me. The laugh that bubbled up inside me came swift and hysterical, and it was with a mixture of tears and hiccupy giggles that I let the fear and horror of the last half hour wash away.

"I'm sorry," I said, hiccupping loudly as I wiped my eyes on his shirt. "I don't know what's come over me. I held it together in front of the detectives, but now you get to see the broken version I guess. I'm not quite working properly yet."

Dane pressed a kiss to my forehead. "You're not broken, Lola, not in the slightest. You're mine—however you are. Whatever comes your way, from here on out, comes *our* way."

I let my had find his, our fingers locking together. "You and me, huh?" I sniffed. "Together?" When he nodded, I gave a watery smile. "What a relief."

He laughed and held me closer. "I hate to say it, but I think we need to put an end to this. I can't stand to see you this upset. Let me call my lawyers; I'll have them investigate, and we can find out who did this. We can move on, and Andrea will have justice."

"It's such a shame," I said, shaking my head. "No one deserves to die like that."

"I just don't understand *why* they're still looking at us." Frustrated, Dane ran a hand through his hair. "Between the trust fund, her modeling jobs, her ex-boyfriends, and a potential mystery man here at the castle, there are any number of suspects who had more motivation to kill her than either of us."

"Maybe it's someone we haven't even looked at, yet. She could've asked the wrong person to squeeze her new chest, for all we know." I leaned heavily on the sarcasm. "Any *number* of people could have killed her, but instead the cops are determined to find a motive where there isn't one."

"I'm sorry they brought you into this, Lola. They wouldn't be looking at you if it weren't for me."

"Hold on, Dane—I might have an idea," I said, brushing away his worry with a squeeze to his leg. "Do you remember this morning when I had errands to run?"

Dane nodded. I filled him in on my findings with Regina and Leslie Gray, and my theories on Leslie having an accomplice.

"You think if we can find Leslie Gray's boyfriend," Dane said, "we might find our murderous pair?"

"It's a long shot," I said. "But it's something."

"Something is better than nothing," he said. "Let me call Gerard to get a car. We'll begin at once."

# Chapter 25

WORKING SIDE BY SIDE with Dane had its advantages. First, he had a zillion sets of wheels to choose from, and none of them required power by human pedaling. Besides having transportation, he also had a way with computers as well as plenty of connections, which spared us from having to get a perm in exchange for Leslie's address.

The supermodel lived in a wealthy little suburb halfway between the city and us—a place where folks with flexible schedules and bulging bank accounts built looming mansions next to shiny modern ramblers, the neighborhood all sharp edges and odd angles. She could easily commute to the city for any of her fashion gigs, and then return home to the privacy and security of her exclusive neighborhood.

As we quietly pulled into the gated community, I glanced at the clock and noted it'd taken us half an hour to drive here from the castle. Dane smelled rich enough that the security guard at the front didn't bat an eye, despite it being an unfamiliar vehicle and driver.

"Yeah, I don't think I'd have gotten in here on two wheels," I said, watching sidewalks disappear as they gave way to narrow roads pierced by entrances to long, windy driveways twisting into the darkness. "Thanks for coming with me."

"Thanks for coming with *me*," Dane corrected. "We're in this together. I wish you weren't involved, but unfortunately, I don't think there'll be much separating us from here on out."

"Does that mean we're really fiancés?" I asked him. "Are we doing this?"

Dane stared straight ahead, then shifted in discomfort. "Well—"

"I totally understand if you want to back out. If you're at all unsure, say the word now. It'll be easier than if we start telling people, and—"

"I told you I'm sure, Lola, and I meant it. My only hesitation is..." Dane's eyebrows cinched together as he pulled to the side of the road a few houses down from Leslie's address. "I don't have a ring, yet."

I felt a smile grow on my face as he turned to look at me, his eyes hooded by darkness, his hair lightened by the glow of moonlight. "That's it? That's your only hesitation?"

"It's a big one. You deserve a grand, sweeping proposal like in all of the movies you've shown me." Dane swept his hand dramatically across the car, the movement making my smile shine brighter. "You deserve flowers and a ring and fine wine and fancy dinners. It's not fair to just...I don't know, talk about it. I'm so unromantic."

"You are not!" I squeezed his hand tighter. "The romance is in the little things. The way you stood up for me in front of your parents when I was nothing more than your assistant. The way you tease me for eating sweets, but you make sure there are always plenty for me on hand. The way you talk to me and tell me you love me. All of that is romantic."

"Lola, Lola," he says, shaking his head. "You still don't understand. You've never been 'only my assistant'. Since the day I laid eyes on you, I knew I wanted more. I just never knew how to show it."

I could see my arguments weren't helping much, so I laid off and tried a new route. "How about this? We're not fiancés yet. We're not engaged—"

"But we're a couple? We are dating, right?"

"Sure, I'd like that." I drank in the bright gaze of my boyfriend and sighed with the weight of it. It was perfect. "Take a few weeks to think about us—take months if you need, or longer. When you're ready, you can do a grand sweeping proposal if you'd like."

His eyebrows knitted together, and my heart fluttered.

"But you don't have to, Dane—I like simple," I said. "I'm simple."

Dane began to respond, but at that moment, a car pulled out of the driveway next to the address marked with Leslie Gray's number. It was a sporty little Miata, a quick, cute little thing that had Leslie's name written all over it. Literally—her license plate said: LESLIE on it and was surrounded by a frame of sparkly diamonds.

"Conversation to be continued," I declared. "Or not—either way, follow her."

Dane Clark followed her at a distance, well enough that I wondered if he'd followed someone before, or if he'd merely read enough crime thrillers. Then, I remembered that Dane Clark didn't read much fiction outside of the classics.

At my frown, he gave a grin. "Ever since you got me hooked on movies, I've been dabbling in television while I do my running on the treadmill. I picked up a few tricks of the trade from crime shows."

I rolled my eyes. "Of course you're running while watching. Sometime you should just plop your butt on the couch, grab a bag of Doritos, and pop on an action flick. You'll think you've died and gone to heaven."

He didn't look convinced, but then again, he was focused on driving. We didn't have to follow Leslie far; she drove in the direction of the Sunshine Shore, pulling into a community located on a higher cliff than most of the surrounding area. This space tended to draw retired folks with old money. The houses here weren't splashy, but they were grand in their own way, and sturdy. Many were over a century old with nifty little additions and meticulous upkeep.

Leslie parked in front of one house with a particularly glamorous view of the ocean. I expected Dane to pull over and tuck his car behind one of several others on the street, but he never stopped. He kept right on driving past Leslie, and I ducked under the window, though she didn't appear to glance our way.

"What are you thinking?" I hissed. "Where are you going?"

Dane shook his head, mystified. "I don't understand."

"What don't you understand? We have to go back. That's probably her boyfriend's house. We need to find out who he is—maybe he's the one who helped Leslie get rid of the body."

"I know who lives there." Dane Clark leveled his gaze at me as he finally brought the car to a stop on the side of the road, several twists away from Leslie's vehicle. "That house belongs to my Uncle Anders."

"WE DON'T KNOW HE'S involved," I said. "Maybe she's here for a different reason. We don't know they're dating at all. What's your uncle like?"

After a few moments of stunned silence, I'd convinced Dane to drive back around for a second pass at the house. We were just approaching when the front door opened and Leslie stormed out, her purse swinging violently on one arm and the end of a word on her lips that couldn't be anything pleasant.

Dane jerked the car to a stop, and thankfully, Leslie was too steamed to notice anything out of the ordinary. She got back in her car and was speeding off, probably toward home, before either of us could react.

Dane shook his head, still mystified.

"Dane," I said gently. "We don't know your uncle is involved. Tell me what he's like."

"He..." Dane tilted his head to the side. "He's never been married, no children. He's my dad's younger brother, but to my knowledge he's never been jealous of the rest of the family. He owns his own real estate business that provides him with a generous living. To me, he's always been a good uncle. Gave me cards with money on birthdays, showed up for holiday dinners, no drama."

"Does he—did he—ever bring someone along? A date?"

"Once or twice, but it was a while ago," Dane said thoughtfully. "I always did wonder why he didn't date more. He's got a lot going for him, and when he was attached to someone, it was always a young, attractive woman. I guess nothing ever stuck for him. In fact, I suspected I might end up like him, and frankly, I didn't think it would be all bad. He was always a pleasant enough family member, which is more than most people can say about me."

"Stop that," I said with a firm shake of my head. "You're plenty pleasant."

Dane gave a weak smile. "I know what you haven't asked yet. Is he capable of it? Murdering her?"

I didn't react, just let Dane muse on his own question.

"I don't know," he said finally. "I don't know him well enough. He was always around, but he didn't talk much. Maybe that's why I liked him so much."

"Do you think we should go inside?" I asked. "If he's truly a nice guy, don't you think he'd have an explanation for us?"

"Do you like being questioned about murder?" Dane retorted. "Sorry, but I don't think he'd take kindly to being suspected by his nephew even if he's innocent."

I gave him that point. "What if we just swung by to say hello? Heck, you could introduce him to your new girlfriend—say you wanted him to hear about it in person before reporters splashed it across the papers."

Dane tilted his face toward the sky, the glow of light giving his features a sharp, almost supernatural glow, as he considered. "As it turns out, I don't think we have a choice."

"What do you—" I turned my head just in time to catch sight of the man waving from the front steps. "Uh, oh."

Anders hopped down the last step, dropping his waving arm as he picked his way easily over the sidewalk. Strong build, tall figure, limber enough—I hated to think so pessimistically, but I'd come to the snap judgment that physically, he could do it.

He could have worked with Leslie to get rid of the body. Between the two of them, it would've been a simple matter to load Andrea into the car and drop her on the side of the road. My inhalation was sharp when I realized one other fact: As a member of the Clark family, Anders had mostly unrestricted access to the castle.

"Dane," I whispered urgently. "Did your uncle come by the castle for any reason recently—maybe when you weren't around?"

Dane pursed his lips. "He stopped by to discuss an investment opportunity not long ago. He was only there for a minute."

"Were you in your office the whole time with him?"

Dane glanced my way, reading the question in my eyes even as Anders reached the car and stood expectantly outside. Dane gave a nearly imperceptible shake of his head as his eyes glowered with new understanding.

I folded my trembling fingers into a pretzel on my lap and suddenly wished I'd brought along something to occupy my hands. My nerves would be a dead giveaway if Anders bothered to peek in the car and say hello.

Dane opened the driver's side door and stepped out with more grace than I could muster. "Uncle Anders," he said quite pleasantly. "How are you this evening?"

"Fine!" Anders gave a clap on the shoulder to his nephew, then peered good-naturedly through the door. "Nice to see you again, Lola. What brings the two of you around tonight?"

As Anders straightened, Dane leaned against the car and surveyed his uncle. I nearly burst out laughing as he launched into his explanation.

"I just wanted to introduce you to my new girlfriend before the media finds out," Dane said. "Lola Pink—obviously the two of you have met before, but I thought it a more pleasant way to share the nature of our relationship than you reading about it in one of those rags."

"Congratulations!" Anders boomed. "I knew it. I told you so, didn't I, Lola?"

I nodded, remembering Anders's odd perception at Andrea's funeral—his quiet assurance that I had already fallen in love with his nephew. "You called it," I agreed. "Even I hadn't realized it yet."

"That's how it goes, isn't it?" Anders mused. "Just sneaks up on you, and then one day, *boom*, you're in love."

"What about you?" Dane asked. "Seeing anyone these days?"

The change of subject was an abrupt one for Dane, and Anders looked mildly confused at the interest in his love life. "No one particularly special," he said. "Dating here and there—the usual. I'm cut out for a life of solidarity, you know. I almost thought you were headed in that direction too. Good thing you found a nice lady to make you an honest man."

Dane gave a quick nod of agreement, and the two men lapsed into an awkward silence. I sat in the car, debating whether Dane's world was always this awkward, when finally, Anders broke the silence.

"Look, I'd love to invite the two of you in tonight, but you caught me by surprise, and I already have plans to which I'm late. Are you looking for your parents? I believe they're on the back porch having a glass of wine." Anders waved a hand in what appeared to be the general direction of said porch. "What do you say I have my chef prepare us a nice dinner next week?"

Dane fumbled for an excuse and came up empty. "Sure," he agreed. "That sounds pleasant. We'd love to join you—call Mrs. Dulcet with a date and time, and we'll be there."

"Take care now," Anders said, already striding away from the car before Dane had closed the door.

Dane started up the engine, taking an exaggerated time to get the car in gear and fasten his seatbelt. He stalled long enough that Anders pulled away first, in the same direction as Leslie, offering a wave over his shoulder as his taillights disappeared.

"Do you think he's lying about Leslie?" I asked in the ensuing silence. "Your uncle doesn't seem like the murdering type, but..."

"It could be a misunderstanding," Dane said, a slight frown tilting his lips downward. "Maybe Leslie's not dating him at all—apparently, it's not all that uncommon for a woman to claim she's dating someone when she's not."

I cocked my head to the side. "I suppose. Man, you rich people have such different problems than us normal folk."

"Watch out," Dane said, pulling away from the curb. "You're about to become one of us."

"I think you should watch out," I told him. "You marry me, and I might just drag you down to my level."

He smiled, reached over, and raised my palm to his lips for a brief kiss. "Where to next?"

"Home," I said. "I think we need to call it a day and hop in bed for the night. We can get up early and start again where we left off."

"Hop in bed," Dane muttered. "I like that plan."

And then he drove home like the wind.

# Chapter 26

DESPITE MY ENTIRE BODY tingling with the desire to linger in bed, I knew the fun had to come to an end. It was funny how quickly Dane's bed had become mine—become a shared thing, even on my first night in its warmth. It beckoned to me, a soft little cocoon where for six to eight hours a night, we were sheltered from the weight of the world.

It was just us, whispering into the darkness until the wee hours of the morning—holding one another and kissing and caressing and just being together in silence.

It wasn't even the physicality that drew us closer—although that *was* a definite benefit to being Dane Clark's girlfriend—but the vulnerability, the closeness we shared.

Secrets were confided, wishes were made, dreams were voiced for the very first time. Though we'd only known each other for months and had only shared a bed once before, it was already natural between us. Easy and routine and blissful.

"Come on, Lola—time to wake." Dane's fingers trailed down my back, his lips leaving kisses across my neck as he tried to pull me from bed. "It's almost eight."

"Eight in the morning?" I scrunched a pillow tighter around my head. "But that must mean you've been up for hours."

"Possibly."

I peeked out from under the covers and found Dane fully dressed in one of his immaculate suits, his hair arranged, a towel hanging up inside the bathroom. He'd showered already, probably read thirteen papers and put in half a day's work.

"Overachiever," I grumped, pulling myself from bed.

As the sunlight hit my eyes, however, it brought back the searing realization that we had business to attend to today—somber business. Though we'd managed to push the gravity of the situation away last night for a few hours, it had come crashing back to our shoulders, weightier than ever.

"Lola, I've been thinking."

"This is why you shouldn't get up so early," I grumbled. "You do all this thinking, and then I'm way behind."

"But that way, your ideas are fresher." Dane watched me with a tense smile, and when I didn't have a witty response, he continued. "I think I should go visit my uncle alone."

"No—I'll go with you. You said it yourself: We're in this together."

"I know, and we are. But as much as I might already see you as family," Dane said, easing to a seat next to me on the bed, "I'm not sure the rest of my relatives will be so receptive. I am hoping he might be more honest if I go alone."

I hung my head, his logic making more sense than I wanted to admit. "What about safety?"

Dane laughed. "He's family; he won't do a thing to me. Especially not if I have Semi waiting in the car."

"Okay," I said finally. "You'll call me the second you leave his house?"

Dane nodded. "Of course. I shouldn't be gone for more than an hour."

"I suppose I could use the time to call an emergency Sunshine Sisters meeting."

"A what?"

"Long story," I said. "Basically, Babs, Annalise, and I have a meeting spot on top of the water tower every time we have important news to share."

"It's illegal to climb the water tower."

"Well, then we've been criminals since we were in second grade."

"What news do you have to share?"

I blushed, surprised he'd asked. "Uh—"

"Is it private?"

"Sort of. It's girl talk." I waited for Dane to dismiss me, but he never did. Instead, he leaned forward, more curious. "You don't want to tell me?"

I sighed. "Dane! I thought we decided I was your girlfriend. And we talked about getting married."

"So?"

"So?!" I gave him some serious side-eye. "Girls talk about these things!"

"Oh."

"Oh?!" I slapped a hand to my forehead. "If you propose, I hope you know these emergency meetings will happen like three times a week until our wedding."

"Our wedding." He contemplated this, and I held my breath as his face changed expressions. Finally, he smiled. "I like that."

"I love you," I said, pressing a kiss to his cheek. "Go on and do your thing and let us gossip in private."

"I'll call you after. Be safe."

I blew him a kiss as he left the room, and then debated crawling back into bed the second the bedroom door slammed shut. After all, there was no place in the world like Dane Clark's bed, I'd decided. I could live here. I could eat it up it was so delicious.

But I really did have heavy gossip weighing on my chest, so I pulled out my phone and texted Babs and Annalise. As usual, they agreed to a snappy meeting on the water tower, and I was forced to climb from the bed, figure out Dane's own version of the spaceship shower, and dress for the day.

We all made it to the water tower in under twenty minutes.

"So?" Babs asked. "Spill."

"I might be getting married," I told them. "If we don't get arrested first."

"What?" Babs spluttered over her cappuccino. "Tell me more."

Annalise merely stared wide-eyed at me. "Have you gone nuts? Babs, does she have a temperature?"

I quickly caught the girls up to speed on the murder case. Like Dane, neither of them asked if I'd done it, nor did they ask for my alibi. They breezed right past the bit about the detectives throwing their theories in my face, and Babs downright confirmed they had nothing on me from what I'd told her.

I hated to admit that was a breath of relief. Despite my absolute conviction in my innocence and Dane's, the detectives were good. So good they'd almost made me doubt myself.

"Enough with the dark and dreary," Babs said finally. "We've covered the murder, now I want to hear about the pretty white dress and flowers."

"Well, Dane sort of proposed," I told them, and Annalise nearly fell off the water tower with the jerk from her gasp. "But not really. Listen! Don't freak out."

Babs squealed and giggled and laughed and clapped along with the story of how Dane and I had gone from personal assistant, to girlfriend, to almost fiancée, and back to girlfriend in the span of about twelve hours.

When I concluded, I had a huge grin on my face. Annalise still looked shell-shocked, and Babs remained skeptical.

"You're holding out on us," she said, pointing a blood-red talon at me. "You said you spent the night at Dane's. Usually, you say you spend the night *at the castle*. Does that mean..."

As she trailed off, I grinned, giddy with the memories. "And not just the night!" I added in a squeaky whisper. "Most of the day."

Finally, Babs looked properly shocked. "Okay, honey, details. AS-AP. Before I die. How was it?"

While Annalise recoiled and Babs pressed for more, I skimmed over the naughtier contents of my day with Dane, giving just enough to satisfy Babs and not quite enough to traumatize Annalise. By the time that story was finished, we sat in silence on the tower.

"Wow," Babs marveled. "I can't believe you took *so long to tell us.*"

I cringed. "I know. I'm sorry, but I couldn't deliver this sort of news over text."

"When's the wedding?" Babs asked. "How will you pick a maid of honor? Do you have a flower girl? What color are you thinking for bridesmaid dresses?"

"We're not engaged! Though, if we're heading down that path...I suppose those are good questions." I sat back against the water tower and flicked my shades down as I sipped my cappuccino. I'd chosen a girlie pink fashion for today, since I'd needed the burst of brightness with Dane off to confront his uncle. "No, no. I can't get ahead of myself. We're still in the middle of this murder investigation mess, and we have to find out who is responsible before either of us get locked up."

"Aren't you waiting to see what Dane finds out from his uncle?" Annalise pointed out. "I don't understand why you don't just cooperate and wait for the detectives to do their job. Obviously, it's a high-profile case. They'll sort it out soon enough."

Babs and I stared at Annalise. "Um," Babs began. "Because she's a target?"

"They don't believe me. Even I have to admit the timing of everything seems really strange," I offered. "I'm not guilty, but I don't want to twiddle my thumbs and just hope it all gets sorted out. Maybe if I ask around, it'll stir up interest and the real murderer will make a mistake."

"Yeah, last time you did that the real murderer went after you." Annalise stood up, tears heavy in her gaze. "Excuse me for wanting to trust the police—the ones who are *paid* and *trained* to protect us."

"Annalise—" I started, but she cut me off, shoving a trembling finger in my face.

"You're—you're Lola Pink. You're my friend, not a cop, and I don't want to see you hurt. I can't watch you do this again, Lo. I'm going. Please try to keep yourself alive, or there won't be a need to pick a maid of honor because there won't be a bride."

Annalise flipped down from the water tower, slithering and jumping with sleek, animalistic grace, until she reached the bottom. There, she swiped a hand across her eye and set off in the direction of the circus tent where she was due at practice in half an hour.

I stared after her, forlorn, until Babs rested her hand on mine.

"I can't do all that sweet flipping business and storming away, or I'd fall on my ass," she said. "Plus, these heels would crack if I landed on them the wrong way, and they cost me the better half of my last paycheck, but I do agree with her on one thing, Lo. We don't want to see you hurt."

"I know." I sighed. "I know, and I don't want to get hurt, and I don't want Dane to, either—but you ladies weren't there yesterday. It was horrible being questioned by the police like we were a pair of conniving murderers. We're not. We'd never! I'd never. Dane would never. It's—it's impossible!"

By the time I finished, my voice had risen to an alarming level of volume. I'd been hollering loud enough for Mrs. Fredericks to pop her head out of the house below and wave upward, her LuLaRoe leggings a bright pattern of hearts and polka dots today.

"Why are there only four legs dangling from the tower?" she asked. "Where are the skinny legs? We're missing two."

"Annalise just left for practice," Babs called back. "Good morning, Mrs. Fredericks. I really like how your leggings match your eyeshadow. You make that outfit pop."

Old Mrs. Fredericks gave us the thumbs up. "Cinnamon rolls will be done by the time you two get down. I'll pour you both glasses of milk."

Once the honorary fourth member of the Sunshine Sisters popped back in her house to check on the oven, Babs turned back to me. "What do you say we climb down, have a cinnamon roll, and by that time Dane will probably have news for you."

"I should get going," I said. "Tell Mrs. Fredericks I had to get to work. Maybe she can donate my portion to your coworkers."

"Where are you off to, Lola?"

"I'd rather not say."

Babs fixed me with her no-nonsense stare. "I'd rather you did say, and I'm winning this battle."

"Fine, but don't try to stop me; it won't work," I warned. "I'm going to pay Andrea's ex-boyfriend one more visit. There's something he said that I'm not clear on."

"Didn't he throw a vase at Annalise's head last time you went?"

"In his defense, she opened the door after he launched the vase. It was poor timing."

"I'm just not sure you should go over there with him throwing his shit across the room."

"I saw him at Andrea's funeral," I said. "He was pretty wound up, and I got the feeling he was truly upset over her death. I just need to ask him about one thing he said. He mentioned he thought she was seeing someone. He thought it was Dane because he'd followed her to the castle one night."

"You think Andrea was seeing someone at the castle—apart from her business with Dane?"

"I don't know, but that's what's bothering me. I mean, I suppose it could be Anders—Dane's uncle. He has been to the castle before, and it's possible they met there."

"Why would he kill her?"

"Maybe Anders was dating Leslie *and* Andrea at one point, and when he tried to break things off with Andrea, things got a bit physical and he accidentally clocked her, only to find she didn't wake up. Pardon the pun, but he'd have killed two birds with one stone—his ex-girlfriend would have been out of the picture, and his current girlfriend would get a huge leg up in her career."

"Extreme," Babs said. "But then again, I don't understand the lives of the rich and famous."

"If Anders doesn't admit anything to Dane—and why would he?—we'd need some evidence to offer the police that's concrete. Right now, it's our word against theirs, and we're as good as sentenced in the detective's eyes."

Babs looked at her watch. "I'll go with you if you can wait an hour. I have a client traveling here for a meeting that I can't adjust. Otherwise, I'd go with you right away."

"It's okay, really. It'll take me five minutes, and I have my phone."

Babs scrunched up her nose. "Fine, but call me in half an hour to check in. If you don't, I'm calling the police and Dane, and not in that order."

"Thank you, Babs."

"I'm donating your cinnamon roll to my stomach," she added. "And if something happens to you, I'm taking your collection of sunglasses. So, please be careful because I don't have room in my closet for all of them."

# Chapter 27

I CHOSE TO BIKE OVER to Ryan Lexington's apartment instead of borrowing Babs's car. The day had turned warm and sunny, and the fresh air was a welcome relief to the crushing worries I'd been harboring over the murder investigation. There was nothing like the thought of being put in jail to appreciate the freedom of the outdoors in a whole new way as I pedaled across the sandy path on the Sunshine Shore.

Biking also took longer, and since I was playing the waiting game with Dane, I figured I might as well burn off some of my nervous energy. I worried about him being alone with Anders, but I also didn't want to disrupt any progress he'd made. He'd promised that Semi would drive him there, and if I trusted anyone to keep Dane safe, it was his loyal tank of a bodyguard.

By the time I reached Ryan's shiny new condo on top of Mr. Reynolds's old grocery store lot, I was feeling an odd combination of determined and chipper. I *knew* that neither Dane nor I was guilty, and I sensed we were close to finding the real murderer. There was no way I'd let either of us be framed for a murder we didn't commit—if I could only poke enough holes in the police theories, they'd *have* to drop the investigation against us.

It was with this new resolve that I faced Ryan's building. As usual, the security guard was oblivious to my presence, so I made my way upstairs without a hitch. As I knocked, I hoped he had the answers I needed. Unfortunately, it appeared he wasn't home.

I waited for a few minutes, knocking several more times, but there was still no answer. Easing onto my tiptoes, I tried to peek through the peephole to no avail. After one more futile attempt to knock, I heaved a sigh and decided to cut my losses and try back later.

Resigned to wait for Dane's return at the castle, I let myself out of Ryan's building and climbed back onto my bike. I pointed my wheels toward the winding road along the shoreline that'd lead me straight back to the gates of Castlewood.

Route 1 didn't have a designated bike lane, but it had wide shoulders and plenty of space to share the road. Plus, it had the best views and the shortest distance between Ryan's condo and the castle. I cruised along at an easy pace, alternating between bouts of deep thought and no thought at all as I gazed over the ocean and the waves lapping against the shore.

I was engrossed in the crystal blue water when I first heard the screech of tires. The car came out of nowhere, swerving toward me as I careened out of the way—just barely managing to stay upright on the bike as I skidded toward the edge of the road that ended in a cliff over the water.

I'd just regained my balance when, to my horror, the car shifted into reverse and shot backward at me. I pedaled wildly forward, but I didn't have enough momentum to escape unscathed. While the car didn't touch me, it grazed my back wheel, denting it in a way that left it unusable.

The impact sent me sprawling. I hit the pavement with a hot skid that had my skin burning and my eyes tearing up in shock and pain. Not only had the asphalt been warmed by the sun, but little pebbles dug into my skin while sand pinched at the open wounds. I was bleeding and skinned from head to foot, aching all over.

My mind snapped to attention at double the pace as the door to the car swung open and a pair of shoes stepped out. A set of hands reached for my wrecked bike and, with a hefty grunt, the man tossed it off the side of the cliff. I could only let out a low moan of dismay as I heard it clank against the rocky ledge on the way down.

"Hi there, Lola," a deep, rocky voice said. "Were you looking for me?"

"Ryan!" I gasped. "What are you doing?!"

His eyes narrowed as I pulled myself to my feet and faced him. The same temper that'd flared up from him over and over again was back, raw and exposed in an entirely new light. He wasn't here for a chat this time; he was here to kill. *Again.*

Ryan pulled a gun from his pocket. "I don't have much time, so I'm not messing around. Get behind the car."

I glanced behind me, stalling—hoping and praying for a car to chance upon us and be the guardian angel that would save my life. But no cars sounded, and only Ryan's laugh drew my attention back toward him as he shook his head.

"Nobody is coming for you," he said. "Andrea wasn't a fighter either. It made things simple. Painless. I promise the same for you if you cooperate."

"Is this where you did it?" I took a step forward since I couldn't see another alternative. I was dismally unarmed, and I couldn't outrun a gun. My phone had clattered to the ground when I'd fallen. It was my only hope.

Ryan watched my eyes as they fell to the cell. He nimbly stepped forward and, with one swift kick, sent it sailing off the cliff. "Yep," he said in answer. "This is the lucky spot. Move it, Pink, or this is going to be a lot more painful than it needs to be."

"How'd you get the paperweight?"

He threw his head back and actually barked with laughter. "Fittingly enough, Andrea got me access."

"Why on earth would she do that?"

"During one of the rare moments when she remembered she was supposed to love *me*, she invited me to visit her on set at Castlewood," he said with a shrug. "By then, it was already too late. I knew she was seeing someone else at the castle, and I figured it was the boss. She wouldn't settle for anyone less."

"So you snuck into Dane's office and stole it?" I asked, keeping my eyes peeled for a rock—something, anything that could be used for a weapon. "If you and Andrea were broken up as you claimed, why did it bother you if she was dating someone else?"

"She just didn't *know* she loved me." Ryan smirked. "For years she strung me along. We were engaged twice. But then she kept meeting someone else—someone richer, more famous, more...whatever the hell she was looking for. I was never enough, even though I was supposed to be. We were meant to be together, but somewhere along the way, I'd become her sloppy seconds. After all I'd done for her, she never wanted me for more than a few free meals and a warm bed in between her other conquests."

"I'm sorry, Ryan, really," I said. "That is a terrible feeling, and it wasn't fair of her to treat you like that. But you didn't have to kill her. And even if you did, why frame Dane?"

"That bastard has more money than any of us. Andrea drooled over him—salivated over what it'd be like to have someone like that love her. Wouldn't it just be poetic if the one thing Andrea wanted more than anything—Dane Clark and his billions—brought about her end?"

"But he didn't kill her. He barely knew her. *You* killed her, Ryan."

"Because of him. Dane made sure I would never be enough for Andrea," he mumbled, leaning closer and smelling of smoke and booze. He'd been hitting the bottle again, though he wasn't drunk—just slightly buzzed for confidence. "Honestly, everything would've worked out *fine* if you didn't insist on poking your head into Andrea's business. Now, I'd like to finish things. There are two ways we can do this: You can jump, or I can push you. Your choice."

I felt sick to my stomach. Violently ill. If Ryan got his way, I'd never eat another of Mrs. Fredericks's gooey cookies. I'd never call an emergency meeting of the Sunshine Sisters on the water tower, and I'd never wear a fluffy white wedding dress and marry the man of my dreams. I'd never...I stopped, wiped the tears away, and looked at Ryan.

If I had any say in the matter, Ryan wouldn't get his way.

I wasn't going down without a fight.

"Fine," I whispered, scanning the area one last time as I inched toward the edge of the cliff. "I'll jump on my own. Just give me a second."

"I'll start the countdown at three," he said, stepping toward me, lowering the gun so it was pointed toward the middle of my back. "Move it, Miss Pink—*two*. And *one*..."

# Chapter 28

I DIDN'T HAVE A FOOL proof plan. I didn't even have a good plan to avoid dying. The best plan I could come up with was to 'stay alive' and that wasn't exactly brimming with specificity.

But when he said *two*, the target on my back seemed to glow red, begging for him to pull the trigger. I began to panic. My time was running out, and if I didn't do something, I wasn't going to make it out of here alive.

On the count of *one*, I took action. I leapt away from sure death on the cliff and lunged for cover behind the car. Ryan didn't fire immediately, which was exactly what I'd been counting on. It would probably be easier for him to make my death look like an accident if I didn't have bullet holes riddling my body.

I ducked behind the car and scurried to the back of the vehicle. My afternoon had turned into a game of cat and mouse, which was better than the game of *Lola jumping to her death*.

"Don't do this, Pink," Ryan said, his voice a soothing whisper that could lure a girl to believe he was sincere. Though it would've probably worked better if he wasn't holding me at gunpoint. "I can't let you live, but we can make this friendly. Simple. I don't want to hurt you—it's just that you're in the way. You need to disappear."

I hadn't found much in my quest for weaponry, but I did scoop a few small stones from around my feet and tossed them to the other side of the vehicle. The noise was enough to pull Ryan's attention in that direction while I crouched and moved the other way. We circled the car like a pair of boxers in a gruesome dance.

We'd rotated so that my back was to the cliff again and Ryan's was to the road, the car a barrier between us, but we couldn't stay in orbit.

Sooner or later, I'd have to take a stand, or he would get sick of the game and just shoot me.

In order to take a stand, I'd need a weapon. Glancing down to where my pretty blue Angelo shades had fallen after my tumble from the bike, I knew they were my only chance. Reaching for them, I snapped one of the arms off the frame, hard—so hard the plastic formed a jagged sort of edge, and I was left with a somewhat flimsy, incredibly rough, shank. That, plus the element of surprise, was going to have to be enough.

I counted out the seconds as Ryan's feet inched toward the nose of the car. My hands began to shake, my heart pounding. The second his foot rounded the curve of the hood, I made my move.

Leaping forward with a bloodcurdling scream, I plunged my makeshift weapon straight toward his stomach. Ryan flinched and stumbled backward, teetering close to the edge of the cliff as I barreled after him. I continued my forward momentum, screaming like a maniac before following up with a knee to his private bits, connecting in a way that took the wind from his lungs.

A visceral reaction kicked in as he curled over on himself, the gun clattering to the road as he groaned in primal pain. Though athletics were not my forte, I lined up the most perfect football punt I could visualize and sent the gun cartwheeling into the abyss.

Ryan's eyes widened in alarm for the first time since he'd run me off the road. His expression flicked to one of shock, then melted away to the cold-blooded look of a determined killer.

"Enough with the games, Lola," he said. "It's time for you to die."

I cried for help as he came at me—a loud and startling yell that I prayed someone—anyone—would hear. My heart sank when I got no response. Ryan had selected a widely unused stretch of road, and luck wasn't on my side this morning. Not yet.

I dodged his attack and sent another knee toward his groin, but he was ready for it. He not only protected himself, but he caught me in a horrible embrace and used my momentum against me. Together, we hurtled toward the edge of the cliff.

At the last second, he pulled back to detach himself from me and administer the final shove that would send me over the side and tumbling to certain death.

But this time, *I* was ready.

While he lined up the hit that would be the figurative nail in my coffin, I prepared, as well. He came at me, his arms stretched forward in a pushing motion, and at the last possible second, I ducked and flattened myself to the ground. Where I'd been standing seconds before, there was nothing but air. The momentum of a six-foot male on a murder rampage carried him off the cliff as I dove downward and rolled, smacking the road and feeling every inch of my body scrape against grit and gravel.

I continued to roll closer to the edge as I regained the ability to function, pulling myself to my feet in time to glance over and see Ryan holding onto twisted vines and tangled bushes while his feet dangled over nothing but rocks and waves pounding below. I barely had time to breathe in relief before worry *for* him crashed over me. I'd only wanted to escape—I hadn't wanted to cause Ryan's death.

"I'm going to get help," I called after him with urgency. "Hold on—I can't reach you!"

"You *bitch*!"

"Yeah, you're welcome," I muttered as I hauled myself to my feet.

My heart still pounding, I rushed to the car and dove into the driver's side door. I fumbled about for any sort of phone since mine was swimming with the fishies, but Ryan must have kept his in a pocket because there was nothing in the car. There were, however, keys in the ignition.

I rolled down the window as I started up the vehicle. "I'll be back!"

If there were any chance of me saving Ryan by myself, I would have done it. But he was too far down for me to reach, and in the event I did find a way to haul him out of the ravine, he would most certainly kill me before I could call the cops. I'd had enough of the fun and games for one afternoon, so I'd let the police handle the rest of it.

I drove like a madwoman to the nearest gas station a mile down the road and half ran, half stumbled into the facility—still bleeding from a rainbow of grimy wounds.

"I need to use a phone," I said. "Now! Someone's dangling from the cliff up there. Call 911!"

The shocked little man behind the counter merely stood there with his lip puffed out in confusion. "Uh—"

I slid around the counter and picked up the phone, dialing 911. I gave them the nature of the emergency as well as the location, and I threw the names of Detectives Ross and Plane in for good measure. Then I hung up and dialed Dane.

"Lo—" he began.

"It wasn't Anders, it was Ryan!" I cried as soon as he picked up. "Ryan fell off a cliff, and he needs help. And oh, I'll need a ride. My bike is busted. Also, my phone is dead. But I'm fine."

Dane took a full thirty seconds to process my wild ramblings. When he churned through the information, he sounded dangerously professional. "Where are you? I'll be right there."

I gave him the location as best I could, and then I hung up the phone despite Dane's plea to stay put. The poor little man at the counter of the gas station was still processing all that had happened as I returned to the side of the road where Ryan had gone over.

"Oh, thank God, you're still hanging in there," I said, leaning over the side to find him gripping tight to tree roots and sturdy bushes. "Don't let go. Help is on the way."

Ryan looked up at me, a change in his features from when I'd left him. His eyes had gone dull, his lips drawn into a painfully thin line. The skin on his face displayed an odd mixture of the palest of whites, dotted with red blotchy spots. His muscles must be screaming with hurt, but he didn't make a sound.

I leaned over the edge of the cliff, sensing a new resolve in him. "Ryan, don't let go. I'm not a huge fan of you trying to kill me, but I don't want you to die. Just hold on for a few more seconds. Wait—do you hear that? It's a siren. That's the emergency crew coming to save you."

Ryan looked up at me with a blank stare. As brakes squealed to a stop behind me, I couldn't tear my eyes away from him.

"Ryan, no—don't," I whispered. "Hold on!"

But it was too late. Even as I screamed, he'd already made his decision. With a shake of his head, he released his grip.

And then he was gone.

# Chapter 29

"DAMN, YOUR BOYFRIEND has a lot of expensive crap." Richard's opening sentence after arriving at the castle was about as elegant as I'd come to expect from him. "Must be sweet living here, huh?"

"It's not a hardship," I said with a smile of understanding. Although Richard and I couldn't be more different in so many ways, we did have one thing in common: neither of us had grown up in this sort of luxurious environment. I could appreciate his wonder of it all. "Can I get you something to eat?"

"Uh, yeah." Richard's eyes flicked from an expensive set of silver candlesticks to me. "I'm always up for some grub."

I winked, then pressed the intercom button on the door to the patio where we sat overlooking the sprawling private pool. It was a beautiful day, and I'd chosen to take my work meetings outside. "Mrs. Dulcet—when you have a minute, could you have some coffee and snacks sent to the back patio?"

"Give me just a few minutes," she replied instantly.

Richard's eyes grew even wider. "How do I get myself some of *that*?"

The day after Ryan had gone off the cliff began with a bustle of activity. I had no time to waste despite yesterday's tussle with a murderer—there was a gala to finalize, gossip to share, and a boyfriend to reassure. Seeing as Dane would've preferred I stopped working entirely to 'rest' and 'recover', we had come to a compromise.

Instead of giving up work entirely, I agreed to hang around the castle as much as possible. An easy promise to make, seeing as my bike was still totaled, leaving me with *walking* as my main method of transportation. I'd take my meetings at the castle so Dane could 'keep an eye on me' until I convinced him that I was completely fine. For my first meeting of the day, I'd invited Richard to Castlewood in order to final the details for The Lost Leprechaun's part in our upcoming charity extravaganza.

While the moments following Ryan's fall from the ledge had been filled with horror and alarm, the rescue teams had quickly determined that Ryan's attempted suicide had been wildly unsuccessful. In fact, he'd landed in a thorny bush and wedged himself in a crevice not all that far down. The firefighters quickly freed him, then the cops handcuffed him even faster.

We'd both suffered from a series of scratches and bruises, but the worst injury of all was Ryan's shattered ego. He had *not* been a happy camper as the police tossed him in the back of the cruiser and arrested him for the murder of Andrea Ricker, along with his attempted murder of me, and a few counts of other charges I'd mostly tuned out.

By that point, Dane had arrived, and I'd thrown myself into his arms. The rest of the afternoon and evening had passed in a blur of lawyers and doctors and police testimony. The only thing I could remember clearly was that Dane hadn't let me out of his sight. Not until this morning when I'd demanded a little space in order to resume my scheduled duties.

When Mrs. Dulcet arrived with the food, Richard dug into the spread with wild gusto. I let him eat in peace, knowing how magical it felt to have tasty items appear on a platter with the snap of a finger.

In a way, I understood Richard more than I understood Dane. He'd wanted to cancel the gala, sentence me to bed, and demand a week of nothing but quiet rest.

"Seriously," Richard said, plowing through the cheese. "How do I get this sort of royal treatment?"

I gave a teasing grin. "Fall in love with a billionaire?"

"But..." he frowned. "I love Stephanie."

"I was joking, Richard. Money isn't everything. I took the job here because I needed the money, but I stayed because I fell in love. I would still be here even if Dane lost his company tomorrow and went bankrupt and poor. I love *him*, not his lifestyle."

A clattering sound from the hallway told me that Mrs. Dulcet had approached at just the wrong moment and probably dropped her tray. I thought I heard a sniffling sound, and I wondered if she'd heard me. She retreated quietly, leaving me alone with Richard.

"No wonder the billionaire loves you back," he said nobly. "You kick ass at this romance business."

"Not really, but I guess when it's real, you just know." I cleared my throat, uncomfortable with the switch in discussion that'd pointed the conversation toward me. "Anyway, how is Stephanie?"

His eyes lit up. "She's fantastic. We have our third re-date tomorrow night. She's loved everything you've taught me to do. I can't tell you how much I appreciate it, Lola. I'll never be able to repay you."

"You're already repaying me by letting us rent out The Lost Leprechaun. That's more than enough."

"You're paying *us* to do that."

"Well, you didn't have to give us such a good deal," I said with a grin. "Now, how about we go over the details? The invitations have already gone out, and we're getting RSVPs by the boatload. I have a plan for the decorations here that I've jotted down. What do you think?"

We spent the next several hours perusing the plans and outlining every last detail, menu item, and drink selection. Richard would've stayed at the castle forever if I'd let him. He lingered well after lunch had been served, and Mrs. Dulcet was no help in the matter. I highly suspected that she enjoyed having the little Irish man around, due in no small part to his wild appreciation for everything she set before him. He even gave rave reviews to the tap water.

It wasn't until Babs and Annalise arrived that he finally got the picture thanks to Babs's stern goodbye.

"Good riddance," Babs said, once she'd practically thrown Richard out on the front steps. "Was that little man bothering you all afternoon?"

"He's a lifesaver, actually," I said, and explained our grand ideas to transform The Lost Leprechaun into a venue fit for Amanda Clark. "What do you think about the decoration plans?"

"I think I'm still annoyed," Babs said with a frown. "I mean, the venue sounds great, but I'm still upset about yesterday. I can't believe Dane didn't allow visitors to the castle all *night*!"

"I know, and I'm sorry," I said, wincing. "In his defense, it was a crazy day. After the whole incident with Ryan, he went into protective mode."

"Yeah, but we're your best friends," Annalise said. "We wanted to come and see that you were okay for ourselves. All we heard was that you almost died and Ryan fell off a cliff."

"In case you can't read between the lines," Babs said with a bitter scowl, "we're expecting thorough details even though it's an entire *day* late."

"I know, I'm sorry," I said with a sigh. I quickly filled the girls in on everything that'd transpired on the road between Ryan and me, including my sunglasses shank, my trip to the gas station, and his attempted dive into the rocky waves. "He survived and will be headed to prison. He gave a full confession to Andrea's murder."

Babs nodded, still sullen. "Dane's uncle had nothing to do with it?"

I shook my head. "It turns out he *is* actually dating Leslie, but it's a brand-new relationship. He wasn't lying when he said it wasn't serious. They just weren't ready to tell family and friends yet. Anders told Dane all of this while I was hunting down Ryan yesterday."

"What about the model," Annalise said, "Leslie—is she just a prick?"

I gave a limp shrug. "I guess so. The fashion show is proceeding as scheduled, except my Angelo shades won't be making the lineup in Regina's event, but everything else should go off without a hitch. In fact, the Sunshine Times is doing an article on Shades of Pink—a huge feature!"

"That's great!" Babs said. "It'll be awesome publicity for the store. We just need to get Johnny to hurry along renovations so they can snap some pictures to run alongside the article."

I gave her a playful nudge. "Maybe you can beg him for me. He might be partial to your requests."

Babs wasn't big on blushing, but her cheeks turned a shade of light pink. "We'll see what I can do," she muttered. "No promises."

"I just wish Andrea was alive to see it—to finally have her dreams come true. It's funny. I didn't even know her when she was alive, but I feel like I know her a little now." I held up my fingers a centimeter apart. "She was this close to becoming a superstar. I'll bet this show would have catapulted her career to the next level."

"I'd rather have seen her become a star over Leslie," Annalise said, wrinkling her nose. "But it's too late for that."

"Maybe I can include a line about her in the article for Shades of Pink," I said. "A last little tribute to her."

"*Shades of the Stars*," Babs said with a grin, spreading her hands out and gesturing to an imaginary headline. "I like it."

"I think she'd have liked that," Annalise said. "Her parents might appreciate seeing it, too."

"Don't think I forgot about my initial complaint," Babs said hurriedly, steering the conversation back to its original topic. "I'm still frustrated about not being able to see you yesterday."

"There wasn't time!" I said. "After the police arrested Ryan, I had a quick trip to the hospital. Even though I was completely fine, it took a while to get through the paperwork and the once-over. Then it was a jaunt down to the station to give our full reports to the cops. It was dinnertime before we got back to the castle. I hadn't showered, hadn't eaten—we were exhausted."

Babs looked as if she were struggling to find a good response.

"I don't think Babs is just worried about yesterday," Annalise murmured, reaching out to squeeze my hand. "It's more than that, Lo."

"What are you talking about?" I looked between the girls. "I don't understand. I'm really sorry Dane closed the castle and you were worried, but you have to understand we were exhausted. I fell asleep before dessert—that tells you how bad it was. I didn't have my phone, and all I could do was text you from Dane's to let you know I was okay."

"He can't keep you away from us!" Babs blurted, then looked surprised by herself. "Look, I'm sorry I got upset about yesterday. I really do understand why Dane blocked out visitors, but it made me worry."

"Why?"

"Lola, I really like Dane. In some weird way, the two of you are perfect for one another. But *we* were your friends first, and I'm worried that if you marry him you'll forget about us."

"Babs, of course not!" A wave of shock hit me with her confession. "That will never be an issue! You're not just my friends; the two of you are my sisters."

"I know." A pained look bloomed on Babs's face. "We love you, and we were scared stiff about you yesterday. We weren't coming over to open beers and champagne—we just wanted to see your face and make sure you were okay. It was a little disheartening to hear that Dane had closed off the castle to all visitors and wouldn't make an exception for us. We're your *family*."

"He was just concerned," I said cautiously. "It wasn't anything personal—I swear. I even told him already that if we get married, the two of you would be a huge part of my life. Nothing will change between us, I promise."

"Don't promise that," Babs said. "That's not true. Things *should* change if you're married, and I understand Dane is—or will be—your best friend. That's how it should be. But please don't forget about us."

I felt my eyes prick with tears. "I am really sorry that we made you feel this way. I'm going to talk to Dane about it. I swear, you two aren't going anywhere."

Babs bit her lip. "I, uh—I might have given him a piece of my mind already," she said quickly, looking sheepish. "Sorry. I was a little frustrated last night."

"If you ever feel that way again, just call the castle. Declare a Sunshine Sisters emergency meeting—I'll let Mrs. Dulcet know those are of the utmost priority and to always put those calls through. You're stuck with me for life, and I want you to know that without any doubts."

"Good," Babs said. "Because we do want to see you married and happy; we just want to be a part of it all."

The three of us fell into some sort of a group hug, shared laughter and tears punctuating the conversation until Mrs. Dulcet appeared with appetizers and drinks around the cocktail hour. When she announced that dinner would be served shortly, Babs and Annalise made their excuses and said their goodbyes.

I walked them to the front door and down the stairs, waving as they climbed into Babs's vehicle and pulled away from Castlewood. I was mid-stride heading back inside when a voice called my name.

"Lola, a word?" Dane had clearly walked to the front of the house from one of the warehouses in the back, and judging by the tense smile on his face, he didn't have good news. "I was hoping to find you here."

"Sure. Actually, I need to talk to you, too," I said. "Babs and Annalise just left."

"Ah."

Something flickered across his handsome face, and I briefly wondered if he was thinking of Babs telling him off yesterday. I crossed the lawn quickly and slipped my hand into his, the slight scratches against my skin prickling at the contact.

"Everything is a go for the gala," I said, easing into conversation. "We've got most of the RSVPs in already, and this morning I finalized decorations, drinks, and food with Richard. If all goes well, it should be a very unique event."

Dane's eyes flicked toward me. "You work too hard. You really should be resting."

"And twiddling my thumbs? I don't like to be bored."

He smiled. "Thank you, Lola. For everything you've done."

"There's something else," I said, shifting uneasily under his praise. "It's not exactly a fun topic, and I don't know where to start."

"I have something to show you first," Dane said, as he walked me back to the garage where his collection of sleek vehicles sat under the loving care of Gerard. "I have something for you in here, and I hope with it, you'll forgive me."

"Forgive you?" I frowned. "For what?"

"I assume your *topic* involves the formal complaints Babs lodged against me yesterday," he said, shifting uneasily from one foot to the next. "She was very upset when I closed Castlewood to all visitors last night—without exception."

"Yeah, that's about right. I understand why you did it, but—"

"Please, let me finish speaking before you make any decisions." Dane gave a tense smile. "I have been worried sick all day about us."

"About us?" A pit lodged in my stomach. "What did Babs tell you that made you doubt *us*?"

My frustration was swinging on a pendulum between Babs and Dane. I loved them both with all my heart, and I needed them to get along. That was the only way any of this would work. We were all pieces of one big puzzle, and with any piece missing, my life wouldn't be complete.

"It's not her fault, although she did put something into perspective," he said hesitantly. "I did a lot of thinking about what us being together would mean."

I'd never seen Dane so unsure. He was usually so certain in his decisions that his now-visible nerves were somewhat frightening. My heart pounded as I waited for the other shoe to drop—I just knew he was going to tell me that things wouldn't work, and my greatest fears would be realized, just when I'd thought I'd stumbled into happiness.

"Dane, spit it out," I said. "You're giving me an ulcer."

He laughed, but it was coarse and dry and didn't meet his eyes. "This way."

A few steps further, and he pushed open the door to the largest showroom. I followed him inside, my hand gripped tightly in his despite the sting as we came to a dead stop.

"It's yours," Dane said, gesturing to the bright spotlight beaming down into the center of the room. "I wanted to make it a car, but Gerard and Mrs. Dulcet seemed to think that too big of a gesture. They said to start small and see how you reacted."

A quirky grin wound its way over my face as I studied the display before me. "Uh, a bike? That's the big surprise?"

Dane gave a quick nod. "It's not just *any* bike," Dane said. "It's *electric*."

"An electric bike?" I moved forward and ran my hands over the sleek surface. "I'm going to be the coolest kid on the Sunshine Shore, Dane Clark." I paused in my examination of the beautiful, shiny finish to wink at him. "This is so generous of you, but I'm a little con-fused—why were you so nervous to show me? It's a very sweet gesture and of course I appreciate it. You didn't have to worry so much."

"It's not about the bike," he said softly, pulling me closer to his side. "I know you probably feel stuck at the castle with no transporta-tion."

"I don't—"

"I never want you to think I'm controlling you or holding you hostage. Sometimes I tell people—including you—what to do be-cause I think I know best, but that is not how a relationship works, and I'm beginning to understand that. I want to make it very clear that I only want you to be here because you choose to be here, Lo-la—not because I'm demanding it of you. End of story."

"Of course I want to be here, Dane!" I slipped around so we faced one another. "What made you think I felt differently? I'm here be-cause I love you. I don't understand where this is coming from."

I sensed something bursting from his chest, an emotion he'd held inside breaking free as he let out a shuddering breath. "Babs called me last night," he said, and offered the slightest of smiles. "With some very choice words."

"She told me," I said. "I think she feels bad about it. You have to understand, she likes you, she was just emotional."

"I know she does." He surprised me with the admission. "She gave me a tip, and it made me think. She explained that if I tried to hold you back, to constrain you and impose my rules and keep people from you, that things wouldn't work. That you need your freedom and space in order to grow and thrive."

I couldn't think of anything to say, so I looped my arm around his waist and rested my head on his chest.

"I tend to have a rigid schedule, and I'm used to making decisions on my own without thought for others. I only do what I believe to be in your best interest, of course, but I was terrified I had pushed you away by keeping your friends from you last night."

"I appreciate you looking out for me yesterday, Dane. I know you only meant to take care of me."

"It's not just about yesterday. I don't want to force you to tell me where you're going or demand you work from the castle. I was even *glad* when you were stranded here without transportation because it made you reliant on me, and I liked that."

I gave him a smile and snuggled in. "Dane, we're all human. You didn't do anything wrong."

"I know, but I just..." He hesitated, resting his cheek against my forehead. "I'm worried that I won't be enough. You are so vibrant and brave and free and determined and beautiful, and I'm none of those things. Calculating, maybe, and rich. But that's not enough to make someone love me."

"I don't love you for either of those reasons. I love you because of what's in here." I rested my hand on his chest and wriggled into a proper hug position. "Thank you for caring enough to be concerned, but you don't have to worry." I leaned up on my tiptoes to give him a kiss. "I just want you. Sure, it'd be great if you get along with my friends, too, but it's a process. We'll get there—*together*."

He met my lips with a kiss back, warm and tingling and trembling with anticipation. A rush of relief came on his exhale as he pulled me into a viciously tight embrace.

"I only want to be the wind at your back, Lola, never the..." he hesitated, and I could feel his brain struggling. "What's the saying?"

"I've got no clue."

"You amaze me every day," Dane said, leaving the poetics behind. "I wish you hadn't had to face Ryan alone, but obviously, you've shown the world that you can take care of yourself. I am beginning to see you don't need my help."

"You're right," I said, my voice a whisper across his cheek as I pulled him closer so I could murmur directly in his ear. "I just need *you*."

# Chapter 30

THE MORNING OF THE charity gala dawned misty and gray, a surprising change for the Sunshine Shore. Normally, it'd call for a cozy morning tucked in bed, maybe a sick day called in to the office and some cookies warming in the oven, but not this time.

Despite it being a Saturday, I'd been up at the crack of dawn, wrangling my friends from their beds as soon as it was safe. With some hefty bribes, I convinced Babs and Annalise to join me at The Lost Leprechaun to help get the place organized and decorated for the evening's event.

By the time late afternoon arrived, the pub had been transformed into a quaint space dripping with fairy lights. The oak barrels that served as cocktail tables were draped with dainty white linens, and an army of servers in smart black suits waited in the wings to begin serving appetizers the second our first guest arrived.

Big Richard himself stood behind the thick stone bar, ready to serve guests their choice of Guinness, whiskey, or cider, and a variety of tap beers. It might not be the most elegant or sophisticated setup this crowd had ever seen, but it would most certainly be different. The magical old-Irish feel to the place might even help to loosen the guests up after their normal high-brow society events.

Either way, the venue *had* to be good enough. Time was running out, and we'd have to make do with what we had at this point. A sudden bout of nerves nearly crippled me as I glanced at my watch. Guests were due to arrive in an hour, and I had yet to go home and wash away the day's grime and hard work that had accumulated on my body.

I also needed some rest, but that would have to wait. Though the scratches on my arms had healed to nice pinkish colors, the weariness from the incident with Ryan hadn't yet left my bones. His face still plagued me in nightmares now and again as he hung there, preparing to fall to his death—nightmares that I kept to myself.

I had sent Babs home earlier to shower and change so she could return and take responsibility for greeting the earliest guests in case I hadn't made it back in time. The second she walked through the door in a stunning gold-streaked dress, I gave her a peck on the cheek and hustled home to the castle in a low-profile car borrowed from Dane's collection.

I was in and out of the spaceship shower in record time, relieved beyond belief to find that Mrs. Dulcet had gone shopping for me. I'd forgotten entirely about the fact that I'd be required to wear a ball gown along with the guests, and the butler must have anticipated the lack of foresight on my part.

I found the dress hanging on a stand in the closet, a bit brighter and bolder than I'd normally have chosen, but perfect nonetheless. A vibrant shade of red, it draped softly over my shoulders as it slid down my body and extended all the way to my toes. An elegant lace pattern decorated the top, so subtle it'd be hardly noticeable under the dim bar lighting, but in the brightness of the bedroom, it gave an added depth to the gown that made it breathtaking.

I added a small necklace that swept gently into the slight 'V' in the neckline, and a pair of tiny diamond earrings that Dane had given me on one of our earliest encounters. I couldn't help but smile at my reflection as I fastened them in place.

The knock on the door startled me. A quick glance at the clock told me that the visitor would be forced to keep things brief because I had less than twenty minutes to be back at the gala before the party was truly underway.

Pulling the door open, I was shocked to come face to face with none other than Dane Clark himself. He stood at the door to his own bedroom, his face white as a ghost, his hands secured tightly behind his back.

"Dane? What's wrong?" I reached for him and pulled him into the room. "Why do you look like you've seen the ghost of Clark Castle?"

"There's no such thing," he muttered as he breezed past me.

I raised my eyebrows, realizing he was in quite a mood if he'd missed a joke that obvious. "Okay, sure. What's eating you, Gilbert Grape?"

He raised an eyebrow as if to ask who Gilbert might be, then a flicker of something appeared on his face, and he let it pass. Instead, his eyes settled on me, finally seeing me, and a smile tugged his lips upward. "You look sensational, Lola. You are the most gorgeous woman I could have ever dreamed of meeting."

"You like it?" I asked, giving him a little twirl. "Mrs. Dulcet did an amazing job shopping for me."

"It's not the dress." Dane's eyes never left my face. "It's you."

I stopped my indulgent twirling, my breath catching in my throat as my airway nearly closed off. "Dane, what are you doing?"

He'd reached into his pocket then bent at the knee, his fingers trembling over the black box in his hands. When his hooded eyes flicked up to mine, he'd grown even paler, if possible. "I've never done this before," he stuttered, looking mystified at his own hands. "I'm shaking."

I couldn't stop the nervous giggle that bubbled over. "Well, you only have to do this once."

My laugh shook him from the hazy funk in which he'd been drowning, and it drew out the confident, formal Dane I loved. His fingers slowly steadied, and as he reached for my hand, his eyes raised to meet mine. They were blue, so blue and so filled with love. "You look gorgeous tonight, Lola, but I'm hoping you are missing something."

It was my turn for my fingers to tremble and my heart to pound. I could hardly manage a nod.

"This ring was my grandmother's, and it's maybe not as big as you'd like, but you once told me you preferred simple things. I know we're not on top of a mountain or at an extravagant dinner," he said with a slight pause, glancing at me for confirmation before continuing. "But this moment felt too private to share with anyone else."

Dane took a minute to steady himself, clearing his throat and giving an audible swallow before he let go of my hand, opened the box, and displayed a dazzling diamond that glittered under the first hints of starlight piercing through the windows.

"Lola Pink, I know this is fast. I know we've only known each other for a short time, but I've never been more confident about anything in my whole life. I love you, and I want to begin our life together without wasting another minute apart." He forced a smile, but it was nothing more than a nervous flicker. "Will you marry me?"

"Oh, Dane, of course," I said, falling into his arms the second after he slipped the ring onto my finger. "Of course, I will—I love you, Dane! You didn't have to be so nervous."

"Thank God I never have to do that again." Dane stood, sweeping me up with him as we stood. "I haven't been able to put a full sentence together for days. Ever since I got the ring from my mother—"

"Your mother knows?" I asked weakly. "And she parted with the ring...knowing you were proposing to *me*?"

He gave a gentle smile, color finally returning to his tanned face, the blue in his irises popping against the healthy flush of his skin. "You'll see her soon enough, tonight. I think you might be surprised."

"Oh, crap! The gala!" I glanced down at my ring in shock. "I almost forgot about it. Any chance we can skip it?"

A look of concern fell over Dane's face. "Are you not feeling well?"

"I feel fine! I feel great! I just don't want to leave. I want to climb in bed with you and curl up together for the night—and never leave. And just enjoy being together with..." I raised my head in awe. "My fiancé."

Amusement edged out the concern in Dane's expression, then it darkened to something more basic. The same desire probably burning through my veins as I struggled to digest the reality that he would be mine forever, and I would be his.

He took me in his arms, his hands sliding across the bare skin of my open-backed dress as he whispered into my ear. "What do you say we go show our faces at the party, then duck out early and get started on your plan?"

I let my hands rest against his solid chest and tilted my chin up to confirm with a kiss. "Come on, fiancé. The quicker we get started, the sooner we get home."

"Are you going to let up with the fiancé bit?"

"Nope," I said with a grin. "It's a limited time special—better use it while we have it."

Dane laughed, took my hand, and pulled me away from the bedroom while I floated behind him staring at my new bling. Contrary to what he'd said, the diamond was most certainly over a carat and ringed with two layers of halo. The thing was probably visible from Mars.

"Are you sure you want me to have this?" I asked, tentative. "I mean, I could wear something cheaper for daily use. I have a tendency to lose things, and this looks—no, it *feels*—expensive."

"It's meant to be worn and enjoyed, not hidden," Dane said with certainty. "This is the most reckless thing I have done—asking you to marry me just months after us meeting. You just might be rubbing off on me, Miss Pink. Be reckless, *wear the ring*."

I laughed at his obvious attempt at a joke. "Oh, I love you, Dane Clark."

Together, we climbed into Dane's newest Ferrari. As we roared down the coast together, I wondered if my grandmother had known all along that by leaving behind a money pit and forcing me to face a mountain of problems, I'd summit the peak with a partner by my side and friends on my flanks.

"I'll be damned," I said softly, glancing once again at the engagement ring and then matching it up against the light from the stars. "Dotty knew all along. Here, I thought she'd left me nothing but problems, but I think—in her own way—she was leading me to *you*."

# Chapter 31

THE PARTY WAS A SMASHING success.

At first, I couldn't say if that was a good thing or a bad thing, seeing as most of these charity style galas are an elegantly good time...not a wild, raging bash. But something about the setting—the sturdy Irish pub, the mouthwatering food, and the free-flowing beer turned the night into something one might call a *rollicking good time*.

In the theme of a smashing success, a record amount of charity money was raised for Mrs. Clark's organization. As guests steadily began to depart for the night, one by one they came over to where Dane and I had parked ourselves near Big Richard at the bar—a man far more eloquent than his son. The three of us received one compliment after another on the success of the evening.

I'd even gotten three new job offers and one marriage proposal from a drunken banker who said if things fell through with Dane, I could give him a call. Dane stuck him in a cab with a little too much force, and I couldn't say what sort of address he gave the taxi driver—but it wasn't anything local.

Annalise and Semi were one of the first couples to leave. Semi had the night off since we'd hired other security for the event, and I'm sure the two wanted to savor their free time together. Annalise looked beautiful in a sleek black gown, her hair knotted high on her head. She was as giggly as a school girl as she kissed me on the cheek and congratulated us once again before disappearing in a swirl of black fabric.

Babs left shortly after her, claiming an early morning meeting. Since the next day was Sunday, I figured it was more of an excuse for a late-night visit to see Johnny than anything early the next morning, but I didn't correct her. I gave her a sly wink, however, which she promptly ignored.

"I'm so happy for you," Babs said as she squeezed me tight. "And I sort of love Dane. You know, in the sisterly way—which is why I'm allowed to tell him off when he's being dense. Lucky thing he seems to have forgiven me for the other day. I did apologize to him, I'll have you know. I still claim intense emotional stress caused me to fly off the handle."

"I think he's forgiven you," I said with a laugh. "If anything, I think he appreciated your honesty."

"Good," she said. "Because there's a lot more where that came from. Speaking of honesty, did you know he asked Annalise and I for your hand in marriage?"

"Really?"

"Well, sort of. He'd been wandering around the path on the Sunshine Shore just in front of Shades of Pink, looking like a lost little puppy when I ran into him. He was wondering if you'd want your mother contacted before he asked for your hand in marriage—his words, not mine." Babs laughed, then winked. "I told him that *nah*, you wouldn't care so long as he asked us first. So, he did."

I glanced out of the corner of my eye at Dane. "I am a very lucky woman."

"And he's a very lucky man." Babs squeezed my shoulder. "You two make a lovely couple."

Dane and I hadn't intended to stay until the end of the party, but most of the room had cleared out before we'd even considered leaving. The evening had been a pleasant blur, and I'd been able to spend just about all of it beside Dane. Plus, I'd been asked to show off my ring a million times, and I couldn't get enough of it; I knew the excitement might simmer to a slow burn after a while, so I took advantage of flaunting it every time someone asked.

Mr. and Mrs. Randall Clark sauntered over, somewhat hesitant, to gather their coats near the very end of the evening. As the coat check man disappeared to retrieve them from the rack in the back, Mr. Clark turned to us, offering us both a handshake and a succinct *congratulations*. I couldn't tell if he was happy or sad or anything of the sort. If anything, he looked mildly amused at our engagement, as if he couldn't quite believe it had really happened.

I couldn't say I blamed him.

Mrs. Clark was more reserved in her approach, smiling first at my hand, then at Dane, before she turned the ghost of what was left on me. "I am sorry if we started off on the wrong foot," she said. "I heard what you did to help our son with that horrible murder investigation."

"I didn't do anything he wouldn't have done for me."

"No, I suppose not," she agreed. "But it seems you care about Dane a good deal more than I gave you credit for. I'm...pleased to see he's found a woman sees him for who he is and not what he has."

It wasn't quite a compliment, nor was it exactly approval, but it was a truce. I could handle a truce, and I was touched by the olive branch. "Thank you," I said, and I meant it sincerely. "Was the gala to your satisfaction this evening?"

A true smile finally cracked her features, and she nodded. "It was a smashing success. You really could specialize in event planning, I think, if you're interested."

Now *that* was a compliment, and I glowed underneath it for the next half hour—long after the Clarks and the rest of the guests had left. Dane and I sat alone at the bar, resting in the peaceful quiet.

"I think we need one more celebratory beer." Richard appeared from behind the kitchen doors where he'd been helping prepare the food all evening. He looked satisfied and exhausted as he slung a few leftover drinks into plastic cups—ditching the fancy frosted mugs from the event and plopping them onto the table before us. "Lola, I want you to meet Stephanie. *The* Stephanie."

My head rested on Dane's shoulder as my own tiredness had begun to creep in, but at the introduction, I struggled to a sitting position. "You're the one-and-only Stephanie," I said with a smile. "It's a pleasure to meet you. I've heard so much about you."

Stephanie was a small, lovely woman with a quick smile, brown hair, and rich hazel eyes. Her laugh was airy and bright. She was shorter than Richard, and she outranked Richard on the looks scale by leaps and bounds.

It wasn't until she smiled at Richard that I saw it: love. The sort of love that can't be explained in a paint-by-numbers picture or described in songs. It's simply that inexplicable, all-consuming, senseless sort of love that I'd found with Dane.

Stephanie leaned forward, lowered her voice, and winked. "Thank you," she said with a whisper. "I didn't mind the dead flowers or the boxed wine, but I did *not* want to shoot mini golf on a date."

I winked as Dane's arm came around me and pulled me closer to him. "Believe me, I understand."

In the soft silence that followed, the four of us found ourselves smiling and chatting, easing into the next morning as the moonlight shone still brighter, and the waves lapped still louder against the shore.

Finally, Richard raised a glass for the final speech of the evening. With a resounding *Cheers!* under the fairy lights, we all toasted to love and to Dotty Pink for bringing us together through her odd special talents.

There are those who doubt Dotty's skills, and those who flat out don't believe in magic, but then there are those moments—fleeting, but certain and unforgettable—that lead one to believe it is all there...written in the stars.

# Shades of the Stars!

*IN A SURPRISING TWIST of events, the brightest 'star' of the Sunshine Shore's grand finale fashion show was neither a model nor a designer, but our very own budding shopkeeper, Lola Pink! Photographed with her new fiancé, Dane Clark, it wasn't just the ring on her finger that dazzled the crowd, but her gorgeous collection of vintage sunglasses that stole the show. When asked for comment on the success of the event, Lola Pink said, "The real star of the show is Andrea Ricker, who was the real inspiration for the fashions. Without her, Regina and I would never have connected." And when asked about her engagement to billionaire boyfriend Dane Clark, she giggled and declined comment—but I think it's safe to say we're due to see the wedding of the century sometime soon. Billionaire babies on the way? Stay tuned!*

—Glinda Bright of the Sunshine Times—

THE END

# Author's Note

THANK YOU FOR READING! I hope you enjoyed Lola and Dane as they solved mysteries and fell in love! Stay tuned for *Shades of Sunshine* coming soon! To be notified when it releases, please sign up for my newsletter at www.ginalamanna.com.

Thank you for reading!

Love,

Gina

# Now for a thank you...

**To all my readers,** especially those of you who have stuck with me from the beginning.

By now, I'm sure you all know how important reviews are for Indie authors, so if you have a moment and enjoyed the story, please consider leaving an honest review on Amazon or Goodreads. I know you are all very busy people and writing a review takes time out of your day—but just know that I appreciate every single one I receive. Reviews help make promotions possible, help with visibility on large retailers and most importantly, help other potential readers decide if they would like to try the book.

**I wouldn't be here without all of you, so once again—*thank you.***

# List of Gina's Books![1]

Gina LaManna is the USA TODAY bestselling author of the Magic & Mixology series, the Lacey Luzzi Mafia Mysteries, The Little Things romantic suspense series, and the Misty Newman books. List of Gina LaManna's other books:

Lola Pink Mystery Series:

Shades of Pink

Shades of Stars

Shades of Sunshine

Magic & Mixology Mysteries:

Hex on the Beach

Witchy Sour

Jinx & Tonic

Long Isle Iced Tea

Amuletto Kiss

MAGIC, Inc. Mysteries:

The Undercover Witch

Reading Order for Lacey Luzzi:

Lacey Luzzi: Scooped

Lacey Luzzi: Sprinkled

Lacey Luzzi: Sparkled

Lacey Luzzi: Salted

Lacey Luzzi: Sauced

Lacey Luzzi: S'mored

Lacey Luzzi: Spooked

Lacey Luzzi: Seasoned

---

1. http://www.amazon.com/Gina-LaManna/e/B00RPQD-NPG/?tag=ginlamaut-20

Lacey Luzzi: Spiced

Lacey Luzzi: Suckered

Lacey Luzzi: Sprouted

The Little Things Mystery Series:

One Little Wish

Two Little Lies

Misty Newman:

Teased to Death

Short Story in Killer Beach Reads

Chick Lit:

Girl Tripping

Gina also writes books for kids under the Pen Name Libby LaManna:

Mini Pie the Spy!

Made in the USA
Columbia, SC
10 March 2020